THE WARRIOR WHO CARRIED LIFE

Cara closed her eyes and began to speak the spell of Fire. Her voice became a drone, then seemed to roll and surge like the movement of the waves.

She felt herself shatter into shards and fragments, broken, splintered, sharp. Finally she was able to scream, and from nowhere came a great wind. . . .

At last the wind died. Where Cara once stood was an armored warrior.

He was tall and broad, arms and legs weighted with muscle. He held a shield and a breastplate and a spear and a sword, all of a ruddy color almost like flesh, and a helmet cradled in one arm. His face was handsome, with a clipped brown beard and staring, startled eyes.

"It's worked," Cara whispered in a husky, rasping voice. "By all the stars, it's worked. . . ."

Other Bantam Books you will enjoy
Ask your bookseller for titles you may have missed

The Warrior Who Carried Life

Geoff Ryman

BANTAM BOOKS
TORONTO · NEW YORK · LONDON · SYDNEY · AUCKLAND

This low-priced Bantam Book
has been completely reset in a type face
designed for easy reading, and was printed
from new plates. It contains the complete
text of the original hard-cover edition.
NOT ONE WORD HAS BEEN OMITTED.

THE WARRIOR WHO CARRIED LIFE
A Bantam Spectra Book

PRINTING HISTORY
First published in Great Britain by
George Allen & Unwin in 1985
Bantam edition / January 1987

Bantam Books are published by Bantam Books, Inc. Its trade-
mark, consisting of the words "Bantam Books" and the por-
trayal of a rooster, is Registered in U.S. Patent and Trademark
Office and in other countries. Marca Registrada. Bantam
Books, Inc., 666 Fifth Avenue, New York, New York 10103.

PRINTED IN THE UNITED STATES OF AMERICA

O   0 9 8 7 6 5 4 3 2 1

Dedicated to
My Grandmother
Edna Florence Burn Pascoe
1889–1928

Contents

Chapter 1

The Wells of Vision

Cal Cara Kerig was five years old when she saw her mother killed. Her mother was mad, Cara was told, and madness was a disruption of the universe.

It was in the last days of the Gara han Gara, whose name meant Even Pressure over the Land. There was a long drought: rain did not fall for over half a year and the rice growing in steps up the canyon walls began to die. Cara's mother went to the wells of vision, which were forbidden to women, to find why the drought had come.

"Cara? Cara?" her mother came to her whispering one night. "I am going away, Cara. There is something very important that I have to do. I'll tell you all about it when I get back." Cara's mother was sweet and startling, with unruly hair and an enormous smile and a conspiratorial way of talking to Cara that did not make her feel like a child at all.

She was gone many days. When she returned, she did not look the same. She was even thinner. Cara could see the bones in her shoulders and strings of muscle around her mouth when she smiled. Cara screamed and wept at the change.

"Don't cry, Cara, please don't cry, there's no reason to cry. I've had my vision. I know why the drought has come. It's a wonderful reason. It's because of you."

Cara's father, who was much older than his wife, put her to bed. Cara saw him bar the door. He knelt down in front of her, to look into her eyes. "You must not let her out, Dear Daughter," her father said. "Even if she asks. She must stay here, safe, with us. Promise me?"

1

Cara did not do as she was told. When her father was out, carrying buckets of water to the high fields, she went to the door and opened it. Her mother came out dancing and clapping her hands. They had great fun together. Her mother put on her red wedding dress, and her wedding hat, a crown of brass, with brass flowers on long stems. "Because this is a special day," she told Cara. Together they went down to the rocks, where the women had once beaten their linen clean by the river. Now the women sat huddled in black, covering their faces, staring at the cracked mud that was beginning to bake dry. Some of the men, helpless, sick with terror, sat with them.

Cara's mother began to dance among them, willowy, skeletal, and she began to sing in a high, wavering voice, praising the drought. She sang of great disruption to come, the destruction of the great City down the river, a harvest of blood, a drought of womankind. She held up Cara with her insect thin arms. "Behold," she chanted. "This is the one. This is the one." The village wives covered their ears and fled, leaving only the men, in an angry circle.

"You call the drought wonderful? You praise it?"

"Yes, oh yes, um," said Cara's mother, in her breathless voice. "All the wonderful things I see begin with it."

"You and your madness will bring these things upon us!" the men exclaimed, desperate for a reason for the drought, and a cure.

"Oh, I won't. God will," replied Cara's mother, who had always been strange, and rich.

Men could not kill women, it was said, or the blood would turn into serpents. But the men had their dogs. "Masu! Masu!" the men ordered, and pointed. The beasts cocked their heads to one side, not understanding. Cara's mother called the dogs by name, and petted them, and laughed, and tried to make them think it was only a game, as they snapped at her long red sleeves. Then one of them caught her, and she stumbled in the mud, and fell. Cara started to scream, and the men closed in about her, and pulled her away so that she would not see, but Cara thought they were trying to stop her from helping her mother, so she kicked and wriggled, and bit the hand that covered her eyes, and saw. She saw the dogs burrow their snouts into her mother's stomach and make quick chewing motions until they had a grip on something they could tear. They lapped the blood and whined anxiously for their share. From far away up the hill, Cara's father howled as he ran.

The wedding dress was washed and repaired and returned to them. The brass crown had been polished. Cara's father did not speak of his wife again. He did not remarry either. Cara, who had been a brave and cheerful child became aloof and disdainful. She hated the village. She hated the men. She ached with wishing she had not opened the door. Forever after she felt incomplete and angry, as if she had been robbed of part of herself. She spent most of her time in the library of the house, reading to her baby brother the tales of Keekamis, the Only Hero, that her mother had read to her. Keekamis had gone into the Land of the Dead on a funeral barge carrying the body of his friend. Cara tried to go there too to find her mother. She drifted many miles down the river in a little boat until her father found her. "How far is it until I'm dead?" she asked him. He didn't answer. He rocked her silently, and wept.

A new ruling Family came into power, blaming the Gara han Gara for the drought. The old Family was marched out of the City, and stoned to death. The rain came again in late autumn, heavy from a dull sky, washing away dried mud from the rocks as though it had been blood.

At unexpected times, all through Cara's childhood, until she was an adult, the flavor of her mother's presence would return to her: when she was lonely, just before supper, in the sunset; when she tasted the year's first honey; when she heard someone singing far away in a high, unsteady voice. She could not remember her mother's face. But she knew that, after death, she would know her mother's soul the instant she found it. Her mother's soul was so often with her.

Then the terrible things she had prophesied began to come true.

Chapter 2

The Destroyed Woman

"I was a wolf, for my year," said Sari, as she fussed. She was a plump little bondwoman with fat, shuffling feet. She was wrapping Cara in strips of white cloth, for her initiation. They were on a hillside at night, under a sycamore.

"I hunted with the pack. I had a wolf for a mate, and a litter of wolf cubs too," Sari said. "They come and visit me sometimes, in the full moon."

Cara said nothing. Of course it was a she-wolf, it always was a she-wolf that they turned into. They could never be fierce in their real lives. Cara knew these people. Widows, unhappy wives, tame daughters, they made themselves excited by playing at magic. The villagers called them the Old Women, Kasawa, without strength or standing. Cara had very little respect for the Old Women. She had very little faith in their powers, but she would try anything now. A torch fluttered in the wind, in the dark.

"Now we must wear the hood," explained Sari, as if to a child. "So that we won't see the mysteries, and be overwhelmed."

"Oh, we wouldn't want that," said Cara. She had been told what poor sort of mysteries were to come. Sari's hands hesitated as they tried to push the hood over Cara's head. They arched delicately away from Cara's face. Sari, Cara realized, did not want to touch it. Did she think it was a disease that could be caught? Cara pulled the hood away from her and down over her own head, roughly. Sari wanted the face hidden? Good, so did Cara, and now it was.

The hood smelled of stale food and other people's breath. Cara could feel Sari hover over her, cowed now, and uncertain what to do next.

"It begins soon?" Cara demanded.

"Yes, yes it will. Our mistress is here." Cara could hear slight rustlings in the scrub all around her. "Well, almost here. Her name is Burning Light in the Wilderness. She will come in a haze of fire. Then the demons will inspect you, and then there's the trials, and then we take you to the Sanctum." She made it sound like knitting. "Oh!" she suddenly exclaimed, faintly, and moved away.

Cara sat, waiting coldly and without anticipation. She heard a door slam, somewhere far off down the valley. Someone nearby coughed. Presumably, it was one of the demons.

Suddenly there was a voice in the darkness, an old woman's voice. "Child!" it quailed. "I am Burning Light!"

It was Danlupu. Burning Light in the Wilderness was Old Mother Danlupu. Oh, yes? Cara began to smile. She could see the old woman in her mind, bobbing and quavering, clasping and unclasping her hands, unable to keep them still. Danlupu's spirit was so unsteady, she never could be still. Cara's smile went rueful with impatience. This was the head of the cult? She held on to measured hope only by an effort of will.

"Demons are here," said Danlupu in a high, strained little croak that was meant to be unsettling. "They are all about us, in the air." At that moment, from all around Cara, came a hooting sound, like owls, or children playing at ghosts. "Hoo! Hoo! Hoo!" went the Old Women.

"They will inspect you now. You will feel them tasting you with their little tongues." Come on, nonsense, thought Cara, come on, feebleness. And it came. The demon's tongues were pine branches, and the women whisked her with them, making sounds.

Kasawa, Kasawa, old, feeble. But in the Other Tongue, they had a different name. In the Other Country, across the mountains, they were called the Wensenara. That name meant the Secret Rose. There, they ruled whole cities and lived encircled by fine, high walls. It was not impossible, surely, that some of their spells were real? Spells were only words, rhythms, that unlocked the powers of the mind. Surely then, they depended on the powers of the people who used them. Cara had great faith in her own strength. She was not Kasawa.

"Now you must walk across a stone that comes from the Land of the Dead!" Danlupu whispered. Get on with it, thought Cara, and stepped up on to it, promptly. It was ice. Cara, whose family had been rich and knowledgeable, knew of ice. She could feel the sawdust they had stored it in, under her bare feet. She ignored the cold, and walked. Cold and nonsense. Tuh. She could endure both.

"And now the test of fire," said Danlupu, and led her. Cara could feel the old woman's hand quiver, like a frightened animal. She could feel the heat of the coals in front of her. Aunt Liri had warned her beforehand that if she walked straight ahead, she would find that the embers were only warm. Cara walked, and it was true, but she wouldn't have minded if the coals had burned her.

"She is accepted! She is accepted!" cried Danlupu. Cara felt herself unmoved. The Kasawa would accept anyone, but most especially her. People in the village still remembered what her family had been. The Kasawa would imagine Cara's interest showed that important people valued their knowledge. Cara valued their knowledge. She would try it, and if it didn't work her hatred would carry her on to something else. Her hands were taken again, and then there was a crackling as a screen of dried branches was lifted up. Cara knew she was supposed to duck under them, but she felt a twist of anger, and broke her way through them instead, with her hands and covered head. She felt herself enclosed in a small space. Many hands guided her and made her sit on a block of stone.

"We have a new daughter," Danlupu said, sounding pleased. "She is yet only a Bud, but she will be nourished by the first three spells. She will be warmed by the Spell of Fire, and watered by the Spell of Rain, and coaxed upward by the Spell of Sitting in Air. Then will come the fourth spell. She will learn the Spell of the Butterfly, who changes. She must transform herself into a beast of the air, or water, or field. She will spend one year in that form, learning how the animals live. Then she will return to us as a Rose, a Blossom."

This was worth less than the muck cleared out of the stables, Cara thought. At least muck fed the ground. This fed only silliness. How could they really expect anyone to believe they had all spent a year as an animal? It amused Cara to try to imagine what sort of creature Danlupu had become. A very tall, tottering sort of marsh bird, perhaps, with untidy feathers. But no, Cara thought, any bird inhabited by Danlupu would surely be eaten long before a year was out.

Her hands were on her face again.

Following the lines of hard, swollen scar tissue across cheeks and chin, she picked at the extraordinary peaks of skin, like budding horns, where her lips had been. Enraged at herself, she pulled her hands away, and pressed them between her knees. She did not want to remind the Old Women why she was here. People had stopped calling her Cal Cara, which meant Dear Daughter. They had begun to call her Cal Clicki. That meant the Destroyed Woman.

And how was she destroyed? Her family was as broken as her face, and she could not forgive, and she could not forget, but as long as she could think or feel or move a limb, she was not Destroyed. The very name Clicki provoked a rage in her. The very name Galu made her go still and cold.

Galu, she told herself, as the Old Women chanted. Galu, she repeated, to give herself heart. Galu, this was for the Galu, not for her. Anything that had the slightest chance of working she would bear with, for their sake, for what they had done.

The Galu had come and sliced her face, yes, with knives. The knives were blue with a tinge of yellow along the edges. They must have been coated with an irritant. Nothing else could explain the stinging and the scarring. Yes, but that was the least of it. They had poured bitter oil on the rice in the granary, and set it alight. They fed human blood to the pigs so that no one could eat them, and they chopped at the udders of the goats so that the poor beasts would never again give milk. The youngest and strongest of the bondmen were killed, and their bodies stuffed into the well, or left to bloat in the paddies, so that even her father's fields were tainted.

"We will give you curse enough, old man," the First Son of the Galu had said. "We will give you a daughter whom no one will wed, and sons who cannot work." Then the arms and legs of her two brothers were cut away.

The Old Women were still speaking in a chorus, about flowers. In the dark, under the hood, Cara remembered, though she did not want to.

She remembered the baby brother she had tended in her mother's place, Soriyo, whom she had called Tikki. She had also called him Proud Sailor, or Mast Climber, because he would scramble up the high fir trees on the cliffs. Tikki now sat swathed like a baby again, his face still young and beautiful, his belly growing fat, his brown eyes staring. When she went through the village, bartering their rich carpets or polished tools for food, she would come back to find that Tikki had rolled out of bed onto his back, and, like a turtle, could not right himself. Wandering at night, because she could not sleep with hatred, she would stumble over him, crawling on his belly across the floor to pass water outside the house so that she would not have to empty his pot in the morning. He heard the jingling bells of the Unwanted People as they passed on their way to market. Their wives, in brazen colored dresses, would sell themselves along the road. She saw him shift with impatience then. He had never had a woman. When she tried to stroke his hair he tossed his head to escape her gentle, woman's touch. "Kill me, Cara," he asked her. "It's the only way to deny them what they wanted." Part of her, like a dark undertow, agreed with him. Her other, elder brother Caro, who had her name but whom she had never really known, now lived with his wife's family—the last shame. They shut him away in a shed far from their house. At night, Cara could hear him bellowing in wordless rage, even from her far end of the long canyon. And Ata, Father, who had carried her on his broad shoulders, she remembered him too. He sat up now, not in bed, but tied to his old chair, so that he would not fall out of it. He glared ahead, never moving. "I am the earth," he told her once. "I cannot be moved." She fed him soup, or porridge, and wiped his white and iron-gray beard. She heard the wind wuthering at night in their empty sheep folds.

Now, in the chamber, while the women murmured prayers, her anger came again, with nothing under the hood to block it out. It was sick and old and weary, this anger. She had known what would happen; she had seen it coming; and she had told them it was coming, her brave and handsome, foolish kinsmen. Farmers, they were farmers. Despite the family history, what did they know of fighting? Woman, they had called her, girl, what do you know of war, and the answer was, more than they did. In the library that was her inheritance from the days when the Village by Long Water was a fortress, Cara had read about what they faced.

The Galu had succeeded as Family to the Gara han Gara, whose name meant Even Pressure over the Land. No one knew what Galu gro Galo meant. They had appeared as if from nowhere, promising an end to the drought. It had seemed even then to Cara's father, that if they had the power to end the drought, they had the power to cause it as well. Year by year the tribute they demanded increased. For fifteen years, the villagers paid it. Finally Cara's father, and others after him, had refused.

Cara remembered the gathering in the library of their house. It was a meeting for the men, but Cara had come.

"The Galu are the ruling Family of the City," she had told them. "They have all the Fighting Schools of the Family under them—the Men Who Swim like Eels, the Men Who Are Baked . . ."

There was a murmur of amused tolerance. "A woman's words," said Hasepi, her uncle and her father's rival. "Do you counsel that we leave the village, Cara?"

"Yes! Or pay the tax, even if it seems impossible, if you are not willing to take the great steps that are necessary to defend us!"

"Cara, this is not your province," warned her father.

"If you are not going to pay, then provide for defense."

"The river is barricaded, and watched," said Hasepi.

"A wooden barricade? They have boats with iron prows. And how many men walk the barricade at night? Five? Six? How many of them show up? How many of them are asleep? If you want to blockade the valley, you must use stone, like the old walls."

"And flood the lower fields? That is my land, not yours, you are talking of."

"And it is my father who leads this rebellion, and the Galu know that."

"You have a willful daughter, Eskigal. Rely on those who have experience, girl, not words in their heads from books."

"The only experience you have of war," said Cara, tears welling up in her eyes and anger blocking her throat, "is setting dogs on women!"

So the Village by Long Water had waited in its widening of the canyon, pastures and orchards on the higher slopes, paddies on the lower, and rows of houses cut into the rock of the sheer white cliffs.

The Galu descended from above, at night, carried on the backs of the Men Who Advance like Spiders. With them had also come the Men Who Cut Horses, and the Men Who Are Baked, and the Men with Wrists of

Steel, and they were led by the Son of the Galu. His name was Galo gro Galu, and no one knew what that name meant.

No one, that is, except Cara.

She could see his face now. She would never be able to forget it, a smiling face, as white as the underbelly of fishes, with blue veins visible under the skin, white hair in oiled waves, beardless. He had smiled, smiled with dead, gray teeth, and wore long brown robes, like a woman shut away for menstruation. He wore no armor, no armor on a raid.

When they came, Cara was sleeping in her bed. She still remembered the warmth of her room, in its last moment of security. She heard a noise, like the hissing of cats. Very suddenly she was wide awake, listening. There was a slight clattering of metal on stone. Arrows, thought Cara, and a bondman dropping his sword. She was surprised at how quickly she moved. She threw off the quilt and stumbled through the lightless corridor to her brother's room. "Up, Tikki, up," she said, shaking him. "It's come." She grabbed his sleep-warmed arm; he stooped to pick up something; and she pulled him into the corridor to run to the last room where there was a secret cellar. Then as suddenly as if there had been an explosion, the only door in or out of the Important House burst open and warriors and torchlight spilled into it.

Tikki lunged forward, armed only with a sickle. A man coated in armor that should have weighed him down spun lightly around Tikki, and coming from behind hugged his throat and grabbed his sword arm.

"Into that room, Dear Daughter, or he dies," the warrior said, with a smile in his voice.

There was a loud shout from farther down the corridor. Father! Cara thought. She thought they had simply struck him down. Then she heard him shout again. "Get out of my house! Villains! Men without souls!" They pulled him along the corridor in his nightshirt, a broad shouldered, bearded old oak of a man. His great brown legs had little lines of wrinkles just under the swelling of the muscles of his thighs.

They were herded into the room, Cara's own room, with its ancient fresco of a feast, and its reed mats, the dried grasses she had put in a vase that morning. Beyond her windows in the night, there was already fire, and unearthly shrieks from the animals. In her room stood the Men with Wrists of Steel, their armor in ringed segments that made them look like worms. There were the Men Who Are Baked, as she had read of them. Their skin was a caked, yellow scarring that felt no pain and resisted the slashing of swords. Their skin was cracked around the joints and their faces were like loaves of bread, with only wisps of hair and little eyes like currants. Her elder brother, Caro, and his shivering child wife were pushed into the room last of all, and then the soldiers parted into ranks and the Son of the Family, as silver as early morning, strode into Cara's room with his dead gray smile.

"We are not here to kill you," he said. The smile was fixed and was turned toward each of them in turn. "If we kill you, the village would benefit. It would inherit your lands and this house. We are not here to benefit this village. We are here to make it work for us. You will help us do that. You will always be with them to remind them what happens to rebels. You will horrify them for us." The smile turned to Cara's father. "We will give you curse enough, old man. We will give you a daughter that no one will wed, and sons who cannot work."

"We cannot live, you take so much!" her father roared. "Do you want us all to die?"

"Eventually, yes," replied the Son. Then he said, "Start with the daughter. He must see his whole life demolished, step by step."

Cara's arms were gripped and she was pulled down. She felt fury that her human soul should be overcome by animal strength. She could not move. She could not fight. She would not scream, she promised herself. She would not cry. Death in any form had to be faced in the end. The soldiers held her on her own bed.

Tikki's arms were smooth and thick, with beautiful workings under the sheen of his skin. The arm with the sickle broke free and slashed the neck of a Man Who Is Baked. A warrior with a horse's tail hanging from his helmet turned and with a casual swipe of the sword cut through Tikki's arm at the shoulder. It hung, held by a few ligaments and skin. Tikki gaped, unbelieving. With a brisk wrench the arm was removed and white powder was thrown over the wound. A warrior bound it with white strips, as Tikki watched, held up on his feet.

Cara's mind went dull. The Men Who Are Baked creaked when they walked. They creaked when they came toward her, creaked when they lifted up thonged skirts. Their genitals too had been burned away. Cara heard the unbuckling of armor behind her.

"No," said the Son of the Galu, a rise of warning in his voice. The warriors paused, and relented. "Yes," he said in approval. "I do not like that," he said. "I only like the knife." Then the knives had come. So skillfully wielded were they, that Cara would never have children.

A grinning face, like Death itself.

His first name, Cara had learned, in a tongue more ancient than that of the Other Country, meant "slug" or "worm." Gro meant simply "inside." His last name, Galu, the Family name, had made her breath catch when she understood it. It was the final, deepest reason for her being here among the Wensenara. The name Galu meant "the Secret Rose."

"Cara? Cara?" Someone was calling her name. She felt herself helped to her feet, and the hood was tugged away from her head. Her ruined face felt naked, as if the nerves were still exposed. She blinked and looked about her.

She saw the Sanctum of the Wensenara. It was an old, disused feed bin hollowed out of the rock, with a few daubs of paint depicting the sign "Ama" for Mother. The ceremonial hood looked like something used to keep pots warm. It was being turned over and over in Aunt Liri's hands. It was Liri, her mother's sister, who had first suggested she join the cult. She beamed at Cara now, swollen it seemed with pride and excitement. And there, to Cara's surprise, was Latch, her own bondwoman who hated her, and her maiden sister, Hara. They watched her, tight-lipped and pinched in the face.

Mother Danlupu told her the Spell for Fire, and Cara repeated it. It was childishly onomatopoeic, a sound like crackling wood. "Do not say it too much. The very stone will burn with it if you are not careful," Danlupu warned. The Spell for Sitting in the Air, a humming noise, and the hissing Spell of Rain came next.

"Now here is the last. Here is the most important. Without success in this, it is written that the Bud will never blossom into the Flower. This is the Spell of the Butterfly, who changes. You must spend a year in the wilderness as another kind of beast, to learn another way of living."

Cara listened and tried to remember. This was the one she had wanted. The spell was very long and repetitive, like a lilting song in a strange language. Cara stumbled over it, trying to remember. "Yes, dear daughter," Mother Danlupu said, "it is difficult. So very difficult, these lessons, but try again." Cara's face was no longer able to express emotions as subtle as irritation. She repeated the spell again, perfectly.

"Go out into the fields, child. Think over what you have learned here tonight. Remember that you have been accepted by the Wensenara. Let that give you strength. Practice, and when you feel you are ready, come to us, and flower."

That was all. Cara felt the women relax around her.

"You feel different now, my daughter. You can feel strength inside you," smiled the old woman, her hands doing a pleased little dance. She clasped them, to keep them still.

"I always feel strength inside me," replied Cara.

"Will you become a bird, sister, and fly?" asked gentle Liri.

"If I did, it would be a hawk," said Cara. "But then hawks must spend all their time hunting for food."

"She could be a fish," said Latch. "She could be as cold as her heart then. She could live in a well and dine off the flesh of my husband and son. As she did when they lived."

"Hate the Galu for their deaths," replied Cara. "Sister," she called Latch, and tried to smile, the aperture of her mouth widening only slightly over skull-like teeth. Even Latch shuddered and looked away. Cara's face had become a weapon. "No," Cara continued. "I want to be a beast of the field. I know what beast it is."

"A wolf," said Hara, scornfully. "Of course."   .

"Oh, it is much more fierce than that," Cara answered. "Though it hunts with dogs." Then she added, "I will try now."

"I do not think that would be wise," warned Mother Danlupu in a voice that was meant to be insinuating and unsettling.

"Why, Mother, are you afraid that the spell doesn't work?" Cara asked. She closed her eyes, and began to speak it. "Lalarolalaraleenalaralaralokilararolalaraleena . . ." Her voice became a drone, which seemed to roll and surge like the movement of waves.

"You are trying too much, daughter. You will disappoint yourself!" Danlupu warned, and looked around, helplessly, at the others. "You must start with the spell of fire!"

"Of course, she wants it all right away. Everything she ever wanted, she always had, right away," said Latch, with relish, drawing her poor robe and shawl around her. "She only comes to us in misfortune. You see how she disdains us. She only wants her wealth back, to lady herself over us again."

"Let us hope she fails," said Hara. "Then she will go away."

Their words seemed to fade into silence. Cara felt only a settling at first, a calming and soothing as the words spiraled round and round in her throat and mind. Then the circles seemed to spread and echo, like ripples in a pond, bound and rebound. Somewhere distant a voice was saying them correctly, but inside her head the words grew all confused and merged into one sound, a sound like thousands of people speaking at once. Cara felt herself grow dizzy. She felt herself sway from side to side as if the hollow in the rock were a ship at sea.

She felt something heavy inside her as well, a gathering weight, like water behind a dam. It was her hatred. With each turning of the words, the weight seemed to turn over on itself and grow. Suddenly in her mind there was an image of a rock that had begun to roll down a hill. The hill steepened, and it rolled faster and faster, picking up dust and debris as it tumbled, growing larger and gaining strength and speed. She became frightened. She tried to stop the stone, but she could not. She tried to stop the words, but the voice somewhere else kept saying them. Everything inside her pitched and lurched and shuddered, the ground fell away before her. Ahead was a precipice. The stone was the size of a temple and it spun out into empty air. Cara tried to scream, but found that nothing in her body obeyed her any longer. She could feel herself falling, everything in her rising up toward her mouth. The ground was suddenly before her, coming up insanely fast, like a fist. She hit, and felt herself shatter into shards and fragments, broken, splintered, sharp. Finally she was able to scream.

The Old Women heard it, a thin, wheedling wail, and from nowhere there was a great wind deep inside the chambers of the cliff. Dust was whipped into their faces and their robes rose up and lashed them like whips. Hazily, they saw Cara stand up, steam issuing out of her gaping mouth.

Then she exploded.

She was torn apart as they watched: great jets of blood and splintering of bone, hair and scalp dancing freely, the teeth flying apart, the skin lifting up like wings. The mass of it hung in the air and swirled, heart opening out, lungs blossoming open like red flowers, ligaments and strands of muscle circling upward like seagulls in the wind. Then suddenly it all began to collapse in on itself again, liver and intestines scurrying back as if for shelter, the rib cage closing like a trap, the skin wrapping itself back around again and healing, and finally, from nowhere, something that some of them thought for a moment might be the shell of a giant tortoise closed over the skin. The wind died, and there before them stood an armored warrior.

He was tall and broad, arms and legs weighted with muscle. He had a shield and a breastplate and a spear and a sword and a helmet cradled in one arm. His face was as regular and as handsome as Cara's once had been, with a clipped brown beard and staring, startled eyes. The warrior stared at them, and the women silently gaped back at him.

Cara's thoughts settled back slowly, like dust. She was Cara. She was here. Her whole universe was a different shape. The movement of air on her arms, the feel of the sandal thongs on her calves, the light reaching her mind through eyes that were in different positions and that would not focus: all her information was received through channels that seemed distorted and swollen. She looked down dizzily on an impossibly broad chest. How did a chest like that work, what on earth could fill it? Her whole body felt heavier, yet quicker, more instant: great splayed feet and broad, veined hands. Yet somehow the great bulk was less stubborn or long lasting. Hanging nestled between her legs was something that felt like a small new animal. The thought and feel of it paradoxically excited her, and it began to swell.

"It's worked," she whispered in a slow, rasping voice. "By all the stars, it's worked."

She wanted a mirror. She wanted to see that weight of flesh that meant she could kill, the weight that would make her safe in the world outside the canyon. Her thick hand, with clumsy fingers like sausages, padded around her face. It was bearded and larger, but she knew also whole and smooth again. She chuckled to herself and the sound, rising deep out of that bloated chest, startled her and made her jump. She laughed at it again. "I am a man!"

A man could walk the roads and not be kidnapped into bondage as a whore. A man could take up arms and fight, and if he knew better what needed to be done, other men would listen. He could get into the place that Cara needed to get into. A man could take revenge, where she could not.

She took a step forward. The whole world rocked and limped and twisted, as she fought to make the limbs work in the way that she was used to. That worried her. She didn't have time to learn to walk all over again.

"You didn't expect that, did you?" Cara demanded of the Old Women, relishing now the booming of her voice. "Kasawa. You thought I'd fail as you did, didn't you?" She took another step and found she could make her unsteadiness look like a swagger.

"Cara?" Aunt Liri called her, horrified, wondering, saddened. .

"Yes?" Cara answered, and turned to her with difficulty.

"What are you going to do? Do you know?"

"I know exactly," Cara replied, and began to walk again with her ponderous careful stride across the room. "Exactly." The thrill of the idea made her smile even broader. "Take care of my family, while I am gone, sister." Without looking back, she walked into the darkness, which swallowed her.

The Wensenara blinked at each other.

"Well!" exclaimed Mother Danlupu.

They gathered up their skirts and left in silence. To talk at all would be to admit that nothing remotely similar had ever happened to one of them.

What sort of power was it that could turn flesh and blood into shield and sword?

Chapter 3

The Little Thing That Feels Large

The Men Who Live like Foxes sprang out from the rocks, from within the very face of the cliff it seemed, along the narrow track. Cara had no time to draw her sword or to retreat.

She had wondered what she would do in her first fight. "I wished myself to be a warrior," she had told herself, as she walked through the night and day toward the village of Deeper and Wider. "If I am a warrior, I must know what to do."

Her masculine arm did not hold her shield up in front of her like a wall. Unbidden, it swung the shield horizontally through the air. "What am I doing?" Cara thought in horror. Then she understood. The shield's edge struck the first of the Foxes across the eyes and forehead. He staggered back; she had gained time to draw her sword. She spun around, for she had heard one of them land behind her, the shield righting itself in time to block a brutal blow from an axe, though her arm went numb and aching from the force of it. There were four of the Foxes, dressed in a mixture of armor and finery and furs; they surrounded her; her back seemed to tingle with its own vulnerability. She swung at the axeman, not knowing if her sword was even long enough to reach him, and missed.

"He's green! He's green!" the axeman exulted.

"Mine!"

"Mine!"

Cara felt a burning pain across the back of her legs. She swung at the head of the man beside her, but he rolled quickly out of her reach. Wounded, unbalanced, she fell. She saw the ground coming up for her; she saw her sword and tried to turn it away from herself so that she would not land on it; she felt skin scrape free from her wrist. She was sprawled, open, on the ground. Desperate, she tried to push herself back onto her feet, or drag herself to her knees, but her legs would not move. Then a heavy boot planted itself on the hand that held the sword, and the weight of a man landed on her back and put a blade along the side of her neck.

"Oh, no. Not so soon. Not so *quickly*," she thought, sadly.

"You're much too fine and lovely a lad to be wearing such armor and not know how to fight," the Fox on her back whispered in her ear. The Men Who Live like Foxes dwelt in burrows and did not wash with water; they burned fungus and sat in the smoke to kill the lice. It was said that they did not live with women, preferring the company of men. She smelled damp earth and burrow smoke on him. "We just want your armor. Strange stuff it is too." Whenever his weight shifted, Cara felt a grating pain across her calves.

"My legs," she whispered.

"Well, if you tie them up you might stop the bleeding. You might even be able to walk to the bondhouse."

"Shouldn't stay there, though," another one of them said. "Better to live in a burrow, with us."

Quickly, neatly, they rolled her over, two swords at her throat. Her shield was plucked from her, and the sword; her breastplate was peeled away, and her fine, thick-soled sandals. They left her barefoot in a shirt and loincloth, bleeding in the road.

"It's a shame," said the tallest, slimmest of them, cradling up the armor. He wore fine traceries of gold as earrings, and a scarf of lace around his throat. "He is lovely. But we couldn't trust him with us, could we."

"Your scarf," begged Cara. "For a tourniquet?"

"Tourniquet, eh? Well, we rich sons do know some big words." But the Fox stopped. "Well," he said in a quiet voice. "As you are so beautiful." He passed Cara the windings of lace. "A fair exchange."

They leapt over the edge of the cliff, and were gone.

Cara sat up, and turned her legs to look at the wound. The flesh across her calves was purple and split open, but the cut was clean and the bone had not been splintered. She understood the Fox's kindness. He had used the blunt back of the axe. "I will not weep," she told herself, as she tied up the wound. Blood seeped through the lace, tracing intricate patterns of fruit and flowers. Then, using her arms to climb up the rock behind her, she managed to stand. The pain was not as terrible as she had feared it might be, except when her feet moved from the ankle at the first step. She went dizzy and nearly fell again. She found, however, that if she kept her feet absolutely flat, lifting them up like plates of meat from the thigh, taking tiny steps, then she could bear it. Fortunately it was late afternoon, cooling with long shadows; she had slept through the worst heat of the day. A bondhouse, they had said. A bondhouse would mean a large farm. All the land here was desert, gravel, and rock. A farm would have to be on lower ground, by the river, nearer Deeper and Wider, from where the boats left. How far away, how far away was that? There were only six hours of light left. She began to walk.

If the ground was even slightly uneven; if her feet dragged, or if she shuffled, then she could feel more flesh tear, and her nerve ends seethe with pain. Each time it had to be a clean lift, up and then down. Sometimes she had to stand still, to let the pain subside. She stood with her eyes closed and waited; she could not risk sitting down. "For my father, who is like the earth," she whispered at each step. "For my brother who starves. For my brother who crawls." The shadows lengthened, and the lace went black and caked; her feet blistered from the heat of the ground, then started to bleed as well. Finally as night came on—night that would be so terrifying because it would mask the road and the precipice beside it—the track dropped away in front of her in a zigzag down the rock, and she saw the ribbon of the river, a slate gray reflection of the darkening sky, and the irrigation canals like patterned mirrors around the fields. She saw a long house with people in the yard drawing water and bringing in wood. She saw the house, and the steep slope and realized she could never walk down to it.

"Hello! Hello!" she shouted with her new voice, and it cracked and went harsh. "Help! I cannot walk. Hello!"

She listened to her own forlornness in the wind. Finally she fainted and fell.

Pain shot up from Cara's legs and through her whole body, wakening her. "Ah. Ah. Ah," she gasped, and sat up in the darkness.

"Duhdo duhdo genzu," whispered a slurry voice that smelled of stale breath, nonsense words that had come to mean an offhand apology. Whoever it was stumbled off in the darkness to a door that opened out onto a darkness which was only slightly less impenetrable. Cara saw the stars in the sky, before the door swung shut again.

"Oh, no," Cara groaned. Now she was awake with the pain. She lay on a blanket on a hard stone floor. Already her fingers had found holes in the cloth. She knew enough of bonded life to know that someone had probably died on it. From all around her came the serried noises of people sleeping. She had seen such bondhouses before. There would be, she knew, two rows of partitions made probably of hanging blankets. Between them, whole families, exhausted, thin, and ill-clothed, slept on the stone. There would be a small shed some distance away for people to die in, and a trough between the stable and the bondhouse for what were called, in Cara's language, Gifts to the Earth.

A baby started to cry. Its mother did not wake. Someone groaned and turned over, but the infant still wailed, untended. How many hours more of this did she have, Cara wondered, the pain in her legs, like fire smoldering in embers, how many more hours of hunger, fierce thirst, and a need to pass water? Cara decided to move. She tried drawing up her knees, keeping her feet in the same position and pushing up with her arms, but beyond a certain point the pain was too great. She could feel the risk of further damage. Finally she twisted over onto her stomach and rose up onto her knees. She made a sudden lunge, bringing her feet up under her, accepted the stabbing pain, and then stood. With her new flat-footed walk, she carefully picked her way between the rows of sleepers, and out through the door of the bondhouse.

There was silver in the east, above the cliffs. Very far away a dog was barking. The air seemed as sweet as flowers after the bondhouse and was delicately cool and clean. It was going to be, however, another savagely hot day. The bottom of Cara's feet were now as badly damaged as her calves; yet she would have to walk. She knew better than to stay any time in a bondhouse.

Across the pavement was the main house, and inside that, the kitchen. Cara could see the flickering of candles through a small low window, and smell the smoke, and hear the clatter of pots. Suddenly there was a shouting, loud, that was quickly subdued. Cara limped toward it, and ducked under the low desert door through walls as thick as her legs were long, into the steam and heat of the kitchen.

A bondgirl was slapping two children as hard as she could across the face. "Damn you took it. Damn you took it," she hissed at them in a frightened voice.

"Our Ata told us to get in first," said the boy, who was not crying. His face was small and hard and blotchy.

"Your Ata can wait his turn," the bondgirl said, glancing at Cara with embarrassment.

"Morning, Sir," she murmured. Bondpeople liked to give each other the treat of aristocratic address.

"Good morning, Lady," replied Cara, remembering that.

The girl ran a hand that was quivering across her face. "I've got no pots to cook," she said, near tears. "I didn't shovel ash all morning for you," she told the children. Smiling in victory the boy stood on tiptoe over the fire wall to nurse his pot of rice. Women standing around the two fires looked at Cara with sullen interest, hugging little black pots to themselves. The place smelled of rancid goat's milk and damp wool and smoldering dung cakes and steam. Cara was already drenched with sweat.

"You'd best sit down, with your wounds," said the girl. There was only one chair, and it was occupied. "Move off," said the bondgirl, to another girl her own age. "The Sir is wounded." The other girl, puffy-eyed, silent, stood up and stumbled away, obeying the laws of hospitality.

"There's no food to offer you. I'd give you some . . ." The bondgirl's voice trailed off. "You must be hungry." Cara lowered herself, carefully, into the chair, and felt a wave of relief. Then she saw that the girl needed it more. She had to lean on the table, and her black hair fell straggly over her face, which was pale, almost translucently white, even in the orange light of the candles. She swayed where she stood.

"My 'Ta will be angry. Without his breakfast."

Cara tried to lift herself off the chair, to give it to her, but found herself rooted to it, unable to move. "I'd give you the chair, Lady, but . . ."

The girl only nodded. "They could give us *something*," she said, hatred harsh in her voice, and jerked her head toward the rest of the main house.

Is this what Latch felt, Cara wondered. The wood of the only table was thick, for the chopping of vegetables and meat. There were no vegetables or meat. Cara saw only the bags of rice the women wore jealously around their necks. Cara's family did not treat their people like this. They gave the bondmen their own places, small houses at the foot of the cliff, and gave them the same food to eat as the Important House. Surely that made a difference?

"They've got you too," the girl said, dull with exhaustion and hopelessness.

"Me?"

"Hmmm. They'll put things on your legs to make them worse. Don't take anything from them, not even water. They'll say you owe them money then, and that you have to work it off, and they'll give you just enough food to live on, and say you owe them for that too. If you try to run away, they cut the strings inside your legs. Or set the dogs on you. And you were off to see the world. It's a shame." Then she added in a sleepy voice full of wonder, "Your bandages are made of lace."

Cara looked at the face with a woman's eye. Desperately tired, but pretty; pretty but coarse, harsh, lips too heavy. Nice high cheekbones. Her dress was rough knotted wool, grainy and oatmeal colored. She had not tried to dye it with berries as the other women had, a patchy purple. The girl was drifting off to sleep on her feet, as Cara watched.

"Were you born here?" Cara asked, suddenly, to wake her up.

"I think we were somewhere else when I was younger. My Ata. My brothers." The girl's lips curled in loathing. She glanced down at Cara's naked body without shame.

"What about your brothers?" Cara asked. The girl shrugged and scuffed her feet and went silent.

Cara understood somehow that she had been beaten at times and that at times, in a house full of men who could not buy wives, all together under one rough blanket, her brothers would have used her for sex. Cara found herself asking, "When I leave here, will you come with me?"

The girl gave a bitter shrug of a laugh. "You? With your feet burned through, and no clothes, and your legs like that?" The face softened a bit. "Duhdo duhdo genzu," she murmured.

What Cara felt was at first indistinguishable from pity. It was an ache in her heart that suddenly seemed to extend to her loins. The pale flesh seemed suddenly beautiful. Cara wanted to stroke it, to feel how smooth it was. She smiled at her new predicament. This was, she realized, how a man felt. Cara glanced down at her own legs—brown and muscular and covered only with a trace of golden hair and a small loincloth. She thought the legs were beautiful too.

"Sit down," Cara said to the girl.

"On you?" the girl asked, her lips curling again, slightly.

"There's nowhere else. You're falling asleep," Cara reasoned.

To Cara's surprise, the bondgirl relented. She settled slowly, like an old woman, on to Cara's lap, and nestled her head on Cara's male chest. "Young beautiful Sirs," she murmured. "You all turn into spiders." Then, in an even fainter voice. "It's the work."

The girl was still asleep when her father found her. He was a pig of a man, if pigs are ever thin and wiry and desperate, with long grizzled beard "Where's my food, girl?" he demanded, his anger kept in check by the presence of the strange young Sir who, even wounded, looked large and determined enough to throw him bodily out of the house.

"She fell asleep," Cara warned, dislike in her voice.

"A man's got to eat, Sir," said the girl's father, stepping forward, stepping back, nervous, resentful, broken.

"Does she work all day in the fields and then do morning and evening in the kitchen?" Cara asked, her voice still cold.

"Well, she's a woman," shrugged the man, made uncomfortable. Then a light came into his eyes. He became a caricature of cunning. "And a hard worker, too, Sir. I think you'll find it's not sleep that's making her sit on your lap. No, she's a rugged hard worker, and does as she's told." Even he had to add, out of truthfulness, "Usually."

"I want her," said Cara.

"Oh, well, what are we talking about?" said her father. "I hope you mean only a decent marriage, Sir. That there is my only daughter, and a valuable worker for me and my sons. My one real treasure, Sir, my pleasure and my comfort." He added, darkly, "There'll have to be a dowry."

"I'm as poor as you are," said Cara.

"Well, no marriage," said the man. "And me and my sons can make sure that there will be nothing else, either." He was bargaining, merely. He waited for Cara to make an offer. He leaned down and whispered, "As a matter between us, I can tell you, Sir. She goes on the blankets." The straggly bearded, sallow little man pulled back, a meaningful glint in his eyes.

That if nothing else would have made up Cara's mind. "You don't understand," Cara answered. "I'm not buying her. I'm taking her. If she'll come."

"Tuh," said the man with a shudder of fear and laughter. He looked for support at the women ringed round the fires. They were fascinated, now. "You? Take her? With nothing but a shirt and a loincloth to you? My daughter's worth more than that." He stepped forward and pulled her arm.

"Get up, you bitch's hole, sitting on the pegs of strange men when I'm asleep! Get up and get me food."

Cara's arm encircled the girl, and held her, and would not let her go.

"Who are you, pushing and pulling?" she suddenly yelled at them both.

"Your father wants his breakfast. You are going to stay in this chair and rest." Cara had to fight to hold her. "I'm going to cook it."

The girl stopped pushing against him. "You are?"

"Yes. If you'll get off me."

Mouth hanging open with surprise, the girl stood up. She looked helplessly at her father. "Well, if he wants to, Ata." She sat down, and with the strangeness of what had happened, blurted out a laugh. The other women in the kitchen crowded round to see the beautiful stranger with his funny walk fill an old square pot with water from the cistern. The girl's father seemed to swell, and put both his hands on his hips in a kind of relieved swagger. "Well, I must have left myself behind in bed this morning."

The fires were piled behind two waist-high, horse-shoe-shaped walls. Amid the embers, pots rested precariously on stone columns. None of them were empty. Deftly, Cara jammed a large branch within the horse-shoe and hung her pot from it.

"Well, he's practiced enough at kitchen work," said a woman with birdlike arms and hanging belly. "Maybe it's your sons he wants to marry." More laughter, even from the girl on the chair.

"I don't think women should work harder than men?" Cara said, as a question, looking into the eyes of the old woman. The truth of it struck the woman's face, and the laughter fell from it. True enough, the face gestured silently to a friend.

"Your rice, girl," Cara asked, holding out her hand. "Come on, I'm not going to steal it."

Her face quickening with some new emotion, the girl reached down into the front of her dress, and lifted out the tiny knitted sack. Without looking to her father, she passed it to Cara, and she was smiling, with hope, though her eyes were wide and sad. He father, at a loss, tried to look amused and victorious.

The rice was boiling when the farmer came in.

"Keri, you're not in the fields," he said, simply.

"It's this man, Sir," said Keri, the father. "He's distracted my daughter, Sir, so that she wouldn't cook, and now I'm late and I haven't had my breakfast yet."

"Then you shall have to work without your breakfast, won't you?" said the bondbearer.

"Yes, Sir, yes, Sir," said Keri, dipping as he spoke.

"I shall bring it to you in the fields, if I can," said Cara, over her shoulder. "Or perhaps your daughter will." Her legs were starting to throb again.

"You're working," said the bondbearer to her. "Good. Legs don't look so bad. Perhaps you'll be in the fields tomorrow." The bondbearer was a heavy man, with bowlegs, wearing what his workers wore, except that he had all of it together: the heavy white robe that could be bound up around the waist for wading through paddies, trousers to the knee, shoulder straps for his sandals, a wine bag, and a broad round hat made of reed that hung down behind his back. In one hand, coiled, was a whip.

"I'm not going to be your bondman," Cara told him.

"Aren't you? Then how are you to pay for the food you've eaten?"

"I have eaten none of your food, and as for a stone floor and dirty blanket, all I owe you for that is gratitude."

"I don't do a trade in gratitude."

"Then you won't get any. Not from me. You must do a trade in other emotions."

"Certainly not in insolence," said the bondbearer. "Not in my own house. Get out and walk with your wounds, if you're able. No boots. No clothes. Tuh." He jumped up onto the table, sat on its edge. "I can give you boots and clothes. And food, oh yes, even you cannot do without food, young Sir. I'll give you these things, and shelter from the sun. And you work for me only long enough to pay for them. You look strong enough, apart from your legs. You should be able to work it back in no time. You'll need to rest, you know, rest to heal. No one's going to give you that for free. Except your own family. From the sound of your talk, they no doubt once would have. But I don't want to delve. Take your choice. Food and shelter in exchange for an honest man's work. Or out, now, I'll not keep you." He looked at the girl. "That rice is done," he said. "Take it to your father."

"But . . ." she began to protest. It plainly wasn't.

"It's done because I say it is," the bondbearer said.

"The girl stood, still weary, hand on her knees to push herself to her feet. Then she strode to the fire and grabbed Cara's arm.

"I'll go with you," she whispered, fiercely, her eyes hard and hungry, encircled with dark baggy flesh.

Cara was going to tell her no. The bondbearer was right. She couldn't walk, she had no shoes, she had no feet. She could hardly stand any longer in front of the fire. She was weak with standing, and hungry, ill with hunger. The bondbearer would come after them, and Cara could not run. Cara was going to shake her head, say no, I cannot take you, I cannot take myself.

"Move, girl!" the bondbearer said, suddenly loud, sensing victory.

There was only one small window in the kitchen. Suddenly, as if it were a pursed mouth between bulging cheeks, wind blasted through it. A cloud of dust slammed through the kitchen door like a fist. The farmer turned and hid his eyes; the girl cried out. Cara felt a nestling, almost tender like the snout of a pet, in her right hand. Shielding her eyes, she looked down. There, point resting on the floor, was her sword. It bumped against her hand again, insistently, and Cara took it up. With a humming noise, like the spell of Sitting in Air, her shield floated in the air through the door toward her.

"Come on, girl!" Cara bellowed and grabbed the bondgirl's hand and pulled, squinting against the dust and wind.

"A sword!" the girl shrieked. "But how? But how?" She did not see Cara pluck her shield out of midair. Together they hobbled across the kitchen, the girl inserting herself under Cara's shoulder, to help.

"The Law! The Law!" the bondbearer shouted, rising to his feet. Outside, chickens that had been let loose for a morning peck were being blown across the stone, balls of clucking feathers, and there were crashes from inside the main house as things were blown over.

Walking out of the desert, came Cara's armor, breastplate, and helmet uninhabited by a body, but in their proper places, the boots walking by themselves. "What manner . . ." Cara began, and then understood. The armor broke into a run to meet its mistress. It met her, and spread, and enveloped her, and suddenly boots protected her feet, and a helmet covered her head.

"Magic!" The girl laughed, thrilled by her luck. "Magic!"

The bondbearer stared in his doorway, stunned, watching the two of them stumble away across the yard to the gate. Staggering under Cara's weight, fighting the wind, the girl pulled it open. The two of them slipped away. A spear followed, all by itself. It hopped on one end. The farmer watched in disbelief, until the gate fell shut and the wind died. Then he roused himself.

"Kawa! Harig ban Har!" he roared, running with heavy ungainly strides toward the stables.

The road from the farm was absolutely straight, all the way to the river, with irrigation ditches and paddies on either side of it in tidy patterns, flat and steamy with only wispy borders of reed in which to hide.

"Who is he calling?" Cara asked.

"The men who train the dogs," said the girl in a voice that suddenly sounded small, and she felt Cara go still and icy beside her. "What other magic do you know?" the girl asked.

"I can fight," Cara said, without much hope. "Get me there." She pointed with her sword to a narrow track that ran along a bank between the paddies. It would be better to face the dogs there than on the wider road where they could be more easily surrounded. They tried to run, with an awkward pumping motion, limping, hopping, along the road to where the track turned off it. Bondmen working in a line across the ricefield stood up to watch them, their faces in shadow from their broad hats, wriggles of reflected sunlight playing on their faces.

From within the compound of the house there came an agonized baying, as if the beasts were in an extremity of anguish. Then a kind of squealing snarl in chorus.

"They're off the leads," panted the girl, bearing a good part of Cara's weight. "If they grab you, they'll never let go, until the master tells them. Go for their eyes then, poke them out with your thumbs. If one of them gets me, kick him in the balls. If it's a bitch, stick it up the rear."

"Front legs?" Cara asked.

"If you can get both at once and pull them apart hard, they die, yes. If you can do it without having your throat torn out. Their hearts stop."

"You've seen this before."

The girl simply nodded. They stopped on the track, and turned, and stood back to back, and Cara passed the girl the shield and the spear. "They'll hit me first. Try to fend them off, like with a stick. The shield's got a sharp edge, use it like a club."

The gates of the farm swung open, and the dogs poured out, tall, gray, shaggy beasts, with barrel chests and long thin black legs that moved in great loping strides, black eyes, flapping ears and tongues and black lips drawn back from fangs. Men in thick leather aprons and gloves followed the dogs, and the bondmaster, holding his hat on his head as he ran. The workers in the field called warnings to their friends, and stood up straight, hands by their sides.

"Will they go for them as well?"

The girl shrugged. "Not usually. Unless they run."

Only on the other side of the road, catspaws of wind disturbed water on empty peaceful fields. "I'm sorry," Cara said.

"Better to die free, eh?" the girl said, but it was a question.

They heard whistles and shouts. Two of the dogs had become confused, and peeled away from the pack, plunging down the bank, into the water of the ricefields. The nerve of some of the bonded people broke, and they ran, mud clinging to their feet, sucking them down. The dogs leapt from one row of rice to the next, where there were roots and plants to give them support. Cara counted the remaining dogs: eight left. They turned in a pack, like a dark stream, from the road onto their narrow path. Cara saw, glancing at the ricefield, a dog launch itself onto a bondman's back, jabbing its teeth into the back of his neck. The man's head was held underwater.

"The dogs killed my mother," Cara said. She wanted someone to know that.

"And mine," whispered the girl.

Then the dogs were on them, close and fast.

"Not this time," Cara promised herself. "Not this time. Not again." A dog leapt toward her.

Cara's sword seemed to launch itself in an arc, slicing across the dog's neck. A dying weight struck Cara in the chest, and she felt an almost gentle brush of cool, moist teeth against her neck, as she wiped the weight away from her with her free arm. She drove the sword down, into the back of another dog's neck. The sword struck between two vertebrae. Cara felt the whole muscular body shudder and twist, and begin its death jitter, flanks twitching. The sword would not come free. Teeth sank into Cara's shielding left arm. Twin, needled vises closed around both of her ankles. The dogs had her.

Behind her, the girl gave a little cry, not of terror, but surprise. Cara could not turn; another dog was clambering up over the backs of its mates to get at her. With a sudden ringing clang, the shield, floating in the air, struck it across the head, splintering bone, then sailed, humming, back around to the girl. With a wrench, the sword came free. Cara swung backhanded at the beast that clung to her left arm, cutting open its belly. She slammed the sword down onto the backs of the dogs who held her ankles, back and forth, back and forth between them, opening gashes over their rib cages, but their mouths still gripped her. Another dog leapt.

Cara felt her helmet eased from her head. Then suddenly it dived, with its pointed crest, ramming itself into the gullet of the dog who was leaping for her, and she understood finally that she could control it. She punched with the helmet, pushing the dog farther and farther back. It choked, and coughed, frothing up mingled blood and saliva. The clenching around one of her ankles loosened and she kicked her foot free.

There was a sudden, bitter stinging across Cara's sword arm, and something like a dark serpent wrapped itself around her wrist and held. It was the whip. At the end of its taut length was the bondmaster. The two remaining dogs, spinning in circles about themselves, wriggled back miserably to their masters. The beasts had never faced people with weapons.

"You'll pay for my dogs," the bondmaster bellowed, red-faced. Cara took the sword with her ravaged left arm. "And you'll pay for my dead workmen! We'll sweat it out of you! We'll sweat it out of your whore!" Cara flung the sword, and it shot, whirring, through the air, and jammed itself into the bondbearer's open mouth.

The sword hung out of it, like a long tongue. The bondmaster, suddenly silent, stared in surprise, and let go of his whip. He gagged, trying to breathe, blood crawling out of the corners of his lips. Cara could feel, as though the sword were the tip of her fingernail, the spinal column of the man's neck. "Hawwak do Kerig," she murmured and pushed the sword with her mind through the cord of nerves. Very suddenly, with the cut, the bondmaster collapsed, raggedly, and rolled down the bank.

The sword extricated itself, and sprang free and tumbled back into Cara's hand. "Let us go," she challenged the dogmasters. They knelt, pulling their dogs to them and stroked them, and whispered to make them less unhappy. They did not want to lose any more of them. As the stranger and the girl passed them, they did not look up. The evil eye.

"Who will be bondmaster now?" one of them asked the other, in fear. Without a master, the workers would drift away. Who would dig the ditches then, and harvest?

The girl was very surprised when, half a mile down the road, the warrior beside her began to weep.

"Flesh of my flesh," mused Cara, resting beside the great river, plucking the tip of the sword with her finger. She could indeed feel it, dully. The sword and all her armor were not made of metal at all, but something smooth and slightly pink, flecked with white.

It was twilight, the sun gone, the sky pink and blue, and the river quiet and deep and rippled with many colors. Rice was simmering in her helmet over a small fire. The girl was coming back through the dusk, with the lace scarf beaten clean on the rocks to wash Cara's wounds. "There's fish in the river," the girl announced as she climbed up the side of the bank. "We can eat fish for free." She knelt down beside Cara, and began with a certain playfulness to daub the arm where the dog had torn it. "You can rest on the boat," she said. "You can rest all the way to the City from the Better Times, and heal."

Oh, this is strange, this is strange, thought Cara, looking fondly up at her, smiling with desire. All she wanted to do was lie with the girl, pull up the rough undyed wool and feel the softness of her legs and slide herself into the warmth that was between them. All she wanted to do, as though the center of Cara's being had shifted down to the bottom of her loins. Even food seemed remote.

"What is your name?" Cara asked her. Cara herself still responded to the depth and resonance of that voice.

"Stefile. It means Three Sleeps. I don't know why. And yours?"

"Cal Cara Kerig," Cara replied without thinking, and realized her mistake.

"Dear Daughter of the Important House?" the girl repeated in amusement, and giggled.

Cara took a deep breath, and then slowly, calmly told Stefile all of the story that she understood herself. The girl jerked away from her at first, and fell sullen and silent, picking at the grass, and asked pained questions. "I thought," she said, scowling, "I thought I felt something like that."

Then the idea began to amuse her. Eyes fastened hard on to Cara's, she ran her hand along Cara's thigh, and under the leather pleats of the skirt, over the thong that held the loincloth, to meet Cara's physical sex. The girl giggled. "Well, there's nothing wrong with that," she said, smiling, and with a practiced movement, pulled it free. Both she and Cara looked at it with rapt attention; Cara had been too embarrassed to look at it herself. It seemed such a small, pink and brown thing to look at, even now that it was swollen and veined, with a head and a mouth. Stefile ran her hand gently up and down it, and to Cara at least, it felt enormous. Stefile's face pressed close to hers, forehead to forehead, eyes meeting, and crossing, and they turned away, blinking, with a laugh.

"If I hadn't seen the magic, I wouldn't believe you. I would think you were mad," Stefile whispered. "Maybe you are."

There, on the bank, where any passing boat could have seen them, Stefile squatted over Cara, and raised her skirts, and lowered herself gently down, guiding Cara's penis into her. With a sigh, they each lay down, or back, and didn't care.

Chapter 4

Violence Begets

In the center of Hapira Izamu Pa—the City from the Better Times—stood the Most Important House, where the Family lived.

The walls of the Most Important House had once been as blue and as perfect as the sky. Now the tiles were falling off in great patches, and brown scrub grass grew in the mortar between the bricks. There was no gateway through the walls of the Most Important House, no door or portal. On the ground in front of it, on a red, embroidered mat, sat the Man Who Drinks Poison.

His flesh was gray and swollen; his eyes were puffy, hooded slits, as in a mask.

"I have come to learn how to fight," Cara told him. The Poison Man stared back at her impassively. It seemed to Cara that if she pressed his face with her thumb, the imprint would remain.

"Is the girl with you?" the Poison Man croaked, in a rasping voice like the bark of a dog whose vocal cords have been cut. If he spat in an enemy's eyes, the enemy went blind. If he touched a wound, the wounded man died.

Cara answered yes. Hidden like a serpent's tongue, his eyes seemed to flick up and down Cara's body, and Stefile's also.

"You both look strong enough," he admitted. Both? He spat on a cube of red wax. It began to sizzle and melt, and he motioned Cara to put out her hand. Was this a test of strength, Cara wondered, a trial by poison? If so, she could not be seen to falter. The wax danced hotly on her skin, and the Poison Man pressed his ring into it. The wax cooled and hardened, bearing the ziggurat seal of the Family. "What School?" the deadly man asked her. "Shadow? Fire? Horse?"

"I have no thoughts," replied Cara, which was a lie. Cara knew which School she wanted, but a supplicant could not offer to join it. It was for the Poison Man to offer and for her to accept. "But I do not want to be a Man Who Is Baked."

"No," said the man whose touch was death, and it seemed to Cara that suddenly there was something very sad in his face. "No, my beauty. We will not bake you. We will send you to the Warrior Angels."

Stefile gave a little cry of delight, and took Cara's arm, and nuzzled her cheek. It was said that in the Better Times, even their enemies did not have the heart to kill the Warriors Who Look like Angels. The Men Whose Beauty Blinds, they had also been called. The Angels rode white horses in parades and served the Family in the inner house as guards and decoration. That was why Cara wanted to be one of them. It would bring her closer to the beating heart of the prince she wished to murder.

Stefile knew that. One night beside the river, she had asked herself if she wanted to go on, to exchange her old life for a brief and wild, desperate one. The answer had been yes. Since then she had traveled down the Great River and seen Hapira Izamu Pa with its vine-covered market and the giant public fountains roaring like waterfalls in this desert land. She had seen the satins and the little ebony boxes in the stalls. Now she was to live in the Most Important House, and be the woman of a Warrior Angel, and help to kill the Son of the Family. That was life enough for anyone, however short. And there was Cara too.

Cara was like no one Stefile had ever met. Cara was kind, and educated, with the soft, smooth manner of an Important Person, as if he, or rather she, were a prince herself. A sorcerer prince on a dire mission. Stefile smiled at herself—oh dear, it was all dreams come true.

Except that Cara would keep insisting that she was a woman, and act like one in ways that Stefile could never quite identify. Sometimes this made Stefile cross and confused; sometimes it made her smile.

The Poison Man stood up with a grunt, and took a deep breath, and pumped out of himself, rib cage flexing in and out, a series of whoops and squeals and shrieks. Both Cara's and Stefile's faces fell, and the Poison Man turned and, for the first time, grinned at them, pleased with himself and the noise no one else could make. "You must climb up," he explained. There was an answering cry from the top of the wall, and a rope ladder was unfurled from it, slapping against the tiles.

The Poison Man took out of a pouch a bar of metal that moaned at his touch like a bell. His fingers came away from it a silvery black, and before Cara could shy away, he marked a quick sign on Cara's forehead—the hieroglyph for Angel.

"You will not thank me for sending you to the Angels," he said, still smiling. His bloated lower lip hung so heavily that his mouth was always open, and he had to suck the saliva back in through his teeth. "Do not be fooled by beauty. Do not be fooled by ugliness, either." He held up an arm for them to ascend. "You have your future," he said.

Eager to see over the wall, Stefile climbed the ladder first. She was near the top, when suddenly a man with yellow skin and no face lurched over the parapet and reached out at her. Stefile squawked in anger and fear, and swung on the ropes. The man laughed heartily, through a mouth that was a tiny, hardened circle of burn. "Do not worry, Lady, don't be frightened of *me!*"

"I'm not," replied Stefile, angry, and pulled herself over the parapet without his offered help.

The Baked Man was utterly naked, rubbing his skin with a block of lard. "Where are you going, Lady? Sir?" he asked, and gave them directions, pointing with a fat, flaking finger. "Follow the Row of the Eagle until it crosses the Row of the Sky." They looked out over the Most Important House.

It was stark noon, the sand-colored brick bright against the blue sky. Rows of courtyards were ranked in straight lines off into the distance, the walls between them all the same height, as bare and geometric as a honeycomb, except where they had begun to crumble. Inside the courtyards, against the walls, were buildings. Domes of brick swelled lopsidedly out of the roofs, and the vents of air ducts clustered like flocks of birds. One enormous courtyard was a park, with a lake and grass and trees and grazing sheep. Above all of it, like a giant crown in layers, rose the ziggurat, where the Family were supposed to worship. It also was plain and undecorated. Here, there were no smiling, beatific portraits of kings, radiant and powerful and unpleasant, to frighten people into surrendering their grain. Here, where the Family lived, there was no need.

The Baked Man lowered the ladder for them down the inside wall. "Duhdo duhdo genzu," murmured Stefile as she began to climb down. "I am sorry, Sir. I was surprised."

"Oh! I was never beautiful to begin with." The Baked Man could not smile, only nod, up and down, quickly.

The first courtyard in the Row of Eagles was full of blacksmiths and bakeries and food stalls. Beyond that, through a gate marked by a pair of wings, Cara and Stefile entered the School of Spiders.

The Men Who Advance like Spiders were sliding down translucent webs from the top of high scaffoldings. They swept down low across the courtyard, screeching like birds in black lacquered armor. They carried scythes and sliced through the heads of rows of wooden dummies.

The Row of Eagles led through each of the Fighting Schools. In the School of Shadows, men fought in tandem with nimble, life-sized puppets, attached to their arms and legs by gleaming rods. The Shadows duplicated the movements of their masters, and could double or treble the size of an army. The bobbing heads were the peeled skulls of enemies.

"Caro!" Stefile called, using the male form of the name, as Cara strode on. "Caro, I want to see!" She had to trot after her, holding up the dirty edge of her dress from the ground.

"And I want to get there quickly," Cara replied, low voiced, and Stefile realized that even Cara, who she thought could do anything, could be anxious about what lay ahead.

Finally the Row of the Eagle met the Row of the Sky. The pitted worn stone over the gate in the adjoining wall showed a sun and crescent moon in clouds.

This courtyard was different from all the others. The walls were washed with immaculate red, and the pavement was an unmarked, blinding white. The sun over the gateway had also been painted white, and the moon yellow amid deep indigo. At the far end of the courtyard stood a kerig, a grand house, with bay trees on either side of the great carved doors. In the center of the courtyard, a mulberry tree grew out of a tub of brick. In its shade, a man in white sat cross-legged, his eyes closed. As Cara and Stefile began to approach him, he opened his eyes, and stretched out his legs. He watched them balefully, as if in warning. It was a peculiar garment he wore, loose and spotless, that seemed to stretch with his movements. It was almost a robe, except that somewhere just above the knee it began to be bound around his legs with white strips, so that it worked like a pair of trousers. He was barefoot, and wore a bracelet around his left ankle. In his golden hair, laurel leaves were intertwined.

Cara and Stefile turned and smiled at each other. We both like the same men, Stefile thought. She glanced between Cara and the Angel, and decided that Cara was the more beautiful.

The Angel was middle-aged, she saw when they drew closer, and had a fierce, exacting, leonine look to him that was not warming.

"Why do you smile?" he asked them.

"Pride," Cara replied.

"Then prepare to lose it," the Warrior Angel said, and looked away from them in something like disgust. "He sent you to be an Angel?"

"Yes."

"Poison in his eyes. He thinks everything not swollen or scarred is radiant. You are better than your girl, I grant you. Your legs are thin."

"He was wounded, he's been healing!" Stefile exclaimed.

"In a fight?"

"Yes," Stefile replied, emphatically, angry.

"Then he is not much of a warrior, is he?" The Angel stood away from the brick of the tub, and began to strut, still looking away from them. "You might of course develop. We will not turn you away. You will stay with us for one month. At the end of that time, all of us will vote on whether you stay or go. We vote on your wife as well. If she is your wife."

"Why?"

The Angel finally looked back at Cara, blinking with the self-evidence of the answer. "Because both of you must live with us." He inspected Cara. "What is beauty?" he asked.

"That which is pleasing," Cara replied, meaning that he was not, despite the sleek workings of his forearms and the grandeur of his face.

The Angel, unmoved, signaled with a grudging frown that the answer was acceptable enough. "A retreat is not pleasing. It is sometimes necessary. Then it must be done so quickly that even the enemy admires it. A blow must be beautiful. It must be quick and clean and kill at once. Armor is ugly. Swords are ugly. Only the human form is beautiful. It must dance in battle, unaided. And it must win."

Suddenly he strode forward, eyes hard, meeting Cara's. "Do not mistake, boy from the fields. Beauty is not womanly. It is not cowardly. It does not lose. We are the best fighters here. The other Schools know that. They fear us. They engage each other, but not us because we always kill them." He relented somewhat, relaxing, and turned away from Cara, and began to strut again. "The Men Who Cut Horses are stronger, but they are brutal, merely. They are not slow, but neither are they fast. The Shadow Warriors are the ugliest; they are clumsy; we tangle them up in their metal coils. The Baked Men cannot be hurt, like the Men with Wrists of Steel, but they are not aggressive enough to win. The Poison Men come closest, but they rely on it too much; they are undertrained. We break them open like rotten fruit." He gave a quick, joyful smile at the thought. The smile went hard and threatening as he spoke to Cara. "If you stay with us, boy from the fields, with your"—he glanced at Stefile—"one-dress bondwife, we will make you nimble enough to climb up panes of glass and hang there for hours if we want you to. We will make you fast enough to run across the top of flowing rivers. You will know beauty alive when you see five arrows flying through the air toward your heart, and you catch them all."

"In my teeth or with my bare feet?" Cara asked, weary of all this boasting.

"If we wish it. Yes," replied the Angel with a hard, little smile. "You are hungry. You will eat with us, and join in the training this afternoon. Now we are washing and praying. We wash our entire bodies before we eat. I think you'd better wash too. It is a ritual. You will learn such rituals are important. My name is Haliki."

Stefile chortled, somewhat deliberately, at the silliness of the name. Haliki meant, literally, Sir Hero.

Haliki looked at her, up and down. "Haliki," he repeated. "You will not be able to do very much around here without me. Now go and wash."

There were rooms where water fell on their heads. Cara and Stefile were very grateful for it after their travels. They followed the sound of mass murmuring into a hall. There, deep within the brickwork, cool and shaded, were rows of wooden tables, with centerpieces of white fleshy flowers and white berries. Butterflies flitted among them, and there were candles to give a rich orange light. From somewhere came the cool pattering of a fountain, and the rattling of paper leaves in the air ducts.

The last of the Angel Warriors and their wives were filtering sedately to places along the benches. They all wore white, spotless white that had been freshly put on. Flowers were entwined in the hair of the women; jewelry, thick plain gold bands in layers, hung around their necks.

Cara and Stefile found a gap along one of the benches and sat together. The food, raw fish and raw salad in red clay bowls, was out of their reach.

"Friends or masters, we thank you for the food," said Cara, with country politeness. No one moved. "We have arrived after a long journey. We have had no breakfast."

"Hisho, dear friend, would you like some more fish?" one of the women said to a Warrior across from her.

"No, Klara, thank you. Would you like some yourself?"

The woman answered yes, and the bowl was passed to her and glances at Cara carried meaning. She had been given a lesson in manners. Here, one did not ask for anything directly.

"Dear friend, would you like some more fish?" Cara asked the woman.

"No, thank you," replied the woman, with a half smile, and looked away. She was not going to offer.

"Then you will not mind if I take some," replied Cara, and stood up, and arched across the woman and took both bowls.

As if it had been a signal, everyone else at the table began to pass everything that was on it to Cara, in contempt: flowers, spoons, bowls, the salt keeper, pitchers of water. They pushed the heap forward until some of the pottery spilled on the floor and broke.

"Is that enough?" the woman asked, with cold amusement.

"Yes," replied Cara, and began, out of anger, to eat directly out of the serving bowl with her fingers. The man across from her groaned.

"We shall simply have to break that too when it is finished," said the woman, airily.

"Tell me," said the man. "What sort of creature eats like that?"

"The kind that has to sit with its consort at table, because it knows it is out of place."

Stefile felt her uncut black hair, stringy with water in front, dry and caked with dust behind, and pulled on it. Very gently, Cara reached up and took her hand, and lowered it gently again to the table. With exaggerated ceremony, she poured Stefile some water.

A question seemed to hover in the air between the Angels, and then receive an answer. As one, they stood up, gathering their robes about them, making inconsequential conversation as they moved to other tables. Stefile and Cara ate alone at the long table.

The Warriors resumed training in the late afternoon when it was cooler, and half the courtyard was in shadow. They rinsed their mouths with mint in milk, and removed their robes and dressed in loose clean garments. They went out into the yard carrying parasols to preserve their complexions. The women hid away from the light, in their rooms. No one spoke to Cara or Stefile, so they sat together under the mulberry, the lowering sun in their eyes.

"They are pigs! Pigs!" said Stefile, murderously, near tears. "I will kill them!"

Cara tried to take her arm, but Stefile pulled it away in anger. "No one has ever spoken to me in that way. I tell you I may be a bondwoman who has always lived among bonded people, but I have never seen the lowest of us forget hospitality and true good manners like these people. We always give strangers food if we can. It is a good duty, and if their ways are different from ours, we look at the person beneath them."

"We will go," said Cara, and stood up. "Come on. We cannot stay."

"No," said Stefile giving her head little shakes. "What about what you have to do?"

"We will find another way."

"We will stay and kill their prince, eh?" Stefile's gaze was intent and fierce. "That will push their beauty back down their gullets. May the Family kill them all in revenge." Her feelings got the better of her. Her voice began to waver, and she stood up, abruptly, and swept her dress about herself, like the highest lady of the highest house.

"Thank you, Lady," Cara said, and Stefile walked quickly away, shoulders hunched, back toward Cara. Tears, Stefile had been taught, were part of your naked soul escaping; it was bad to let anyone see them. Cara understood that, and did not call after her. She walked back into the kerig. The Angels sat straight-legged, heads resting on their knees, backs arched.

"They will break you if they can," said a voice, and Cara turned.

Behind her stood a middle-aged man with a broken nose and a pot belly. He did not wear clean white robes, but a brown loincloth. He did not carry a parasol; his skin was dark from the sun. "And if they break you," he continued, "they will send you home, for you are not strong enough. And if they do not break you, they may simply dislike you."

"Who are you?" Cara asked.

"I am Galad. I am the trainer. Am I wrong in thinking you are a new candidate?"

"No, you are not," Cara replied, and asked with a nod at the Angel Warriors, "Do they call that fighting?"

The Angels had begun what looked to Cara merely like a very spectacular dance, with high leaps and spins in midair, and dives toward the ground that turned into somersaults. They grabbed each other by the arms and threw each other in circles.

"It is fighting of the most deadly kind," replied Galad. "You will see, later."

"Are there so few of them?" Cara asked, having counted roughly sixty of them.

"Most of them are in the great house. They guard there three days, and spend one in training."

"And how long, Master, does it take to become a fighter of this School?"

"Three years," replied Galad, "before you know the basic positions."

"And how likely is it that new candidates are accepted?"

"Of every fifty, one."

Cara nodded. "Then we'd best begin." She unbuckled her armor and leaned it against the tub of the mulberry, feeling a certain sense of relief: she need not worry about being accepted by the School; she need not accept its customs or its manners; she did not have time to learn its techniques. She would have her month in the Most Important House, and that would have to be enough.

"The first thing you must master," said Galad, "is the positions. Without accomplishing the positions, you will not be able to perform the movements. This is the first." Galad sat on the white stone, cross-legged, and bent down, and despite his paunch, put his chin on his lap and his forehead on his feet. "And the second," he said without strain in his voice, and arched backward until his forehead touched the pavement behind him.

"Try," said Galad, and Cara did, and of course failed.

"Don't move in sharp jabs," said the trainer. "Move slowly, as far as you can, and then hold it."

The Angel Warriors began to gather around her.

"He has a back like an iron rod. He is a cripple!"

"These country men do too much coarse labor. It ruins them for anything precise. He'd be of more use as a pack horse."

"Or a Carrier for the Family."

"Would you like that, country man? To be a Carrier?" Haliki teased Cara.

"He does not even know what it is!" chuckled one of them.

"Harado, my friend," said Haliki, sounding pained. "For appearance's sake, get rid of this boy's armor, will you. It offends me."

"I should not touch it, if I were you," said Cara, and succeeded in putting her head on her knees.

"A threat?" said Haliki, amused. He squatted behind Cara and placed the edge of his hand along her back. "A blow. Right there. You would open up."

Cara sat upright, and looked around at him. "I merely made a statement of fact. That armor has a mind of its own. I should not touch it."

"Get *rid* of it," said Haliki, wearily.

One of the Angels tried to pick up the sword. It leapt away from him.

"Ah," said Haliki, "Magic. We have someone from a traveling show. What other tricks do you have to amuse the peasants?"

"Are you a peasant, to be amused?" Cara asked. She looked at Haliki as steadily as she could. "I know what you are doing, Sir Hero. Go away and let me learn my positions. As you had to."

"He has heart," said one of the Angels, simply.

"Only because he does not know what he is facing. Watch, magician, and learn who we are." Haliki patted Cara on the back, and stood up. The others followed him, filing out of the courtyard through one of the gates.

"Rest," said Galad, sitting beside Cara. "And watch."

The Angels, returning, carried three huge rocks among them. The boulders seemed to float in the air, the Angels using only one finger each to support them. They were lowered gently; the Angels stood back.

Haliki blew at the stone. "Wawawa," he said, and thrust his hands toward it, palm first. His hands stopped, and vibrated, as if with reverberations. Then, with one movement, he dived for the rock, like a swimmer, hands flattened against each other into a head like a spear. He plunged into the stone, breaking it into thirds. Each third stood poised for a moment, as if in surprise, before rolling apart with a rumble on the pavement. Haliki stood, to light applause.

"They sense the faults in the stone," said Galad. "They sense the faults within the human body. They find the faults in the mind, the hairline cracks in the soul that weaken. Men who attack them with swords end up cutting themselves in confusion. To fight them is to fight air that suddenly becomes a fist. Never fight them. In a fight, you absolutely could not win. Please, country soldier. Remember that!"

Cara tried the first ten positions, as the afternoon faded. In the last red light of sunset, people approached along the top of the broken walls, with a beating of gongs and drums and thin reedy wailings from flutes, and with the swaying of great umbrellas over them.

"Galu," said the trainer, in a flat, guarded voice.

Cara saw how they approached and she knew then that she faced a very great evil indeed. She saw what the Angels had called Carriers.

The Galu rode men, as though they were horses. The first Carrier was a giant, with great heavy arms, and bulky legs and buttocks and sure broad feet. The top of his head had been cut away, to make him stupid and docile. His eyes were blinkered either side of his head, and he champed a bit inside his mouth. The Galu, astride his back, was completely covered in black. Even his face was covered by a lustrous black leather mask, without a mouth. On the feet were spurs.

"Are they women, to hide their faces so completely?" Cara wondered aloud.

Galad shook his head. "Those? They are the Sons." Cara's heart caught, with hope and hatred. "They are only ever seen at night, or just at sunset, covered like that."

"Galo gro Galu?" Cara asked, her voice rising.

"Sometimes it is him."

Behind the first was a second Carrier, who had been born an idiot, with no brain. His forehead stopped just above the eyebrows, and his hair, as though confused by the lack of its allotted space, was clotted and thick and crowded with swirls. The empty eyes were not blinkered, but looked around the world in delight. One of the Galu held up a hand, and the parade stopped, on the wall above the School of Angels. The orchestra, in single file, stopped sawing and bashing and whining. The Galu who rode the mutilated giant dismounted and strode to the edge of the wall and looked down. The Angels paused, and genuflected, and then went on with their practice with renewed vigor.

Cara realized that the Galu was looking at her. Cara bowed, hand on chest. It was a gesture of purest hatred. The Galu, hidden in folds of cloth, seemed to swagger with amusement. Then with deliberation, he plucked away his mask, and smiled down. It was a chilling smile, full of knowledge, and Cara had the sudden, unreasoning fear that the creature knew who she was. She strained to recognize the hateful face. In the light of day it was as white as a frog's belly, and the fringe of hair was not silver but uncolored, like a cobweb, or the hair of an albino or someone who has recovered from fever. The face was squinting with pain at the light, but with a swelling of certainty and purpose and relief Cara saw that it was indeed Galo gro Galu, the Worm in the Flower, the destroyer of her family. She would have her chance, her magic year would not be wasted or forlorn. Her joy was fierce beyond disguise. She grinned and bowed, and grinned and bowed, and the Galu gave her a mocking salute. Galad looked away from her, pondering.

The evening meal was held in the same chamber, with even more ceremony. Flutes played, and at the entrance there were bowls of lemon water which the Angels and their women patted on their foreheads and wrists. There were new flowers on the table and new flowers in the hair, and sheaths of gold cloth over the white robes. As the Angels marched into the chamber, fresh from bathing, Cara heard the distant sound of raucous laughter from the other Schools, and loud rough singing and cheers—the loutish awkward joy of soldiers released like gawping boys from discipline. She looked at the faces around her that were tense and bitter, and she understood that here there was no release from discipline, no relenting of control, no revealing of any weakness.

"You looked slow today," one of them said to another.

"Speed is not strength," was the reply. "But I understand that difference is difficult for you to appreciate."

"Hello, dear friend," said an Angel, perhaps too loudly, clasping the back of his companion's neck. "Surely, you could not have said the things about Haliki that Bovik tells me you have said?"

The returning smile was as sharp as a knife. "I do not know what Bovik told you. But I do know that one often hears what one wished to say oneself, rather than what has actually been said."

This is a dreadful place, thought Cara. How like the respectable grandmothers of the village they were, pretending to confide and comfort, while all the time trying to establish their higher rank. She found herself a place at table, and people moved away, farther down the bench. Cara looked around anxiously for Stefile. Would she come at all?

The bondwoman came from the interior entrance, from the rooms where the Angel wives had hidden away from the sun. At first Cara did not recognize her. Stefile strode in, holding herself tall, carrying her pride as if it were an egg that could drop and break. Somehow she had beaten her road-weary dress until it looked new— the dirt between the thick wool threads was gone—and she had flattened it somehow so that there was not a ruck in it. Her hair, by some peasant festival trick, had been braided and then woven into a perfect sculpture of a flower, a land lily, a graceful horn of glossy black. Tenderly, Cara arranged food near them so that they would not have to ask for any. Back erect, like a princess, Stefile scornfully lowered herself beside Cara, her glaring eyes daring anyone in the room to comment.

"Some bread, Lady?"

"Thank you, Sir."

It was a frugal meal. Crusty bread and water and bean paste and a clove of garlic. As they began to eat, one of the warriors rose, with a lyre, and said, "A song." There was light applause. He began to sing in a high, pure voice, songs of death and murder and all manner of defacement and maiming. "We hung their guts like garlands about the trees. We made their voices wail. All the riches of their bodies spilled like treasure to the ground." Cara pushed her plate away from her. The hideous song went on and on.

"How many of you!" Cara suddenly shouted. "How many of you have ever even seen a battle?"

The singer faltered, and lapsed into silence. There was a horrified pause, because that question had only one answer.

"I'll tell you! None of you have! Not one. There has been no killing here since the fall of Gara han Gara, and that was only the gutting of a sick old man and the stoning of his sons—who you were pledged to protect. If you had ever seen anything like a battle, you could not sing so lightly of murder. You could not say it was beautiful!"

Cara thought of her father, and it seemed suddenly that she would choke. She was weeping, and she stood up, desperate to get out of the room, and stumbling over the bench, strode quickly out of the chamber.

Stefile remained behind. She sat erect, and raked each of the Angels and their women in turn with her eyes. Conversation gradually resumed, light chatter as if nothing had happened, but none of them could meet Stefile's gaze. "Music! More music!" called Haliki, but the next, uncertain song was a love song.

Outside, in the courtyard flooded by moonlight, Cara wept with rage and disgust and remembrance. It was some time before someone, a mere moving shadow in the ice-blue light, came silently toward her. It was Galad, the trainer.

"What you said was the truth," he whispered to Cara. "They will not forgive that."

"I know," replied Cara, drawing in a shaky breath. "I will never be an Angel now, and I tell you I don't want to be."

"You are here for a reason, aren't you?" Galad said.

Cara poised, hovering, and then answered him. "Yes."

"You won't have time to learn any of the Angel techniques. But you have a sword and armor. I can teach you how to use those."

"Thank you," replied Cara. "But how? When?"

"It will have to be done at night, when the others are done. I think you will learn quickly."

"I have not much time."

"A word," said Galad, glancing about him. "If it is Galo gro Galu you wish to . . . meet." The trainer was in an agony of embarrassment. "Then only wear your loincloth."

Cara looked at him puzzled for a moment, and then understood.

"That is why he comes to watch," said Galad, and shrugged as if to cast something off. "We begin now?"

"We begin now," said Cara.

The days passed in a pattern. Cara limbered and stretched, and found that this gave her more strength. It made her more at home in her body. Galad made a show of teaching her the basic lessons of the School. At night, under the clear sky of This Country, he taught Cara sword and shield play. "No, no, don't think," he hissed at her in exasperation. "The moment you think, I can see you go uncertain. Somehow your body knows all the tricks." But it was good to be reminded: never sit with your back to a door, keep your sword on your left side, remember the aim is not to parry but to strike. Strangely enough, Haliki did not interfere with these night time sessions. "Country Boy knows he will not be here long, and he has the wit to see he cannot fight. Broken Nose teaches him ugly warfare, which is all he is good for."

It was Stefile who Haliki pressed mercilessly, calling her Dirty One Dress and Chin Dribble. "Her hands are so rough from work that they draw blood. It is a mystery to me how the two ruffians make love"; and then, "Poor little thing. What a shame you do not have a man to defend you." It was done out of malice, human and inexplicable. During the day, Haliki practiced fighting men with swords. "Do not fight him," murmured Galad. All the time she was there, Cara held her temper, nursing her secret revenge.

Every day at sunset, Galo gro Galu came to look at her.

"When it happens," Cara told Galad, "tell Stefile. Tell her to leave, then, quickly. If she asks where the Galu has taken me, don't tell her. She must get away. We have arranged a place to meet outside the City. Make sure she leaves for there, gets out of the House. Tell her also," Cara added, "that I think of her as my wife."

It was in the third week of Cara's month that the Galu came at night, instead of sunset. He wore only his purple wrapping and his coiled necklace, and he sat on the edge of the wall, an almost luminous white in the night, casting a long moonshadow across the courtyard. He applauded Cara and called out, "Oh, brave, brave, well struck!" and laughed. Cara stepped forward, in her loincloth with her sword. "Good evening, Master," she said.

"Good evening, warrior!" He swung his pale legs back and forth like a child. "Come up and talk to me."

"I am too humble, Master. I must train," replied Cara. "And besides, how am I to reach you?"

The Son of the Family laughed again, a high musical laugh. He stood up and unwound the cloth from around his middle until he was naked, and lowered it over the edge of the wall. "Climb up," he said, challenging, insinuating, ordering.

"Can you hold me, Master?" Cara asked, lowering her eyes from his nakedness, which sickened her.

"I am stronger than you think," the Galu said, with a voice like ice.

Cara could not look around at Galad, out of shame and fear that the Galu would see something between them. "We all live only by hope," she thought to herself. Without looking back she walked to the wall, and with a gathering of sweaty stillness realized that her time had come, that she might not see Stefile again, that she herself would probably die. The Galu certainly would. She grabbed hold of the purple and scrambled up the wall, her sword, sheathed, hanging from her waist. The armor and shield, leaning against the wall, were told by her mind to follow.

"There you are," said the Galu, lifting her with arms like straggly bands of steel. "And here you are." The smile was fixed and the eyes unblinking, as Cara remembered, the Galu hugged her, pressed himself against her, and whispered, "Have you ever loved a man, my warrior?"

Cara told the truth. "Yes, Master."

The Galu chuckled, a low ugly sound from somewhere deep in his throat. "Let's walk," said the Galu, slinging his purple over one shoulder. He put an arm around Cara's waist and padded along the broken walls next to her. His skin was cold, even clammy.

"I cannot bear this," thought Cara, and longed for it to be over, longed to be hidden from sight, safe from eyes, so that she could do it quickly and escape.

"I love night," said the Galu. "It is so cool and quiet and still. Day is too bright and scorching. You like the night too, don't you? Isn't it beautiful?" He stopped to look over at the temple, the ancient ziggurat, looming up in layers over the even, broken walls. "Look at my house."

"It is decaying," said Cara.

"That is why it is beautiful," replied the Galu, and picked up a piece of broken brick with his bare and supple foot, and dropped it over the edge. "I like ruin. Listen. You can hear air move in the grass that is growing out of the walls. I like that too." The Galu brushed the grass with his foot and then stepped back to let Cara admire his nakedness. Cara looked away, but glimpsed despite herself the blue-white, deformed, bald organs of his sex. The Galu chuckled again, that deep awful sound. "Oh! But he is embarrassed. He is modest. Well then, I must cover myself." The Galu did so by pressing himself against Cara again. "He is so warm. It must be the sun." The Galu smiled with his lifeless teeth and kissed Cara; she thought she would gag and she pulled her head away.

"Not here," she blurted out, and glanced about them.

"Oh, my Prince is embarrassed," hissed the Galu, taking hold of Cara's ears so that she could not turn away again. "Where would my Prince like to go?"

"It is said that I will not be selected. I will not be here long. I would like to see the palace."

"He wants to see the Most Important House. Then of course he will." The Galu took Cara's hand, and his fingers were like chilly claws, and he led her back and forth and across the top of the maze of stone, and Cara began to dread that she would not be able to find her way out again. The honeycomb of stone seemed to cover all the world out to the horizon. She glanced back and saw her helmet and shield peering over the top of a wall as though they had eyes.

Finally the Galu led her down a single staircase from the walls into the shadows of the inner house, kerigs around courtyards, like the Schools.

The palace was lit inside only by low guttering torches, and the corridors were stark. There was hardly any furniture, a carved stool, perhaps, against a wall, an old tapestry fallen and crammed dusty into a corner. The friezes had dropped in sections from the walls. Reliefs of armies of marching men were interrupted by breakage, their faces mottled by flaking paint. In one vast, dim, empty chamber were carvings of Asu Kweetar, the Most Noble Beast, winged, god-given. The gouges across the images seemed to Cara to be deliberate defacement. What kind of sacrilege was it to deface the most beautiful creature? The legends called it The Beast that Talks to God, and every child yearned to see it in the sky. What kind of sacrilege was it to reduce the Most Important House to this state? As they walked, Cara heard the fluttering of wings and the scuttling of delicate little claws. There was the hooting of an owl, and the sudden, heart-stopping swoop of bats toward and then away from Cara's face.

In front of the door to Galo gro Galu's chamber an Angel stood on guard. The Angel was Haliki.

Haliki began to laugh. "So little Dirty One Dress has something new to learn," he said, grinning.

"Haliki will not mock my Prince," said the Galu, stroking the hair on the nape of Cara's neck. "Haliki will not laugh too long, either."

Haliki mastered himself. "Yes, Master," he murmured, but his eyes followed Cara, glistening with amused delight.

"It does not matter about me," Cara thought, feeling the presence of the Angel Warrior behind her. "If I have to die to kill the Galu, it will be worth it." She followed Galo into his bedchamber, and the door was closed behind her.

The room smelled like an abattoir, and was dark, no windows. A single candle burned on the floor amid encrustations of wax. This room too was bare, only pillows and cloth on the floor. The Galu stood, expectant. Before she would have to do or see more, her mind benumbed and determined, Cara drove her sword straight into the chest of Galo gro Galu, where she hoped his heart would be.

The Galu groaned, and rolled his head, and looked at Cara with eyes that seemed to shiver.

"Oh, not so *soon*, my love," he cooed. "You will ruin it. Slice slowly."

Cara could not understand; she thought she had misheard; she thought the Galu did not yet realize he had been struck. Then the Galu stepped toward her on the sword, eyes full of yearning. Stepped forward, and then stepped back. Forward and back, forward and back. Blood welled up into his mouth, and down his chin, and he licked and swallowed it.

"Ah! Ah!" squawked Cara, in horror, and tried to wrench the sword out of him. The Galu smiled and reached up, and took hold of the hilt, and passed it to her. Then, like a yielding virgin, he settled down onto the pillows, and licked his fingers, and smeared the blood down his belly. He fingered the edge of the wound, gently, in delight. Cara struck at him, clumsily, to make him stop, to wipe away what she was seeing. She cut him across the shoulders and face.

"That's it. That's better," said the Galu, and smiled. This time the teeth were red. "I know who you are," he said, and gasped. "Dear, Dear Daughter. I know who you are." Darkness was spreading out evenly all around him, seeping across the cloth. "Look," said the Galu, with a voice like the dying wind.

There was a sudden crackling noise and the Galu groaned again—merely groaned—and writhed on his bed, and with a sound like the splitting of logs the wound in his chest broke wide open from the base of his throat to the bottom of his belly.

Great petals of flesh, thick, black, like a flower, erupted out of him. Cara watched, uncomprehending, as stems rose out of the midst of the petals, rustling, bearing on their ends three clear, crystalline globes like jelly with spiralings of gold flakes within them. The Galu was still alive. "The Secret Rose," he whispered. A bubble of blood burst in his mouth, and he looked up at the thing with love. "Beautiful. The Secret Rose." His eyes went staring, and then glazed.

"No," said Cara, rejecting. "No. No. No. No. No." And she began to beat the sword against the stone, not knowing why, only knowing that what had happened was monstrous and wrong, only knowing from the Galu's face that this and nothing else was what he had wanted, knowing who she was. The great black petals shifted and sighed, and bestirred themselves, reaching out, settling over him, quivering, alive, inhuman, inhuman as the Galu were inhuman, whatever they were.

Cara backed away from it, eyes gaping, and felt her way out, opening the door.

"Finished?" a voice asked behind her. "Was it a surprise?"

Haliki stood behind her, grinning. Cara could not answer him. "There's blood on your sword, Country Boy. I'm going to have to kill you."

Wake, Cara, wake, she told herself, and she lifted up her sword with what seemed nightmarish slowness. Haliki laughed at her, and with a malicious grin spun his arms completely around from the elbow, like blades, in the air. Then, without a twitch of movement in his legs, he casually flung himself at her, hands outstretched, and Cara felt a flutter about her head, and she was enveloped. There was a sound like ringing metal, and crumpling pain across her chest. But she was alive.

"Ouch!" yelped the Angel, nursing the edge of his hand. Cara's armor hugged and protected her. The Angel's eyes were fierce, and hard. "Magic. I would have thought you had seen magic enough tonight."

And suddenly he was spinning through the air toward her, a whirligig, arms and legs moving with mindless speed, and Cara danced backward away from him, trying to follow the rolling and ducking and weaving with her sword to strike him, and suddenly there was a hard line of pain across her arm. Her own sword was buried deep within it. The Angel's face was suddenly right against her own, with a smile like a box full of teeth, and there was suddenly a smashing and rending in the center of her body and she felt her heart judder, and stop, and clench, and begin again. She couldn't breathe. She thought of her sword—lift it up out of the arm, swing with it. But the sword was gone. Where was the sword? The Angel's grinning face returned. The tips of his fingers flicked at her solar plexus.

Cara felt like a pile of stones that had suddenly come apart, and she rolled to the floor, and seemed to lie in pieces. Her fingers felt thick and numb, and they tingled as they did in winter when she plunged them into warm water. Her legs lay sprawled and leaden. She couldn't move. She could move nothing at all. Even her eyes couldn't blink and the suddenly parching air stung them and made them fill with tears. Her lungs worked, like a trembling rabbit in her chest, and hopelessness spread over her like a stain of blood.

The Angel strutted. "I am going to enjoy this," he said. "I am going to break each bone in you, one by one." His braceleted foot rose over her legs, the heel pointed downward, like a spear.

The blow did not come. Cara's vision was blurred, but she saw him wince, heard his hiss. She saw him rotate his head, as though his neck were stiff, and he stepped back, lowering the heel flat on to the floor. Then he sank to his knees.

Through rainbow refractions of light, and the trembling of tears, Cara saw it was Stefile astride him, with the sword burrowed deep into the back of his neck.

Stefile leaned over him, and whispered into the Angel's ear. "For all your kindnesses, Master," she said in a voice that was chilling with hatred. "For all your gentle words." She gave the sword a twist within his neck and Haliki shrieked, a shrill, high keening cry like an eagle. His hands fluttered like the wings of birds caught in a net, and his tongue lolled heavily out of his mouth. She would not let him fall.

"Know this before you die, Mister Hero," Stefile said. "You were killed by little Dirty One Dress." The Angel moaned in protest, unable to speak. "You were killed for all your bold talk and fancy dancing by a bondgirl of sixteen winters who has never held a sword in her life." Then she ripped the sword out of him and pushed him, face forward, down onto the stone.

Stefile stood over Haliki for a moment, her breath rattling in and out of her, and she wiped her upper lip. Then, with a sudden expulsion of breath, she turned to Cara, droppd down beside her, and jammed the sword through the thick wool of her dress. Furiously, she jerked it across the bottom, cutting away a strip of cloth. Muttering peasant spells of healing, she tied the cloth across the wound in Cara's arm. Cara was suddenly able to blink and clear her eyes.

"Can't move!" Cara said, choking on her tongue.

"Oh, my poor love. Where are you hurt?"

"Get me up!" Cara cried in terror, seized by the unreasoning conviction that if she did not stand up now, at once, she never would again. "Get me up, now!" Stefile quickly felt along her legs for breakages, then unbuckled the armor at the shoulders and lifted it away. Warmth returned to Cara's arms, and she flailed them, helplessly. Across her chest, over her heart, was an enormous bruise. Stefile's fingers rippled across her rib cage. "Get me up!" bellowed Cara. "Now!"

"All right, all right. Sssssh!" Stefile stepped around behind Cara, and lifted her up by the arms, and dragged her back toward the wall. "Cal Cara, you're always getting yourself cut up. And I'm always having to carry you." She grunted with the weight and tried to pull Cara up, to prop her against the wall. Cara's clumsy arms tried to reach around to climb up it; Stefile ducked underneath them and pushed up. There was a stinging and then an ache down Cara's thighs, and then fire seemed to pour down all the nerves in her legs and along the bottom of her feet. Hesitantly, she made them accept some of the weight.

"How," Cara asked, "did you *find* me?"

"The armor and the shield led me. They came back for me. The sword just came into my hand. Can you stand? Oh, Cara! I have killed the chief of the Angels! I must be either a very wicked or a very powerful woman."

"Both," replied Cara, with a grateful, spasmodic smile.

"Did you kill yours?" Stefile's face was bright and tense and expectant.

Cara's smile stiffened. Horror and remembrance fell over her. Unable to describe or to account for what had happened, she could only nod yes.

Stefile gave a little snarl of pleasure, and clenched her fists and shook her head and did a little dance, kicking with her feet. "Oh, Cara. Then we're free! We've done it!"

Cara's eyes were haunted, and she shook her head.

Stefile was stilled. "Why, what's wrong?"

Cara tried to say, but found no words. She only pointed with the sword that was somehow back in her hand, toward the room of the Galu. Scowling, Stefile turned and climbed up the steps toward it.

"Don't go in!" warned Cara.

Stefile pushed the door, and it swung back across widening darkness. What was beyond it made a crackling noise, sharp and evil, like a rattlesnake. Stefile stepped back, hugging her stomach.

"What is it?" she asked quietly.

"I don't know! But oh, Stefile, he knew who I was! He wanted it to happen, he made it happen, he loved the sword, he lay down for it, and that thing came out of him, and he called it the Secret Rose!"

Stefile took two steps toward her, and then stopped. "The name of your cult?"

Cara only nodded.

"What does that mean?"

"I don't know!" wailed Cara, near tears.

Stefile looked at her, wide-eyed, solemn. "We have to get away." She strode back to the body of Haliki. "At least we have only killed one man, then. That lessens the sin." She rolled the Angel over, knelt beside him, and closed his staring eyes. There was no libation to pour, no offerings she could make to appease Haliki's spirit. "Don't follow me, Mister Hero," she warned it. "Or I will do something this terrible to you again."

Stefile thought very quickly of the life to which she could never return, and the life she had entered now. They had done something to the Son of the monstrous Family and killed the head of a Fighting School; the Angels knew their names and faces. Wherever they went, the fear of discovery would follow. They would have to travel to places where they were not known, where their families were not known. They would have to live any way that they could. They were outlaws. How could everything change so completely?

"This life is mad," she said simply. Then she gathered up her one dirty dress, and stood, and took the outstretched arm of her lover, and together they ran out into the darkness.

Chapter 5

Dear Daughter of the Important House

They had to live wilder and faster. By the time they reached the Village by Long Water, they rode horses that they had stolen. Feeling themselves to be reckless and outside the law, they foolishly dressed like it. Instead of the plain dress of common folk, they had taken the rich garb that Stefile had dreamt of, plundered from the same caravan as the horses.

Stefile wore a fine sheath dress from Aegoptus, to the South, made from the bleached fibers from the stems of a plant. It was translucent. She had to wear it over men's trousers to ride. She had a tiny gold flower inserted in a nostril, and a crown of gold, and a sword, and a long red cape. Cara was an even stranger sight: a massive, scarred warrior in armor, but with large hangings of jewelry from his ears and neck and arms, and great swathes of lace billowing out from his shoulders and tucked into his belt.

Anyone would know that they were outlaws.

They rode up the great canyon, between the walls of sheer rock that were a blazing white, moving in and out of cool shade, past rapids, where prickles of moisture in the air danced on their skin. They had to cross landscapes of wet fallen rock at the base of waterfalls, where everything was made dazzling by sunlight in mist, and they couldn't hear each other speak for the roaring noise. They made up their minds to go to the Other Country, in the North. The library of Cara's house had books that would tell them about the language spoken there. They made each other very excited, imagining the life they would have there and the things they would see.

Sometimes, though, in the heat of the day, away from the river, Stefile would go morose. "And this year, then. Is it true about this year?" she asked, her voice begging to hear that it was not.

"It is, Stef. True."

Stefile could not really imagine it; she could not really believe that her handsome friend had once been a woman and would be one again. She gave the reins of her horse a sudden, uncalled-for flick that meant bitterness. Either it was true, or Cara's insistence meant that she was mad, and Stefile could accept neither. "Well, can you make yourself as you are now, again?"

"I can't, no, the spell works only once."

"So what happens to me then?"

"We can only decide what to do when it happens," Cara said, gently. "Only then."

"How long is that? Until then?"

"Through this winter, to the end of next summer."

"How will it happen?"

"I don't know, Stef."

"I have followed you, I have come with you. I don't believe you."

"I don't believe it either, sometimes," said Cara in a quiet voice.

It was nearly dark when they entered the Village by Long Water, passing the first house, Manu Norig's. The air was full of the smells of cooking; low talk came out the windows through which candlelight flickered on warm-colored walls. They came upon Mala, a girl Cara had known from childhood, carrying water from the river. Without thinking, Cara greeted her. "Mala! Hello!" The girl glanced up at the armored man and his blazoned doxy, and looked down, her face closed tight, and began to walk very quickly. Cara remembered then, and clicked at the horse to move on. Mala heard the sound, and broke into a run, dropping the bucket. She slammed and barred the door of her house behind her.

As the darkness grew, so did the darkness of Cara's thoughts. It was fine to talk of adventure in the Other Country; it was fine to see her village again, but inside her house, as enduring as death, awaited the ruins of her family, the desecrated bodies of her father and brother. They rode past the rocks where cloth was beaten clean by the river; they rode up a hard, gravelly track, to the base of the cliffs and around the corner of a giant wall of rock.

"My house," said Cara in a faraway voice, yearning for the house of her past.

"That is where you live?" asked Stefile, in wonder.

The Important House was hewn out of the rock, midway up the cliff face, a line of dark windows under an overhang of limestone. Beside it, a kind of ceilinged yard had been hollowed out, with pens and stables within it for the animals in winter. The yard was empty. Two ramps of stairs made a zigzag up the face of the rock to it. There were buckets on pulleys, down to the well that no one drank from now. Around the well, below the house, clustered the round stone huts of the bondmen, and spreading out below them in layers of grassy ruin were the rice paddies down to the river and up the other side.

It was a sad, slow ride up the steps, forward in one direction, back in another. The house seemed not so high off the ground as Cara remembered it, or so grand. Within the shelter of the rock it was already night, though the clouds above the opposite side of the canyon were still pink. They put the horses into the pens.

"Do you want me with you?" Stefile asked.

Cara thought, and answered honestly. "No, Stef. Stay here. I don't know what I'm going to find."

The candles were in the old place, with the flints, just inside the only door. Cara struck them and the old kitchen flickered in ghostly light. The great round cistern, the fireplace that filled the yard with smoke, the old gray table. By the door was a row of heavy shoes that had not been needed since . . . Cara broke off the thought in haste.

"Who's there?" called out a voice, a strange voice, quavering in fear, that Cara at first did not recognize. She did not ever think of her father as being afraid.

"It's me, Father. Cara." Her male voice sounded deep and close by within the rock. A new misgiving came upon her. Had Aunt Liri told them what had happened? Had he believed her? Would he even know Cara for who she was? Steeling herself for that, and for what she would see, Cara went into the next room.

It was her father's favorite room, the library, the only room in the house that had windows in two directions. She held the candle over her head.

Her father and brothers sat strapped, limbless, to chairs, and their bandages were filthy and they were riddled with what looked like sores and their hair was matted, and their ribs and the sinews of their necks showed straggly through the skin, and the place stank of urine. On her father's face was a long fat vein that looked like an abscess.

"Where is Liri? Where is she?" Cara wailed. "I told her to look after you! I told her to feed and wash you! Where is Liri?"

"Liri? Liri cannot come near us," her father raged, with feverish eyes sunk in a hollow face. "No one can come near us, for what you have done!"

"Oh, Cara," said Tikki, in a small sad voice.

"Abomination! Abomination! Man-woman! Witch! You brought this on us!"

"Brought what? Father, what's wrong?"

She moved toward him, to hold him, comfort him, untangle his knotted hair. "Get away!" he roared at her.

"Cara! Don't come near!" Tikki wailed, and they writhed and twisted and shrugged in their bonds, trying to rock the chairs backward. "Don't come near us!" Tikki whispered.

The vein in her father's face seemed to throb; what looked at first like two rows of metal thorns emerged through the skin. They glinted in the candlelight, encircling flesh, closing. The flesh disappeared, and out of her father's face another tiny face slid out. It grinned, befanged, a visage like a child might model of a human face in clay, with tiny eyes that blinked. From all of the sores, across the once handsome shoulders and breasts and bellies of her family, from behind their ears, out of their nostrils slipped things as thick as a finger. Worms.

Cara's male voice bellowed, harsh with horror, and she stepped back, moaning, shaking her head. "What is it? What is it?" Stefile called from outside. She ran into the room, and stopped, and fell utterly silent. Cara, shivering, found a chair. Stefile stood behind her, clasping the back of her neck.

The worms looked at them, blinking. The worms spoke.

"We do not want to do this," said the worm in her father's face, in a high, piping voice.

"Forgive us, mistress," said another.

"The Galu make us do this," said a third. "We were their enemies, and this is how they punish us."

"But we must eat to live," said the worm in her father's face.

"Do not come too near us. Do not sleep in this house, or we will find you too. When your family dies, do not carry them out. Leave them, or we will slip into you as you bear them."

"How . . . long do they have to live?" Cara found herself asking them.

The worms turned to each other, and then looked back. "Sometime yet, mistress." Cara's father groaned, and shook his head. "We try not to pierce the vital organs for as long as we can. We try to make it last."

"We are sorry, mistress."

"We are sorry, sister."

"We were human too."

"They came in the night, Cara," said Tikki. "They covered the floor. We couldn't escape."

"How many nights ago?" Cara asked, and Tikki told her. The worms had come the night she had tried to kill the Galu. This was their revenge.

"What are the Galu?" Cara demanded. "What manner of thing?"

"They walk like men, mistress," pleaded the worms, in fearful, squeaking voices.

"They look like men."

"But they are not?" Cara demanded.

"Oh, do not make us answer that! We must not answer that! If we do that, they will punish us again."

"How could they punish you more horribly than this?" Cara asked, her voice controlled and even.

"The Galu can always think of something worse," whined the worm in her father's face.

"If you tell me," Cara said, "I promise to set you free."

The worms looked at each other, back and forth, and nodded their heads. "They walk like men, but they are not. Their love is different. To have sons, they must be murdered, out of hatred, by the children of God. If they tempt the fallen children so, then a blossom rises out of them, bearing three eggs, which grow into their children who are exactly like them. The Galu cannot change. They can only grow more numerous."

"Which they are doing now."

"You were not the first."

"They love killing," said the first worm.

"They love pillage," said another.

"They yearn for the knife," said a third.

"They will bring ruin."

"Cara," said Stefile, gripping her shoulder. "Cara, we must be away. You heard what they said. They will come for us."

"Yes," said Cara in the same, flat, damaged, weary voice. "Yes, yes, yes."

Outside, in the yard, four of the Old Women stood, arms folded.

"So, Cara," said Mother Danlupu, and tutted. "You return to see what your precipitous spells have done."

"Casting yourself as a great sorceress," said Hara. "You have caused a great disruption."

It was Latch whose eyes were hardest and most steady with hatred. "What a fool you look," she said, her smile arching with disgust at the earrings and the lace and, of course, at Stefile.

"Is there no pity?" Cara asked. "Then you are smaller than the worms. Even the worms have pity." She drew her sword. "Get out of my house," she said, calm, heavy.

"Abomination!" whispered Latch, smiling. "Abomination," they all whispered together, "Abomination," and made signs against her, to keep away the evil things that followed her path.

"Or would you rather sit in my father's lap!" Cara suddenly roared, and grabbed hold of the nearest, old Danlupu, and pulled her backward by both of her frail arms toward the house. Danlupu shrieked in terror at actually being seized, and bobbed birdlike and helpless in Cara's grasp, and began to weep. "Where is your Kasawa magic now? Where are your mighty spells?" Cara raged, and shook her, and the old woman began to beg.

"Cara, stop, please, she is old!" Stefile begged.

"In! In, and sit among the worms!" Cara held the old woman above the ground and her legs pumped in the air.

"Cara, please!" shouted Stefile.

Cara threw the old woman to the stone floor of the yard, and sat on her, and pressed a sword onto her throat. "What are you to the Galu?" she demanded.

"I don't know what you mean!" the old woman wailed.

"Their full name means 'the Secret Rose,' they become the Secret Rose, and 'Wensenara,' your name, means the same thing. What are you to the Galu?"

"I know nothing about the Galu!" the woman wept, wretched.

"When we came to offer help!" Hara's voice shook with indignation.

"Brave warrior to strike at old women!" hissed Latch.

"Hah!" cried Cara, and slapped her stingingly with the flat of her sword, and Latch shrieked and clutched

her side, convinced she had been cut. Her sister
gathered her in her arms and pulled her away.

"Out! Out! Out!" Cara raved and hauled the old
woman to her feet and flung her after her friends, who
were running now, down the steps, sobbing with fear.

Silence. The sound of wind up the valley and the
distant sound of weeping. Very suddenly, Cara sat down
on the stone.

"Cara?" whispered Stefile. "Cara, Cara, Dear One.
We can only leave. Come on." She tried to pull, but Cara
was unmovable, and staring.

The wind in the reeds by the river made sounds like
a sleeping child. All along the valley were lights in windows, as dim as fireflies, except around Cara's house and
the houses of her people, which were dark. There was no
moon, only stars, but they were bright enough to show
the river, winding as it always had, and to cast a line of
silver along the top of the opposite cliffs, as large and
familiar as the memories of her father. From somewhere,
far away, someone began to sing in a high, unsteady
voice.

Tears spilled suddenly out of Cara's eyes. She had to
gasp to get her breath back, and she stood up abruptly
and strode to the corner of the yard, to the stables that
still smelled of animals, and pressed her face into the
corner, caressing the stone with her forehead, and she
wept, helplessly.

"Oh, Cara," said Stefile, and tried to comfort her,
taking her arm, but the arm was as beyond comforting as
the stone. "Cara, don't weep. Weeping never does any
good. It is bad to weep."

Cara simply turned to her, eyes bulging and wet,
and screamed. What else was there to do but weep? She
tore the earrings from her ears, and the lace from her
shoulders.

"Oh, Cara," whispered Stefile, and softly held her.
"Peace." Cara writhed in her arms, to fight off easy comfort, then succumbed to pain and implacable reality, and
rested against Stefile. They stood together a long time,
in silence, as darkness progressed.

Finally Cara was able to speak. "She saw it."

"Who?"

"Ama," replied Cara, and staggered away from the wall, pulling Stefile with her to the edge of the court- yard. "All of it," she said in a faraway voice. "The Galu, the murders, and that in there. None of us understood, none of us knew what she meant. We thought she was mad." Trembling, as if with weakness, Cara sat, slump- ing clumsily, legs dangling over the edge of the cliff, as she had when she was a child. "The harvest of blood," she said. "The drought of womankind. The City is going to be destroyed, Stefile. We didn't understand. I don't think she wanted us to, then."

She stared ahead, unblinking. "They made us bes- tial, Stefile. They drive us. They make us as bad as them. We kill them, and they rise up three times as numerous as before. They are not born of women, there are no women among them, they do not know of family and love and mothering. They only know the knife, and ruin and silence. They will grow and grow and grow, and we can't fight them. If we fight them, we make them grow."

"Cara. My hand. You're crushing it," said Stefile, carefully, for Cara was beginning to unnerve her. Cara loosened her grip, and moved the hand to her lips, to kiss it. Instead, distracted, she began to mumble it in her mouth, taste its living saltiness. Fraught with wizardry and grief, she was seeing a picture in her mind.

She saw a field, a wheat field she somehow knew, far away, and it had been burned black, and an army marched across it, an army of Galu, in perfect grinning ranks, each with a fixed, identical smile. Humankind was in danger of being replaced.

"It's not a question of revenge, Stef. It's not a ques- tion of escape. There is no escape. We have to stop them, now, while they are still small."

"We can't do that," Stefile said, dreading another mission, and let a light blow from her clenched fist fall on Cara's shoulder.

"We have to. We're the only ones who know."

"How, Cal? How can you fight something you can't allow yourself to hit?"

"We could tie them up. Lure them, trick them, into a cage." She looked up at Stefile, blinking, confused, but no longer distraught and staring. The look reassured Stefile enough for her to become cross.

"Oh, yes, and who will you have to help you? How many times will they be fooled? How will you stop their brothers coming to untie them? Threaten them with a sword? And what about Haliki? He knew. What if all the Fighting Schools know, and are with them?"

"It will . . . have to be a new answer. The answer is there. It already exists. My mother said there would be an answer. I think she said I would find it." Cara tried to clear her mind, but it kept coming back to violence and entrapment. She felt a need to dissolve all her old ways of thinking. She said simply, "I need a vision." She stood up.

"Oh, *Cara*," said Stefile in sudden fury. "Yes, you are a man, I suppose, to go down the wells."

"My mother went to the wells. She had a vision." Unaccountably, Cara began to feel almost cheerful.

"That vision," said Stefile in weary scorn. "It is stupidity. The men march off into the hills, and starve themselves and drink nothing, and boil themselves in steam until they give themselves a fever, and then they say that they have seen things. To no one's surprise but their own. The vision means nothing. It is babble. Even my brothers have had a vision."

"What did they see?" Cara asked, suddenly amused.

"Oh! One of them became a tortoise, and lived in the mud. The other saw himself as a huge peach, which was eaten."

"It sounds like a kind of truth."

"The kind of truth in dreams and children's stories."

"There's truth in those." Cara's face was mild, almost smiling. "I'm going, Stef."

"I know," replied Stefile, rueful, with misgivings.

They led the horses back down the steps, with hesitant cloppings of hooves against the stone, the beasts snorting with unease in the dark. They rode most of the night, up the valley, along the cliffs, to the wells of vision, where the sons of the Village by Long Water went to become men.

They slept at the bottom of a well, a shaft cut deep into the rock, to avoid the attention of prowling beasts. In the morning, they built a fire in the pit and covered it with stones, and when these were blue-black with heat they poured water on them from buckets, lowered from above. With a hissing like a thousand serpents, the steam rose. "You will be very sick, and I will have to carry you again," Stefile said, and climbed the ancient rope ladder out of the well, leaving Cara below to await her vision.

Cara could hear the air move across the mouth of the well, and through the fir trees around the rock. The sun moved overhead, filling the well with hot light, and hot steam wafted over her skin, bringing forth pimples of moisture, as if from the skin of an orange that has been squeezed. It began to trickle down her in streams. "All my skin is weeping," she thought blearily. She had had no food since the morning of the previous day. Stefile had rice balls to eat. Cara could almost feel them in her mouth, plump and moist and chewy. The hunger would bring the vision more quickly. She poured more water on the stone, and watched the droplets dance with the heat.

In the center of Cara's head was a slow, sluggish dullness. She was tired, deeply exhausted by hatred and suspense and mourning, and violence and too many wounds, and by magic, the will it took to stay in the warrior shape of a man. Fatigue was a coiled lump within her. She wanted tranquillity. She wanted safety and solace and a chance to mend. She wanted light.

She saw light in the steam. It seemed to be dazzling, more bright than the sunlight in it. She was drifting, in and out of sleep, on the surface of sleep, where there are dreams.

And suddenly it seemed as if she were on the river. A loud, cheerful, piping little voice was calling out her name. She was hidden in a boat, behind reeds, and it was hot sluggish summer, slow clear water, not roaring spring. "Sssh," warned a smiling voice above her head, and Cara laughed, giggled a hearty, girlish chuckle. A dragonfly buzzed near her head, and two great white warm hands enfolded her. Cara turned and looked up at the sheltering, kindly, pale presence, the face dim and undefined, that she could never quite see.

"Ama," she whispered. "Ama."

Suddenly there was a shriek of joy and release, and Cara started awake, and in the blazing mist, rising out of it on its hind legs, a white horse reared up, and tossed its white mane, and shrieked again. It spun about itself in excitement, and trotted around the perimeter of the well, white tail lashing, and it halted in front of Cara, blinking with dark, kindly eyes. Cara held out her hand to it, and it shyly advanced, head down. Cara felt its gentle muzzle in her palm, flinching and soft and warm. She felt the surge of its breath, in and out. Summer wind. The sound of reeds.

And a high unsteady voice began to read to her. "Find the seventh cavern," it began, and Cara knew at once what it was reading. "Find the seventh cavern, with the door of carved stone." Cara saw herself, slim and naked and pubescent as she once had been, climb onto the white horse's back.

Suddenly she was riding the horse, flying on its back, through the steam of clouds. "Go through the door, the carved door, and through the doors, the seven doors, beyond it, the doors in the hall of stone." Cara heard her own adolescent voice read them too, as she had read them to her brother Tikki.

The horse plunged down through rock, brown stone that seemed to part for them like the bead curtains in Cara's room. "Find the seventh chamber and the casket made of lapis lazuli, and in the casket you will find the story of Keekamis Haliki, hero, and the things he did in the Better Times."

Cara saw the casket, and her heart caught. It was blue as the sky, with hints of green, glimmering with light reflected on its carvings. Her heart rose to her mouth as the lid of the casket rose. In a row, like bricks, were the seven tablets of the Book, the One Book, the truest copy of it, long lost, made by Keekamis Haliki himself in clay.

She read it again, and it seemed that she understood the story for the first time, understood the loss and confusion Keekamis Haliki felt when his friend died, how he mourned not just for him, but for all of humankind doomed by the Serpent to die, and how he rode—rode a white horse—down into the underworld, and met the Serpent, and learned how life and death and love came into being, and how the Serpent hated all three, even death, which was its only creation. She read about Hadam and Hawwah, the Father and the Mother of humankind and how the Serpent deceived them, in the Garden that had been the world. She read how Keekamis wrested the Flower from the Serpent, the White Flower that was Life, that would return life to humankind and all the beasts, that was all that remained of the Tree of Life. She read how he had fought the Serpent, and won the Flower, and then lost it again when he slept. She read very quickly, knowing the words.

Suddenly Cara was pulled through chilling mist, as icy as the breath of winter, and the white horse's breath caked its muzzle with a frozen, opaque sheath.

And Cara approached the coils of the Serpent, saw them clenched around its prize, and she saw the Flower through all of the Serpent's folds, like the sun through light cloud, clearly defined and bright. The layers of coil were rendered clear by its light, like jelly. The light reflected from the jewellike scales in many colors.

Cara's heart cried out for it, for the Flower was beautiful, the Flower was peace and kindness and flowing talk and music and good harvests. It was flocks of birds rising into the air, and clouds of blossoms on apple trees, and women's breasts, and the bursting forth of water and life; the light tread of feet, the mouth ready to smile, the eyes dilating with interest and response. It was the gamboling of calves in fields when released in the spring, the eagle sheltering its young under its wings. It was the love of wolves and the smile on the face of the dolphin, inexplicably loving humankind. It was the gift of words, the gift of fire, the gift of mind. It was life, eternal life, obdurate, unworried, steadfast, always blossoming outward, never closing, always bearing fruit.

The lid of the casket closed.

Cara was back in the pit, bereft of the Flower, and the sun had moved, and everything seemed dark and shriveled and sour, like fruit that was rotting.

The white horse was walking backward, into the stream, a tear on its veined, fleshy cheek.

"Don't go," murmured Cara. "Please don't go yet." The horse shook its silent head, eyes on Cara, and was lost in the mist.

Cara screamed. She screamed for water and for what the world had become, screamed for what had been lost and for humankind, who died, and for herself who was primitive and deadly.

Stefile came down for her, calling her name with worry, and Cara collapsed against her and wept.

"I told you it was folly! Was it terrible?"

"No, no," Cara wept.

"It looks like it. Moon-faced! Look at you! Here." She passed Cara a waterbag. The water in it was hot from the sun, and poured out of Cara's mouth as she guzzled it. "I don't suppose you got your answer."

Cara broke off drinking suddenly, and wiped her mouth and forehead. Panting for breath, she scowled in thought. "Yes," she said, warily at first, and then with more certainty. "Yes, Stef, I did. I did." She let water slop out of the bag, over her head.

"Then why the weeping?"

Cara let the water run off her. She turned to Stefile, with haunted eyes, and opened her mouth to try to explain. "I can't tell you, Stef," she said. "Come on. Help me up."

"Up? You're staying there to rest!"

"I'll sleep on the horse." Cara struggled to her feet.

"On a horse? You haven't eaten!"

"On the way, too."

"Where? Where are we going?"

"To the Other Country. To the Wensenara. But I have a promise to keep first." So saying, Cara turned and began, shakily, to climb.

They returned to the Important House. Cara wandered through each of its rooms. She had a tender, dazed look to her that Stefile found annoying. She wanted this horrible business to be brisk, but Cara seemed to be saying goodbye to everything. "Sister! Sister!" the worms joyfully cried out when Cara entered the library. She went through each of the books, stroking the pages as she turned them. Stefile did not understand books. They frightened her and made her feel angry that other people should know how they worked. "Hurry up!" she said. "It's the dregs of day already, and I'm not sleeping here!" Cara silently passed her three books. Stefile left the room, trying not to look at Cara's family, and packed bedding and clothes in a fury.

Cara laid out bowls of food and jugs of beer on the library table, and her father's favorite books. She stabbed the books with a knife, to kill them, and stabbed her father's heavy boots and his most handsome coat. "You will walk again, Ata," she promised him. He did not reply. "If hungry people come and eat the food before you can, try to forgive them. Don't haunt them. I will come back with more."

Her father, stone-faced, turned his head, knowing what was to come, unable to look at what had once been his daughter. Caro, who no longer spoke at all, sent back by his wife's family in a cart like night soil, glared at his sister balefully. Tikki's eyes, tortured and dim, looked into Cara's, and he nodded silently that, yes, this was right, this was the only thing to be done.

"How old do you want to be?" Cara asked him.

"Ten," he replied. "When we were children and Father was young. Meet me beside the river. We will play a game then, in the reeds."

"Yes. Yes," she agreed. "Perhaps that will be soon, eh? I hope so. Father. Caro. I can't kiss any of you. I'm sorry."

She poured pitch over them, arms extended away from her body, in case the worms could leap. "Yes, Sister, yes!" they cried out, gleefully. Cara lit a torch that had also been soaked in pitch. She did not look at the faces of her family as she touched them with it, tenderly, like a flower, until the flames caught. Then she turned and ran out of the house, stumbling out of the doorway, fumbling for the horse's reins. "Away, away," she ordered the beast, and pulled it, laden with bundles, down the steps.

The fire spread across the broad chests of her kinsmen and trickled down the legs of the chairs. Cara could only cover one ear. She could hear behind her the squeals of the worms as they were consumed and set free. She heard no other sound. For her sake, her family would not cry out as, behind her, all her childhood burned.

Chapter 6

The Other Country

Cara spent each night along the way hunched over a book, near the fire that she had set alight by words alone. Three Sleeps, Stefile, looked over her shoulder, scowling slightly. "How can those chicken tracks mean anything?" she demanded.

"Some of them are pictures. This one here is the sign for peace. It shows a woman under a roof."

"Doesn't look like that to me," complained Stefile.

"It was first made long ago. It has changed with much writing. These marks here are signs for sounds. You can write the word for peace with them too, only the writing then is different for each language."

"What good does it do you, this reading, then?"

"This book is teaching me the language of the Other Country. The sound signs will tell me how to make the right noises. That is of use, surely."

Stefile shrugged with resentment, and huddled into her furs. "You will teach me how?" she asked in a small, angry voice.

"When there is time," Cara promised her. "When there is time."

They had to travel along the foothills of the Dragon's Back. The Northern People lived there. They were smaller and more pale than their conquerors to the South, and they moved deftly in smelly goatskins along the narrow paths. The Northern People were unfriendly, and spoke Our Language in a strange way. Cara and Stefile could not understand what they said; the directions they gave to the trails were sullen and short and misleading. The gates to their fortified houses were not opened when Cara and Stefile called; the travelers were not given food. This was a mistake. Cara and Stefile killed their goats, and stole their mules to carry the packs, and rode through the night to escape, beyond reach. They rode west, toward the lowering sun, slanting orange light through the needle-leafed trees. They rode over squelching boglands and back up on to rocks. Bells rang across great distances, from the necks of the grazing sheep, and there were sudden wafts of billy goat scent as they wormed their way along the paths.

They came at last to the Unwanted Way, which led through the mountains. It was held by the Unwanted People, who guarded gates and demanded payment for passage. The lace and the jewelry Cara and Three Sleeps offered was more rare to the Unwanted than they pretended. They also demanded some of the dried goat meat that Stefile had made. "Eat your horses," they told Cara. "Eat them when they die of cold, but sleep inside their bodies first. They will give you one more night."

"What about thieves?" Cara asked.

"Hmm. No thieves. We keep it clear. That's why you pay."

The Unwanted People attacked Cara and Stefile as they slept that first night by the Lonely River. A sword and a suit of armor, uninhabited by a man, drove them back. Word spread upstream that the warrior and his woman were protected by sorcery. Cara and Stefile were left alone after that, with the seasonal chill.

It was getting late in the year, into autumn, and the nights in the narrow mountain pass came early and stayed long. Cara and Stefile awoke the first morning in darkness, and lay uncomfortably on the sloping rocks for a very long time before deciding, finally, to move, still in darkness. They traveled after that through the night. The Unwanted People watching from their high shelters saw them take turns sleeping on a horse's back while the other led, walking with the reins. Before them, to light the way, was a flickering tongue of flame. It burned alone, in midair.

By day, the stone was gray and cold and bare. In the shadows were patches of unmelted snow. On the lower peaks, snow was a gray and white speckled film, and beyond those, on the great single mountains, snow was a thick, flawless, creamy coating.

"When the Dragon wakes, the mountains will stir," Cara recited from the One Book. "The snow is his icy, sleeping breath."

"The mountains here look like clouds," Stefile said.

They ran out of food before they were through the pass. They did not want to eat the little mule that carried their tent and furs; the horses would have to carry the things then, and they would have to walk all the time. They spent three miserable days and two nights without food, wondering if the Unwanted Way led anywhere; if perhaps they had not strayed into some sorcerous trap, a pathway without end, in winter.

When they finally came upon the Unwanted House, suddenly around a bend in the river, they did not feel any leaping of joy within them. They were too tired. They saw a wall across the pass, a dull gray snaking of stone down one steep slope and up another, and in its midst a small house, a mere heap of stones itself, and a gate. Cara and Stefile did not expect the Unwanted to feed them; they did not even ask. Cara drew her sword, but did not need it. The gate was open. The gatekeeper watched them pass, his face resting like a wrinkled pouch on his hands. He had been told to let these two go through.

Cara and Stefile paused on the trail, and looked down. As far as they could see, falling away in layers of hill and valley, was forest, more needle trees, and nestled everywhere among them, like pieces of broken mirror, lakes with rocky islands.

"Is this the Other Country?" Stefile asked, in disappointment. It did not look in any way extraordinary. Perhaps the forest was thicker and a darker shade of green. She looked behind her, twisting on the blanket that served as a saddle. "And that was the Dragon's Back." She blinked, stupid with fatigue and dirt and hunger. "We didn't even see the Wordy Beast." The Wordy Beast was the name that common folk gave to Asu Kweetar, because it was said to whisper stories to children in the night.

An hour later, beside the road, a large rodent stood up as tall as a man's waist, on its hind legs, to look at them. It had a round face with whiskers and long squirrel teeth and was unafraid because humans did not hunt it, usually. Cara threw her sword at it, and the sword sped fast as an arrow, but more true, and lodged itself in the beast. Cara and Stefile built a fire with trembling hands, and roasted it. Its flesh was stringy and tasted metallic, like old dirty pots.

The first person they came upon was a fisherman, a young boy by a lake. He wore a long, heavy black coat, fringed with goat hair and embroidered with brightly colored yarns. His hide boots were also embroidered, fur turned inward, and had pointed toes that curled upward. He had a trumpet made of horn and a black hood that came to a high peak, but that was pulled back from his blond head. Fishing nets were about his feet. His skin was as pale as milk.

"Ugh. They are all Northern People here," Stefile said with displeasure. "You think the Galu came from here? They are pale enough."

Cara tried to speak to the boy in the Other Tongue. She asked him where the city of the Wensenara was. The boy looked back at her, his face absolutely still. Frightened, his mouth taut, the boy replied. The way he said "Wensenara" was very different, and none of the other words as he sounded them made sense to Cara. He pointed down the road, however, and Cara followed that.

"Did you understand? Did you understand?" Stefile demanded, and Cara admitted that she hadn't.

Huge creatures prowled in the woods at sunset, great fearless loping things, which walked on four legs with lumberings of fatty flesh but could also walk upright, like men. The beasts gathered by the river; Cara and Stefile saw them fishing, salmon impaled on their claws.

"Is that a wonder enough for you?" Cara asked.

"Hmmm. It is different, but not wonderful."

"What were you expecting?" Cara chuckled.

"Oh, I don't know. Something like the songs. The songs are lies."

"There will be marvels," Cara promised. "If I succeed."

They came to a village. The houses were made of wood and were very ornate, a line of patterned carvings along the crest of each roof. The wood was varnished or whitewashed, then overlaid with stylized paintings, silhouettes in red or black of the Serpent, or the Whale or simply of men in log boats fishing with spears. On the side of one of the buildings was an enormous pictograph for the word "Inn."

It was an ordinary house that took lodgers, when there were any. The widow who ran it flung up her hands in excitement when she heard Cara's speech, and bustled them into the house, and sat them down with bowls of rich stew, wiping her hands on her apron. She clattered about on her wooden floor, in wooden shoes, and her cheeks were plump and very pink—Cara wondered if that was because she ate salmon. She sat down with them, bursting with interest, and asked them many questions, repeatedly, until they understood her. She could hardly believe the Unwanted had not robbed them. No one went through the pass now, she made them understand. No one wanted to go to the Desert, which was what she called Cara's country. It was a place full of evil and discontent. When Cara asked her how many bandits there were on this road, the woman flung up her hands again. Bandits, here, north of the hills? Oh, no, there were not bandits here. When Cara and Stefile made plain they had no money to pay her, the woman simply shrugged and replied that she had expected that. The cutting down of a tree and its dismemberment into logs would be payment enough.

As Cara worked at the logs, with wedge and hammer, the next morning, she asked the widow the way to the city of the Wensenara. The woman's happy face went more solemn then. It was not a city, she said, but a mountain fastness. It was called the Wensenari, which simply meant Place of the Wensenara, or the Yahstranavski, which meant the Fortress that Needs No Defending. She drew it for them with a piece of charcoal, on a log, a tall strangely elongated building with many towers. A person could only enter it by being pulled up in a basket, she said. Then she asked, cautiously, why they wanted to visit the powerful sisters.

"Because," Cara was able to answer her, "we want our land to be as peaceful and hospitable as yours."

This pleased the widow, but did not entirely untrouble her. "I hope you do not bring disruption," she said. "I also hope you do not find it. The Wensenara are not evil, but neither are they good." She drew a map to it on the inside of Cara's book, and gave them warm cakes to eat on the way, and stood on her porch, waving, as they rode away.

There were many Inns on the road that ran along the base of the foothills, and a gathering number of pilgrims traveling on it to the fastness of the Secret Rose. There were women in black riding sidesaddle on donkeys led by their families. There were farmers with entourages, and beggars who limped alone on crutches. There were sick people, with rotting feet and simple toothache. There were fear-haunted men who had lost their holdings to a scheming cousin. There were so many of them that Cara and Stefile, who had no money, had to sleep in the fields beside the Inns and work for what was left over in the great cauldrons of the kitchens. In the morning, with the first light, all the pilgrims would leave together in a stream. They told jokes and stories, and sang songs that Cara and Stefile could not follow. The road was never empty.

On a day when the first real bite of winter was in the air, they first saw the fortress. Their breath came out of them as vapor. Stefile tried to blow it in rings, like smoke from her pipe. Through the steam of her own breath, Cara suddenly saw it, a blur of shadow on a cleft of rock, blue and gray, impossibly high on a distant cliff. "That's it," said Cara, quietly. She thought it would take an hour to reach it. It took the rest of the day.

The road wound through a thick forest. From time to time Cara glimpsed the Wensenari through the trees. She saw wooden walkways and ramshackle rooms perched out from the walls on stilts, rows of windows, and golden domes in segments like oranges on towers, with sunlight streaming over them in rays.

The pace of the caravan quickened. The songs died. The pilgrims walked with longer strides, and kept track of each other out of the corners of their eyes. Ahead, Cara could see the end of the forest, as if it were a tunnel. "Hee-yah!" cried a man in a wooden chariot farther up the path, and his mules started forward with spurts of dust under their hooves, and began to trot. "This is it," grunted a man, and flung his bag over his shoulder, and ran. The caravan broke apart. Donkeys were whipped and their riders clung, rolling, to their backs. The plump young woodspeople broke into an intent, stumbling run over the uneven ground. An old woman called out a name, peevishly, over and over.

Leaning over, murmuring to their beasts, patting them, Cara and Stefile kept their beasts to a skittish trot, as people pushed past them. Then someone slapped Cara's horse, hard, from behind, and it bolted forward, and she hauled back the reins, seeing ahead of her the naked legs of the people it would trample, and it tossed its head, and snorted, and danced sideways. "Leave the horse alone!" Cara roared, and looked behind to see who had done it. When she looked around she was out of the forest. She saw the Wensenari, as tall and thin and stretched in its narrow cleft as the widow had drawn it. She saw something else as well.

In the afternoon chill and shadow, all the way up a gentle slope of broken rock, was a vast encampment. There was row on row of tents and lean-tos made of blankets. Listless smoke from many fires hung in the air.

People sat unmoving around them. Beyond the tents was a solid unmoving mass of people in dark Northern dress, thousands of them, waiting for the Wensenara, each one of them ill or old or in some way desperate.

"Oh, God!" cried the man with the bag, and flung it angrily to the ground. All heart gone, some of the pilgrims simply stared at it. Some wept and held their heads, who had been singing just that morning. Others slowed to a despondent, trudging walk.

The people of the encampment rose to their feet.

"Stay there. You stay there. You wait your turn!" they shouted, wild-eyed. They picked up rocks from the ground to throw. The man in the wooden chariot rode on, up the path, as if to plough through the camp. People leapt out of his way, and shouting curses, hurled stones after him. The mules turned, the chariot swerved, skidding sideways into a fire, knocking over pots of water, and riding over the corner of a tent, pulled it down. One of the mules stumbled, its legs collapsing under it, and it was dragged, until its brethren resolutely stopped. The driver lashed them furiously, and shouted. Too late to realize his danger, he looked behind him. The people in black closed over him, and pulled him from the chariot, and snatched at his goods. He disappeared under their hands, which rose and fell, and rose and fell, rocks clenched in them.

"I dealt with the fool who struck your horse," said Stefile, drawing up beside Cara. The men from the camp advanced toward them.

"You go no farther," one of them, bearded and dirty, told them. Cara understood most of what he said. "If you've got a tent, pitch it here."

"How many days do you wait?" she asked him.

"Weeks," replied the man. "There's a line of sorts ahead, but those are the people who have been here longest."

"How many a day do they let up?"

"No one. They take names, help some, maybe ten a day. There is no food here, and no one to sell any. You'd best go back."

Ahead of them, the crowd was withdrawing from the broken chariot. Its driver lay bloody on the stones, half naked.

"I do not come for myself," said Cara, clucking her tongue at the horse for it to move. "I come for my people."

"And I come for my son!" exclaimed the man, and grabbed the reins of Cara's horse. Cara sliced through the air with her sword, just in front of the man's eyes. He gave an involuntary yelp and leapt back.

"Stef," she said, "there is going to be a fight. Be ready." The shield and the spear rolled slowly through the air toward Stefile. One of the men jumped and caught the spear instead, to chuckles and small cheers from the jealous, gathering crowd.

Without Cara even looking around, quite calmly it seemed, the spear began to ascend. It rose up through the air, the man still clinging to it. He gave a laugh of mingled panic and amazement, and started to kick as if to jog the spear free from whatever held it up. It went from twice the height of a man, to three, then four, five, six times, until it was too high for him to let go. From all around them came a stirring of the crowd. The dispirited people who waited, squatting on the stone, stood up and craned their necks. The man stopped kicking.

"Let me down! Let me down!" he called, his voice already far away, but people could see how wild and wide was his stare. Someone stupidly gave a cry of rage before trying to pull Stefile off her horse from behind. With a snarl, Stefile spun around, using the sharp edge of the shield to slash across his arm. He gave a cry and fell back, a great fat man in tatters. He looked at the fleshy gash, and the welling of blood on his arm and tried again. With a dull ringing like metal, the shield struck him full across the forehead, and blood quickly drenched his face. He settled back into the arms of his companions.

"I have killed an Angel," Stefile warned them, though they did not understand Our Language.

"I can't hold. Let me down!" the man on the spear wailed in terror, as high now as if he stood on the moun-

tain. Suddenly the spear plummeted toward the earth.
The pilgrims screamed, and beat each other back to get
out of its way. Just before hitting, the spear pulled up,
and shook the man off, and he fell free, tumbling onto
the stones, collapsing on his own legs which folded under him, and he gave a cry of pain.

"We do not want to hurt people!" Cara shouted at
them. "We do not come for ourselves." She added to
Stefile in Our Language, "We'll try to ride around them
all." The spear floated tamely into Stefile's hand. "We are
Wensenara!" Cara shouted again. "Wensenara!"

The word seemed to spread all around them, like
the wind. Cara tapped the side of her horse with her
heel, and began to move forward. The men gaped, and
drew back, and then parted for her. They had seen the
magic.

"Lady? Lady?" asked a woman walking quickly beside Stefile. "If you are Wensenara, Lady, help me!" She
had no teeth and encrustations about her mouth.

"I'm sorry. I'm sorry. No. Nothing," Stefile replied,
shaking her head.

"Take a message for me, Sir!" someone else called,
to Cara. "My village. There is a plague!"

People followed them, calling them. Cara led many
people around the tents, to the winding rows of waiting
people. "Wait your turn. You wait. You wait!" people in
the line shouted at the newcomers.

"We have been here as long as you!"

There was a sudden general rush. All the crowd
surged forward. The fragile order of precedence was broken; the lines mingled and dissolved; people pushed
back; there were screams. "There is a baby here!" a
woman shouted, outraged. Girls with swollen bellies,
who had waited weeks, wailed in dismay, and gave up
hope, and shook their heads. A fight erupted, a furious
flurry of fists. A hen, escaped from somewhere, ran over
the surface of the crowd, over many heads and shoulders, its wings beating wildly. No one could move. Cara's
heart sank at the disruption she had caused, and at what
it might cost her. She stood up in the saddle and saw,

over all the heads, a wooden table and two women in black behind it. They made sharp, angry gestures with their hands. Those who heard what they said held up their hands beseechingly, and implored them. The women gave their heads short, quick shakes, and gathering up their skirts, strode back away from the table to hangings of thick rope and pulled, savagely. High overhead, and faint, a bell sounded.

Cara repeated to herself, over and over, the spell of Sitting in Air, imagining it as a net holding her and Stefile and their animals. Indeed, very suddenly, her horse was lifted up, and then dropped, with a wobbly, seesaw motion. Its weight was too great. Cara narrowed the focus of the spell, clenched it like a fist around the things that had to be carried.

Like divers in a slow arc, Stefile and Cara rose up from the horses, followed by a clatter of their plates and weapons, and a stream of furs. For Cara, all sound was dead, all movement floating and dreamlike. She saw the people below reach up in anger, a slow stifled gasping. She pulled her feet up under herself, and glided over the top of the table. She stretched her legs out again toward the ground, and landed gently beside the sisters, and all the harsh noise and speed of the world started up again.

"You! You caused this! Go away!" one of the Wensenara ordered her.

"I am Wensenara. I must talk to the Great Mother."

"You will talk to no one." The woman, furious, frightened, turned to the crowd. "None of you will talk to anyone. Go back to your homes. Accept your fates!" Behind her, the ropes were sliding upward. She glanced nervously overhead; a kind of wooden carriage, not a basket at all, was being lowered toward them.

"I am Wensenara," Cara said to the other sister.

"You are a man!"

"I look like a man. Spell of the Butterfly. Lalarolalara . . ." Cara began to speak the spell.

"Ssst! All right, you are a Bud."

"Blossom."

"Blossom, Blossom, does it matter?" The woman strode forward to join her sister. "We will be back. We will be back tomorrow, but there must be order, or we will stay away. And we will see only the sick, no one else!"

The carriage was now nearly down. As suddenly as if wiped by a giant hand, the crowd was swept back, their feet skittering over the stones. Those who fell were held up, and carried along. The Wensenara silently moved their lips.

"We're going to jump into it," Cara murmured to Stefile in Our Language.

Ropes whined through pulleys in the van; it seemed to swing to a halt, and then hover, just above the ground. The Wensenara did not wait for it to settle. Pressing their robes down between their legs, they swung their feet over the sides of the carriage, and nimbly stepped into it.

Stefile knelt to gather up their furs. "Leave them!" hissed Cara.

With a creak and a crackling of rope that rose like lightning all along the distance above their heads, the van began to rise again. The people wailed and pleaded. Hard eyes were upon Cara and Stefile, promising revenge. The carriage rose chest-high from the ground.

"Now!" said Cara.

They leapt forward, grabbing hold of the thick, smooth, varnished edge. As one, the crowd and the Wensenara cried, "No!" Released from the magic that held them back, the people poured forward, and grabbed Cara and Stefile by their hanging legs. The carriage tipped to one side; its bottom edge scraped along the cliff face, and the two sisters were thrown from their feet.

Cara's mind felt like a whip, lashing out, and she felt the sword and the shield and the spear cut and slice and gouge. The weapons made sounds through the air like sudden gusts of wind, and the flock of people below shrieked. Hands let go of Cara's legs, and the carriage seemed to leap free. Cara made to pull herself into the carriage, and met something as solid and real as the cliff.

It pushed her back. It seeped under her fingers and began to prize them off. Stefile squealed in fear, "I can't hold!" Across from them, faces hard, eyes staring, the Wensenara mouthed spells in unison.

Stefile fell. Cara caught her in the Spell of Sitting in Air, held them both. Magic reached out of her, and caught hold of something, and grappled with it, pushing it back, out from under her fingers, away from Stefile. She felt it give. One of the Wensenara gasped, as if in pain or surprise, Cara wrested something free, and with a little cry, Stefile sailed smoothly into the carriage.

Cara felt power rear out of her in rage, like a dragon's head, and the Wensenara were driven back. She shouted in rage, and it was like breathing fire, and the Wensenara turned their heads away, and they were miserably crushed, pushed deep into the cushions that padded the benches of the van.

"Stop it! Stop it! All right!" one of the sisters yelled.

Cara swung up into the carriage and settled, sitting next to Stefile, and she smiled with power. She felt thunderous and channeled, like a torrent. "I don't know what spells you have, my sisters," she said, "but I am beginning to realize that I am a very great sorceress indeed, and that I can probably beat you."

One sister was helping the other to sit up. "Threats will not get you in to see the Great Mother."

"Then tell me something that will," replied Cara. "I am Wensenara. I shouldn't have to do these things. I don't want to. But how else was I to get this far? I could have waited down there for weeks—you would have left me down there. Here is a letter. It explains why I have come. Please. Give it to the Great Mother."

The two sisters stared back glumly at her. One of them sniffed. "Well. We will have to tell her you are here, certainly." With a flick, she took the letter out of Cara's hand.

For the rest of the long way up, they sat across from each other in uncomfortable silence. The two sisters held hands, backs erect, very nearly indistinguishable from each other, their heads covered, their finely lined faces as colorless as dumplings.

"Poor horses," said Stefile, looking over the edge of the van, wind stirring in her hair. The blue shadow of the mountain cut across the valley and the woods. She was thinking of the animals she and Cara had left below. "Those people will eat them, I think." The furs that had followed them into the van wrapped themselves around her, to stop her shivering in the wind.

The carriage hung from two great leaning wooden towers that creaked and groaned and made snapping noises. It was hoisted to the level of a windswept courtyard, teams of Wensenara grinding two large cranks. The women jammed wooden pegs into the cogs of the device, dashed to two other giant cranks, and turning these, wound the arms upright so that the carriage swung in over the pavement. They ran to catch and steady it, saw Cara, squealed, covered their faces and ran away again, their feet making fluttering noises on the stone like light applause.

"It's only a man!" sighed one of their more world-hardened sisters in the van. She shook her head and stepped neatly out of the carriage.

"And he says he used to be a woman," added her sister. She turned to Cara, looking almost friendly. "We'll deliver your letter. Wait here." The two sisters walked off together, very precisely, as though plucking a musical instrument with their feet.

The Yahstranavski was sandwiched between two walls of damp rock. The carriage sat, Cara saw, on what used to be the roof. Other buildings, gray, mottled with lichen, had been built on it, with towers of their own. Alleyways of steps ran between them, leading to other buildings higher up the slope. Beyond all of them, clinging to the sides of the rock, was a maze of small huts and stairways and vegetable gardens under nets.

Stefile wandered to the edge of the roof and sat down. She peered at her feet that dangled over the bulk of the fortress below them, the sheer wall of windows and the bark tile roofs of the extensions. She spat, to watch it fall. Patterns of forest and open ground stretched out to the horizon, lost in haze, and above where the horizon should have been, more mountains rose up, clear, above the clouds.

"Are you really a great sorcerer?" Stefile asked.

Cara sat behind her, hands on her shoulders. "I think so."

"Will you be in songs and stories, then?"

Cara smiled. "If the Great Mother lets me in," she answered. "Yes."

To Cara's surprise, the Great Mother did.

Cara and Stefile were led down, not up, into the fortress. The interior was caked with gold, on the pillars and walls and across the high ceilings; gold in the shape of the clothes that icons of the great sisters wore, gold as in rays about their varnished faces. Gold lamps hung on gold chains; candles blazed all around them. High warbling voices gargled out strange noises, spells in chants, that scented the air, that kept Cara and Stefile on the right path, and that prevented them from touching the gold.

They came to a corridor, lit by windows. The thin light of day seemed suddenly wan and pale. A row of women sat on stools, shelling peas. The sister who led Cara and Stefile nodded, and without a word, one of the women stood and strode with a light step to a door. She insinuated herself through it, sideways, so that the strangers could not see what was beyond it. The woman did not come out again, but the door opened by itself, and smiling, the Great Mother stood within it, hands clasped in front of her. Her name was Epesu, which meant simply "work."

"Come in, come in!" she said, sounding genuinely pleased to see them. She was very young, ruddy-cheeked with fine-grained skin. Her sleeves were rolled up and she wore homely slippers made of string, and a black apron with embroidered flowers. "This is my day room," she said. "I'm weaving." There were many windows in the room, but almost no furniture. There was a loom in the corner and a mat of parchment, and ink and a brush, and piles of paper pressed between blocks of wood. Otherwise the floor was bare, polished wood. The room was icy cold.

Cara and Stefile stepped in, and the entire room groaned with their weight. There was a knothole through the floor, and Cara saw daylight through it, and, refocusing, rocks a very great distance below.

"Hold this for me, please," said Mother Work, casually, holding out a spindle while searching her apron pocket for something. Cara took the spindle. "Wonowonownoahowah," droned the Great Mother, and Cara found she could not move. Her arms drooped to her sides, and she sagged at the knee, barely able to stand. The only thing that did not loosen was her grip on the spindle. Epesu turned her bright eyes on them again.

"This is the Spell of No Wind in the Branches," she explained. "You won't be able to do anything unless I will it. You will answer questions and be able to tell only the truth. Don't take the spindle, girl! Or the spell will fall on you, and I will have to use more brutal means to control him." Easily, the sorceress flung herself onto the air, and it held her, and she sat, sprawled and comfortable in it. "You must admit, girl, I have a right to worry about an armed sorcerer who has forced my daughters to take him into our home."

She was beautiful, but the face was somehow too sharp, with flared nostrils and a mouth like a knife. "You will allow me that?" she asked Stefile almost winsomely, amused and requesting. Her manner was graceful and patrician, her voice modulated by power and education.

"Yes, mistress," replied Stefile, casting her eyes down with shame. Guilt makes hatred of the self; shame makes hatred of others. Stefile's eyes flared up again, full of rage.

"Thank you," replied Epesu, and turned again to Cara. She asked, almost caressingly, "Now. Tell me. Are you Wensenara?" She sounded as if she would understand perfectly if Cara were not.

Cara was only able to jerk her head backward, to answer yes. Epesu's eyebrows rose in acknowledgment.

"You are a very powerful sorceress. Do you know, you bested our most implacable spell of banishment with the Spell of Sitting in Air? But do not mistake, Blossom. Magic is the interaction of the powerful one and the world in which she lives. The magic exists between them. The same person can move mountains one day, and not lift a stone the next. The magic must be right. The world must want it. You are being carried by something very powerful indeed. That is why you are here. Not because of that"— Mother Work chuckled tolerantly—"silly letter. You keep talking about a plague in it, and don't tell me what it is. Tell me now."

Cara tried to explain what the Galu were. The words were slurred, as though they were feet to be dragged. It seemed to her that she cast them, like a long cord from a boat to the bank, and that she watched them arch, and sometimes miss. It took a very long time. Epesu was patient.

When Cara was done, she asked, "Why didn't you want to tell me, your Mother, what it was?" She sounded surprised, almost hurt.

Cara did not want to tell her. The words seemed to come out of her gullet by themselves, like bubbles. "You might be a part of it. Their name. It's the same. As ours, Wensenara. The Secret Rose."

There was a flicker, a sudden startled blinking, in the eyes of Mother Work. "Ah," she said, and worked her hands. "Well, if there is a connection, I don't know of it. I know nothing of these creatures who look like men. Why should we help you?"

The reason seemed so overwhelmingly obvious that Cara's weighted mind could not put a name to it. "I can't think," she wailed, heart-stricken, frightened by her haziness of mind. This was what it was like to be stupid. She felt a sudden panic that the spell would never be lifted, that she would be this slow forever.

"You mean that you cannot invent a reason. That is because of the spell. If there were a truthful reason, it would come to you lightly. You are like those people down there." Mother Work stood, and put both her hands on the small of her back and stretched. "They think that just because we have power, we must use it to help them. They come when it is easiest for them, just after harvest when we are busiest, cooking and preserving for the winter." Epesu went to the window, and leaned on its sill, looking out. "They want us to curse a neighbor, or to cure an abscess in the jaw. You mentioned our name, Blossom. You don't even know what it means. The Secret Rose refers to the secret that everything contains. Every word is really another word that is being used in a different sense. Every action is also many other actions. A spell for good often does harm, because it disrupts the world. A spell to do harm often does good. We try to learn these secrets, and leave the world as we found it. Now. Again. Why should we help you?"

"Because . . ." The reason came to Cara, and went.

"I think you had better go," the Mother smiled.

"No!" Cara shook her head, her mouth hanging open. A line of spittle was flung out of it. There was a plot she had, a scheme, buried deep, a reason, something to offer, *what was it*?

"Because it will give you more power!" she was finally able to blurt out.

"Really?" Epesu sounded pleased. "It would seem to me, daughter, kindheartedness aside, that if I wanted to preserve and expand the power of the Secret Rose, I had best join with these Galu." The smile was sweet, absolutely delicious.

"No," moaned Cara, near tears. "Let me tell you. Let me *think*!"

Stefile stepped forward and snatched the spindle from out of Cara's grasp. The spell fell on her.

"Oh," said Epesu, as if she had stepped in something unpleasant. "Love. Let me warn you, warrior, you move toward me, and you shall crack and blister in spells the like of which no one knows but me."

It was like fog blown in a wind, very quickly swirling away; Cara's mind was clear. She said very briskly, "I want you to send me into the Land of the Dead. If you do that, I promise to bring back to you the Apple that Hawwah ate, that gives Knowledge. You could learn more secrets then."

The Mother laughed, a beautiful, musical laugh, and shook her head, and seemed to look on Cara with endearment. "Dear daughter! *What* makes you think I can send you to the Land of the Dead?"

"Keekamis Haliki rode there on a white horse. I have seen a white horse in a vision."

"Oh, *child*!" said Epesu, and suddenly her eyes were round and angry. "Keekamis Haliki lies! He lies most poisonously, he lies about everything! To send you to the Land of the Dead, I would have to kill you. And I could not be sure of bringing you back. Books! Books, books, books, and dreams. Do you know what the Land of the Dead is? It is the Secret Rose of the Land of Life. It is everything terrible and awful and sad and bad. There is no beauty, there is no hope, there is no change, there is no growth, and at its heart is the Serpent. Prize apart the fresh, sweet, plump petals of life, and there is the mite, and the destruction it has gnawed. You want to face that? Go home, child, go home to your books!"

"Is that what it was like when you were there?" Cara asked, simply. The woman's haunted eyes had told her.

Mother Work stopped, and then chuckled, darkly, conspiratorially. "Good. Very good. Yes," she answered.

"So there is a way."

"By murder. Or suicide. Go home, child, and read your precious Haliki. He will tell you that the spoils of the serpent can be won by neither man nor woman." The moment she said it, Epesu's face froze.

"Which am I?" asked Cara. "Man or woman?"

Epesu was trying to disguise a certain shaking of her hands. "I could kill you, and bring you back," she said. "The risks are obvious." It was, after all, an offer.

"If you do not bring me back, you will not get the Apple."

"If you do not get the Apple, then I will not bring you back," whispered Mother Work, and smiled, and did a curtsy. "And, if there is any trouble when you return, there is always this girl, to keep you to your word." She inclined her head toward Stefile without looking for her.

"She must be left out," said Cara. "You have enough of a hold on me, I think."

"You might return and decide that the Apple is too precious to be surrendered. You have nothing to fear, if you give me the Apple. I certainly don't want her for anything."

"Agreed," said Cara, quietly.

"No," moaned Stefile, and shook her head. "No."

"Can you do it now?" Cara asked softly.

The Great Mother sniffed. "I suppose these things are best done quickly." She drew a small, very shiny dagger from the pocket of her apron, and inspected it. "You'd best make farewells in case anything goes wrong." Cara looked at Stefile, and shook her head with the hopelessness of finding the words to say. "Goodbye."

"Ca—ra," Stefile said in a small voice, as if calling from very far away.

"Bare your neck," said the Great Mother. "You might as well take your armor off. It won't go with you."

"It will," Cara answered her. It had not escaped her notice that Epesu had not asked Cara why she wanted to go to the Land of the Dead. Cara cursed herself for mentioning Keekamis Haliki, who tried to carry back the Flower. Epesu would know that the Flower was what she sought, and had not mentioned it. That meant Epesu wanted the Flower too.

Epesu came toward her with the knife.

"What about the blood?" Cara found herself asking.

"Oh, it seeps out through the floorboards," shrugged Mother Work.

A few moments later, she was surprised to see that the armor was gone. It too had traveled.

Cara awoke on her back, at the foot of the cliff, listening to a sound that was only something like the sound of wind. It was bitterly cold, the kind of cold that seems to gnaw at the tips of the fingers. Cara felt it, but in a curiously muffled way, as if she were only remembering the pain. She wondered if she wanted to open her eyes, if there was any reason to. Finally she did.

Cara thought at first that it had snowed. There were no colors, no greens, no blues. The world was still there, the cliff rising up above her, but the sky and the rocks were a dazzling white. The shadows were black and hard-edged. There was no shading of gray.

"I'm dead," Cara said aloud. Her whole body, lying on its back on the gravel slope, felt as still as ice. So did her mind. She saw no reason at all to move.

Then something leaned over her, defined only by the shadows of its face, the rest of it merging with the white of the sky.

"Cara. Cal Cara," it said with sadness. It nudged her gently with its muzzle. "Come, Cara, up. You have work to do."

"The Flower," Cara remembered, in a hollow voice. "The Apple." She did not want to stand at all. She wanted to rest on her back, lay down the magic and the thing she had to do. The white horse moved her hair tenderly, with its upper lip, coaxing her. Finally, wearily, Cara stood.

The camp about the base of the cliff was gone, except for the ash from the fires, and the people who had died there. They sat around the cold fires, staring, still waiting.

"Cara? Cal Cara?" asked the horse, its great head pressed gently against hers, asking her a heartfelt question. Cara knew who it was, she knew whose soul had wished itself into this shape before dying, taken this shape for Cara's sake, to carry her. Cara knew and didn't care. She felt no love. She was no longer capable of it.

"Do you know the way?" Cara asked coldly.

"Yes," said the horse, pulling back.

"You will carry me?"

"I have carried you before," said the horse, its eyes even blacker than before. "I hope, Cara, that you have made all your plans before coming here, because this is the Land Where Nothing Changes. You will not be able to think of anything new here."

"Take me to the Flower and the Apple," was all Cara said. As single-minded as an infant in the womb, she climbed on the horse's back, and kicked it, to make it move.

Head bowed, the horse picked its way down the slope, the rocks underfoot rattling and clinking like broken pottery. Halfway down the slope, a searing heat passed through Cara and the horse. It burned Cara's legs and made her heart jump as if it were alive, wafted through and across her, and Cara saw it, a ghostly image, roiling and seething, made of a million dancing particles, full of glorious subtleties of light and shade and possibility, and Cara caught a snatch of its voice, rising and falling on waves of feeling that seemed to carry Cara up and down with them, a tumble of love and weariness and despair. "They'll hear us tomorrow," the voice said, still hoping.

It half-pulled Cara off the horse as it passed, crowding her head with a tumult of emotions that confused and hurt her. She opened her mouth to call after it. Then it was gone, and even that desire faded. Everything faded.

"Life passes through us, and we cannot touch it," said the white horse. Cara did not reply. She was already beginning to forget it.

They rode through a denuded valley without trees or grass, past lakes that were still and hard, like glass, unchanging. There were buildings, every building that had ever been in the valley, some of them standing in the midst of each other, in the same place, like layers of curtain. There were no pathways to them, and their windows were blacker than night. There were houses in the ground, one on top of the other.

Dead men sat fishing without lines, staring ahead, unblinking. Dead children stood in the middle of the road, waiting for their mothers; old women knitted without yarn. A middle-aged man, scowling slightly, walked up and down a rocky field, calling, "Sara? Sara, where are you?" A plump woman in all her finery, jewelry clinging to her ears and nostrils like insects, crawled on the stone on her hands and knees. "Oh, how silly," she said. "It was just here. I seem to have lost it. Oh, how silly. It was just here. I seem to have lost it."

There were lovers who held each other in the embrace they gave when they finally met again. A hanged man twitched and kicked and gagged in midair, without gallows or rope, and farmhands tilled fields without grain because they could think of nothing else to do. Cara asked no questions about the things she saw. There were no questions she wanted to ask.

They traveled back across the mountains through the Unwanted Way. The mountain river did not roar; there was no day or night. The horse stepped over butchered bodies that the Unwanted had killed and robbed. They snored, thinking they were still asleep. A young man writhed on the ground like a worm, wailing, "Don't kill me! Don't kill me! Please don't kill me!" forever being murdered.

They came down out of the hills. The horse rode on the unchanging surface of the great river, through the canyon, to Cara's house.

It was full of other people who had lived there, the people in the frescos in Cara's room. Amid the rock of the garden, where her mother's flowers had been, Cara's father was trying to dig with a shovel that could not pierce or change the ground. He was younger and stronger than the last time Cara had seen him. "Oh, Cara, there you are," he said, not particularly surprised. "Tikki's calling for you. He's by the river." Cara's father had his arms and his legs and his boots, but not the pair that Cara had killed for him.

"I promised I'd meet him there," Cara remembered.

"You go on. I have to get on with my work." He looked mildly perplexed for a moment. "I wish I knew where your mother was."

By the river, Tikki was calling Cara's name, over and over. He was a child with white hair. There were no reeds to hide behind. "Cara," he said when he saw her, accus-

ing her in a piping voice. "You said you'd come and play.
I've been waiting here all day."

"I'm sorry, Tikki. I can't play now."

The white horse licked the white hair out of his
eyes. The eyes were only shadows. "You said you'd come
and play," he repeated, in a wan and pale voice. They left
him waiting, his feet rooted by the river. They heard him
begin to call her name again.

Farther along the banks of the river, Caro, Cara's
elder brother, sat surly and miserable, his face darkened
by the shadows of his spots, throwing stones at the river.
They skittered and bounced across it. He looked up at
his sister, and then away, as he always had done, Caro
who somehow had never taken his rightful role of heir to
the house, Caro who now never would. The ribs of the
white horse swelled outward and then contracted with a
sigh. They rode on.

"How much longer?" Cara demanded.

"Soon enough, dear daughter," said the horse.
"Soon enough."

They rode down the river, through the marsh, past
Hapira Izamu Pa, to the sea. They rode across the surface of the sea, which was as white as the sky and indistinguishable from it. Ahead of them, in the sky over the
east, was a glow of silver-blue, like the sun about to rise.

They rode to an island in the whiteness, and like a
bubble all around it was warmth and shades of brown and
beige and gray-green, revealed by a hidden light that
waxed and waned. The horse climbed up from the sea,
stepping up onto the warm bank and into the soothing
air.

"Oh!" moaned Cara in relief, and rolled her head,
drooping in the saddle with pleasure. Her heart and
lungs gave a fitful shudder and were still again. She began to notice things around her.

It was the last of autumn in the garden. Leaves were
on the ground, and the long spindly grass underfoot
crackled like straw. As they neared the center, the colors
deepened, the season shifted. Leaves on the trees
blushed into red and orange. The stalks of the flowers

were green, though the blossoms were still withered. Suddenly Cara and the horse seemed to plunge into a curtain of hanging green leaves on purple, flexible, vicious stalks that whipped back into Cara's face, which could not be cut. There was a rustle among them, and a whistle of air through feathers, and a bird rose up, shrieking. Cara gave a grateful laugh and felt a sudden coursing throb of blood in her cheeks. They broke through the screen of leaves, into the center of the garden.

It was a field of flowers, light mauve, bright yellow, deep crimson, delicate lavender, with white butterflies bobbing among them. In the middle of the field was a tree, an apple tree in blossom. It was not very large, but strong, spreading wide, with beautiful bark in pieces like a puzzle, and thick shiny green leaves. Coiled all around its branches, as though trying to pull it down, and piled up behind it in a mound, was the body of the Serpent.

The scales of the Serpent were purple and gold and green, all at once, like oil on water reflecting light. The scales of the Serpent reflected light all around them, in ripples, on the tree, on the flowers. Light came from within them. In the center of the mound of the Serpent's body, there, unable to be hidden by layers of coil, clear and simple and lucid, without halo or refraction, undimmed, undistorted, its shape sharply defined, glowed the White Flower, the Flower of Life.

Cara felt her heart twitch again, and her lungs open up, and she felt a chemical stirring as the cells of her body began to process again. She felt the nerves in her mind like branches in a tree, blossoming.

"Ama," she whispered. "Ama. Thank you." Lovingly, she stroked the horse's muscular neck.

The Serpent began to move. Coils slid away from each other one after another, to reveal, in their midst, a woman. A white woman, pale as chalk, with white hair and white nipples, and a white, caked mouth, straining in vain toward something red and yellow in her hand. Coils fell away from her shoulders, and knees, and there was the Serpent's head, resting across her lap. Green, slitted eyes glared balefully at Cara, and she understood her terrible danger.

"It doesn't matter what happens to me now," she reminded herself, and the thought was an immense comfort to her. "It does not matter what happens to me."

"What have we here?" the Serpent said in a voice like metal, which rose in sudden rage. "What have we here?" And his head shot across the field in the space of a heartbeat and reared up, and his huge unpleasant face was level with Cara's own, and she was staring deep into his green eyes. The horse whinnied for the first time, in fear, and stepped back. The Serpent's head was larger than its own, and his breath smelled of dead and rotting flesh. His breath wreathed out of him, icy and vaporous.

"An armed warrior in the garden?" the Serpent asked himself unblinking. His tongue flickered, investigating. "No. Not quite that. And not altogether dead, either. Look behind you, warrior. Go on, look. I'm too interested in you to bite you yet."

Quickly, not trusting, Cara looked behind her for the first time. Trailing behind her along the ground, the way she had come, was a cord of pale flesh, with threads of blood in it.

"I cut it, and you are here forever," said the Serpent, in harsh and bitter glee. With blinding speed, he spun around Cara and the horse, making a circle around them on the ground with his gleaming body. "Now," he said. "Why are you here?"

"I," said Cara, and faltered. "I am here to answer Hawwah's riddle."

The Serpent threw back his head, and roared with laughter, his mouth open wide like a trap, his long white fangs seeping venom. He twirled like a whirlwind, laughing, back to the white woman. "Hawwah! Hawwah!" he rejoiced. "Someone wants to play your game!" With a snap, he settled back in her lap, and gazed up at her in a mockery of fondness.

Hawwah managed a sideways glance at Cara, and a cramped smile, as though impolitically disturbed. Her full attention returned again to the apple in her hand. It was red one side and speckled yellow on the other. Her nostrils quivered with the scent of it, and her head and hand yearned toward each other, but could not meet.

"Oh, come Hawwah, greet our guest. Delight her with your kindness and wit. Wile her, my love, as you do me. Tell her all the things that fill your mind."

"The Apple," said Hawwah, in a little-girl voice. "All I want is another bite of the Apple."

"The first new thing in ten thousand years, and that is all you can say? Your game, wife. She wants to play it. Your clever riddle, love. Remember it?"

Hawwah turned again, and gave Cara a look of idiot knowingness, raising her eyebrows, and narrowing her eyes and laughing a silent but mischievous laugh. Then distracted, blinking, she turned again, back to the Apple.

"Look, warrior," said the Serpent, "at the face of Knowledge. Is it not divinely inspired? Does its variety not enchant? Oh-ho." The Serpent gave a dark and vengeful laugh. "Hawwah can ask a riddle, one riddle, but she cannot answer any. She cannot sing or dance, or open up her legs. Hawwah can't think. Is this called Knowledge? Is it? Warrior? Knowledge?"

"It is called Death," said Cara. "And you made it."

The Serpent howled, and even faster than before, he ploughed his way through the flowers, and pressed his face close against Cara, slapping her with his tongue. "Yesss!" he hissed. "I made it, warrior. But it does not stop me from being weary and it does not stop me from being alone. It does not stop me from being dangerous with boredom." With a sudden spin he was behind Cara, sidling across her back, and around to face her again. "Are you sure you want such Knowledge, warrior? Are you sure you want to sin, like Hawwah?"

"How? How did Keekamis Haliki lie?" asked Cara, still in the befuddlement of half-life.

"If you do not know that, perhaps you cannot answer the riddle," the Serpent said softly.

"I," said Cara, and faltered again, in the same place. "I have come to answer Hawwah's riddle."

"You have said that!" howled the Serpent, and with a shudder fell away from her. "You have already said that! Do not repeat yourself! I am surrounded by the dead. All the world's dead, and every day the world produces more. I'd destroy them if I could, but the dead cannot be destroyed. You are alive. Surprise me! Stun me! Do something new! Answer," he commanded, "Hawwah's riddle."

With a sudden loop and arch and slither, the Serpent wrapped himself around both Cara and the horse. He reared up, lifting them, and the horse shrieked in terror, kicking its long white legs that hung down behind. The Serpent wound sideways, carrying them to the apple tree. Cara distinctly felt him shiver, quake, like Epesu's hands. They were lowered through the apple blossom, and stood in the strong, sweet scent of knowledge.

Hawwah's face had the look of cunning that innocent people have when they think they are being clever. She liked asking her riddle. She liked each word of it, which she was unable to vary. "The riddle comes in two, like all things in life," she said, reciting. "The first part is: what does every woman know that every man does not?"

Cara's heart felt for her. For such a scrap of knowledge had the world been lost. Hawwah, the first woman, had wanted to know how it was that other people came climbing out of her swelling belly. She wanted to know why she was different from the beautiful Hadam, whom she loved and trusted; she wanted to know why they loved. The Apple had told her, for a price.

"Oh, Hawwah, the world has changed. Women kept your secret for a time. But men learned it. We all would have learned it, in time, without the Apple. The secret is this: when men and women do the act of love, their seed combines in the nest of the woman's belly, to make another person. Men learned, Hawwah, and women lost their power over them, to withhold children."

That had been the part of the riddle that Keekamis Haliki had answered.

"Oh," said Hawwah, in a sad, disappointed voice. She had forgotten the hero.

"And the second part of the riddle?" the Serpent said, in a steely voice. His coils were still wound around the horse's belly, and Cara's waist, and he stared unmoving at Cara, save for the tremor beneath his scales.

"The second part of the riddle is: are you a human being? Only if you can answer yes, is the Apple yours."

"Yes," said Cara, with narrowed eyes.

"The answer," said Hawwah, pleased, "is no. The race has been divided. No one person is both man and woman."

"I am," said Cara.

The Serpent was absolutely still. "The bond has been broken, Hawwah. The Apple is no longer ours. Humankind is free to choose again."

Somehow, the Apple was in Cara's hand. She turned it over, red on one side, flecked yellow on the other, and cold to the touch. Hawwah sat, arm raised, lips yearning, her hand empty.

Cara's plan was simple, almost hopeless: to follow in the steps of Keekamis Haliki, and succeed where he had failed—to answer the riddle correctly, to gain the Apple. Keekamis had come to solve the riddle of death, to regain life for humankind. He had failed to gain the Apple, but saw the Flower, and wrestled with the Serpent for it, and won. Exhausted by his struggles, he had fallen asleep, on the road back to life, and the Serpent stole it from him again.

Cara's plan was to win the Apple, as she was the only person who could, and to ask it how to take the Flower. The Flower was what she wanted.

She wanted to give the Flower of Life, not to humankind, but to the Galu.

The Flower would make them immortal. If the Galu were immortal, they could not die, and if they could not die, they could not reproduce. They could be sliced to pieces, and the pieces scattered so that they could do no harm even though they still lived. Her vision had told her that this was the only way.

But she had to sin, to do it.

She turned the Apple over in her hands. Then she lifted it up to her lips, and bit it.

The Serpent gave a shriek of joy, and released her. The Serpent danced. He wove from side to side, grinning. "Hawwah!" he cried. "Hawwah. We are not alone. We are not the only ones now. The only Human has sinned as well. Humankind has fallen again. A Second Fall. A Second Fall!" He wrapped himself around Hawwah, and licked her lovingly with his tongue, and she stared beyond and through him, looking still at her empty hand. "Hawwah!" he railed, his voice curdling. "Hawwah, you are free!"

Cara turned the flesh of Knowledge over in her mouth, trying to swallow. Despite its fragrance, its taste was salty. Finally, she swallowed it whole, and could feel it land, harsh and bitter, in her stomach.

"Oh, Hawwah," said the Serpent, and dropped away from her, as if in exhaustion.

Cara waited for the change. The Serpent waited, watching her now. Cara felt a tug, in her mind. Then suddenly, as if a curtain had been pulled back, Knowledge flooded into her mind. Knowledge burned her, dazzled her, like light, and she screwed her face up against it, and covered her eyes. To understand the Flower, she had to understand everything else.

She saw the Creation, swirling dust and fire, and a shudder of life in the sea. Which was primary, man or woman? The answer was neither: both had grown slowly out of the other animals, and she saw how pleased and tender toward them was God, for intelligence had blossomed like a flower. A part of the universe could see and understand.

Cara saw that it was not woman who had been discontented with the garden and with love and with life. It was man who had hungered for more. Then Cara knew why there was Death, and why humankind had been driven out of the garden, and why Keekamis had lied. She knew who the Serpent was.

"Are you really so happy that we have fallen again?" she asked, pulling back her hands, staring at him with dull eyes, seeping tears. "Father? Hadam?"

It was Adam who had tempted Eve, Adam who was jealous of God and wanted power. He had made his wife bite the Apple so that the blame and the harm would fall on her and not on him. In punishment, God had made him inhuman, made him the emblem of the male organ, to crawl on the ground. And Adam, poisonous Adam, deprived of intimate knowledge of the value of life, murderous Adam, had destroyed the Tree of Life, which kept intelligence alive, and had stolen the Flower of Life. He did it to deny humankind to God. He did it to keep his children to himself. Alive, immortal, humankind would grow and grow in wisdom until it was fully part of God. Death would cut off such growth, prevent its blossoming, prevent the fruiting of Life into Knowledge. Adam denied his children to God, but at the price of murdering them. He kept them in his kingdom, monotonous, dead, unchanging.

"No," said the Serpent, answering her question. "I am not happy." He was bereft of everything.

Cara could almost pity him. She understood evil. She understood how the Serpent could love what he hated, and hate what he loved. His hatred had turned in and in on itself, until it was as labyrinthine and twisting as his coils. His thoughts were a maze of hatred, from which he could not escape, which was of his own making. She understood too how Keekamis had lied, could not bear to bring back this report of his own sex, which marched to war, which had made Death for the sake of Knowledge, understood how Keekamis had moved the blame on to a hapless beast of the field, and on to Hawwah, who had been bitterly betrayed. The Serpent shifted.

"Is that all you know? My son? My daughter? All?" The Serpent's eyes gleamed with expectancy, and for one moment Cara wondered and dreaded what he meant.

Then Knowledge came again, like a blow in the stomach, and she gasped for breath, and doubled over, and whined in a voice made thin with horror. "No."

For Cara knew suddenly that the Serpent had made the Wensenara, given them their spells, solely and only so that she, or someone like her, could be standing there, able to take the Apple, so that humankind could fall again. And there was worse to come. As she was the only person who could take the Apple, so was she, the Paradox, complete, the only person who could carry the Flower back into the Land of the Living. The Serpent wanted her to take the Flower.

For the Flower shone for eternity next to the Serpent's breast, and the Serpent could not die. It reproached him, for eternity. For eternity, his thoughts could grow toward his enemy, show him the dreadful trap he had made for himself. Holy, indestructible, the only fragment left of the living God in the universe, beyond the control of the Serpent, always threatening to break free and drench the world with light again, the Flower was the thing the Serpent loved and hated most. He wanted it destroyed.

The secret of the Secret Rose rose to the Secret Rose, rose up into Cara's mind like vomit. She had been brought here to destroy the Flower. The Serpent had brought her here.

"Ah. Now you see," the Serpent said, with settled satisfaction.

He had made the Galu in his own image; undying and hostile to life. Humankind would give them the Flower to be rid of them; the Galu would devour the Flower and the last light would be absorbed destroying unnecessary evil. The Wensenara, the Galu, who had the same name, Cara herself, and the vision of her mother, all had been part of the same engineering, the Serpent's scheme.

"I will not take it," said Cara, her voice thick with tears. "I cannot take it."

"No?" said the Serpent, smiling. "Won't you? Not you? Not little Cara? Then look. At least, look."

His gleaming folds unraveled, swiftly, layer on layer tumbling away, uncoiling, and the light grew even stronger, stronger than any light Cara had ever seen, but it did not dazzle. The outline of the Flower was hard and pure and fresh, gleaming white, and Cara saw it, a fleshy flower, plump-petaled like an artichoke, with a thorn on each tip. She felt blood rush to her cheeks, and saw the plants of the garden turn toward it, new tendrils, pale and juicy, spiraling toward it. The field grew virulent with colors brighter than Cara had ever seen. All shadows were banished. In that radiance, Cara could see the blade of grass at the farthest end of the field. She could see the twitch of the leaf on the farthest tree. Hawwah's breasts rose and fell with breathing. Her arm for the first time in a million years fell to her side. Her hair was red, and her lips were pink, and her eyes, like her nipples, were dark brown. She stared at Cara, weeping.

"Don't listen to him, daughter," she said. "He lies and lies and lies. Don't trust him. Do nothing he wishes."

Finally the Flower stood completely revealed. A hush fell on the garden. Everything basked in its light, as if in relief, as if all things were in their proper place again.

"Is it not the most beautiful thing?" wheedled the Serpent, in a reedy voice, writhing as though trying to escape from himself. "Is it not the most delightful thing? Doesn't it shine? Doesn't it warm and shelter and preserve and encourage and inspire? Doesn't it love? Doesn't it love even me, the Serpent, the thing that crawls on the ground and wishes it gone, wishes it destroyed, that hates it? Why should it love me? Warrior?" Hawwah moved her hands from her face, and remembering perhaps old love, held out her hands to him, and sobbed.

"Oh, quiet, woman!" the Serpent shouted in his tormented rage.

Cara's face turned away from the light, though it pierced her cheeks, though she could see the Flower just as clearly as before through the flesh of her eyelids. She had a choice. She could leave the Flower here, refute it, wreak havoc on the Serpent's plans. For one moment her heart hardened with determination to do that, leave the Flower. But then the Galu, the other Rose, would spread, destroying humankind. She had to choose. She, Cara, daughter of a farming village of reeds and stone. She felt the whole universe turning, she felt the weight of it, and she was the pivot.

"I cannot make this choice. I can't decide this!" her soul protested to itself, over and over. Ah, her wiser self responded, but if you cannot make such a choice, you should not have come here at all. Did you think to meet the Serpent and to escape unscathed? The Death of humankind, Cara, or the Death of the Flower. You have to choose. There is no escape. Which is it to be?

Her people spoke of God sometimes, but over the dying generations they had forgotten, and worshipped a pantheon of Gods, gods for each hearth and fire, spirits for every river and tree. How could she know what God would most desire? If she took the Flower she would be the merest dupe of Hadam's rage, and if she did not, if she did not, was there any hope at all? She searched with all her new, harsh knowledge, which ached in her breast, for another way. There was none.

"Oh, horse," she said, and patted its neck. "Both of us have been sorely used. What should I do now, horse, Ama, and how can I believe what you tell me?"

The white horse said simply, "Look for the Secret Rose."

Every action has another action at its heart, bad spells do good. The Flower as clear as a lake at dawn still glowed. It was the last piece of God left to the universe and to humankind, one of God's many flowers, the last one left. The others, it was said, were the stars. Cara looked at it and felt peace returning to her. "If I choose wrongly," she said, "the blame will fall on me, and it does not matter what happens to me. I must not fear blame. I must only choose correctly." She looked at the Flower, and knew that, whatever else it was, it was not there to be preserved at the cost of the final death of humanity. As long as Hadam's children lived, however briefly before he took them, there was hope. The Flower, she realized, had given her an answer.

She tapped the side of the white horse with her heels, and clucked her tongue, and the horse started forward, with a slight jump of something that was not surprise. As they passed the Serpent's head, it turned with them. "Are you sure, daughter?" he asked, in a voice that was utterly human.

She nodded. "Do you fear for me, or for yourself?" she asked him.

"For both," he replied.

The horse rode up and over his coils, lurching, its hooves slipping on the scales as if they were wet stone, its head turned away in shame from the Flower. Cara felt all her nerves dancing, her heart and lungs racing with the speed of hummingbird wings, and she reached up for the Flower, the structure of her hand revealed. She touched it, as warm as another human being, and plucked it from the air. The Serpent threw back his head and howled. It was a cry of loss.

Cara's eyes seemed to go clear, clearer than they had ever been before. Each cell on the farthest blade of grass was clear to her, like padding on a quilt; she could see each grain of soil and each seething morsel of life reaching upward on it; finer even than that, the threading particles of energy that really made them up, interweaving in regular patterns like lace, were revealed to her, as though the garden were the most detailed embroidery, with every stitching of its manufacture revealed. She felt a surge of hope and joy, wild and riotous and completely without fear of any kind. She had made the right choice. She held the Flower aloft, like a blazon, and began to ride from the garden, down the steps of the Serpent. She did not bother to look at him as they passed.

"Disruption!" the Serpent shrieked after her. "You bring disruption. You are the Serpent too."

Cara felt the universe change all around her, topple over in one direction, never to rise. The garden burst into its last wild spring all about her. Leaves and buds and blossoms and fruit erupting into life, scampering after Cara, rising toward the light, a great froth of greenery. Great whirring clouds of butterflies were released, their colors winking on and off with the motion of their wings. Orchids opened like arms, great trees creaked forward, grass wound itself around the horse's hooves with the speed of its flourishing.

As Cara passed them, and the light was withdrawn, they withered again, wrinkling, crispening, crackling, breaking, going from brown to gray. Cara neared the island's edge, the horse stepped on to the sea, and she passed out of the island—there was a sense of passing, but no gate—and suddenly all color was drained from the island. Its life went black, obsidian like glass. A booming wind smashed into it, shattering it, scattering the black glass, driving the splinters into the stone. The tree of knowledge was broken, spreading over the ground in a thousand cutting pieces. The Serpent clung to his bare rock, eyes closed against the wind, and Hawwah rocked, weeping, as she would weep forever more, for the garden, for her life.

Wherever Cara rode, however, there was light and color. The white horse swam across a blue sea. Dolphins leapt up out of the water, saluting them. A white wave carried them on to the shore, and everywhere that Cara carried the Flower, the Land of the Dead bloomed, like a desert after rain. There was a revival in the ground. Not grass, but prickled flowers with horny leaves sprang up, a dusty green with pinkish, thorned fruit.

Wherever Cara rode, the Dead she passed gave a groaning cry, and turned and followed her, open-mouthed, their hands outstretched. A great caravan of the Dead followed her, shuffling, silent, hollow cheeked, but ruddy, leaving off their endless repetitions. Some of them held hands.

The Serpent, in fear and loss and bitterness and victory, unfurled himself as a flag across the sky, waving in great folds, his tail rooted somewhere over the horizon. "Change!" he rejoiced. "Anarchy and change! Growth and breakage!"

He sprouted, thousand headed, in fields. He waved in the wind, like wheat. "I am in all of you! All of my children!" he reveled. He leapt out of the eyes of the Dead, and poured out of their mouths on to the ground, to show all the places he could hide. When Cara rode again to the base of the Wensenari cliff, Mother Work was waiting for her, and the Serpent, small and plump like a baby, was nursing at her breast. The perfect lips of Mother Work parted with delight and greed when she saw both the Flower and the Apple, and she faded away, back to the Living, to prepare.

"Cara!" the Serpent's voice called, mocking. From between Cara's legs, the Serpent raised his head and grinned. It was a human smile, with thick red lips too wide for his face, and two white rows of flat even teeth. "You will see me," the Serpent promised, "every time you make love." Then he too was gone.

Cara listened to a sound that was only something like the sound of wind. It was the hollow, empty sound of loss and regret.

"Get down, Cara," said the white horse, "I cannot follow you."

It looked at Cara with its great black eyes, wind stirring its mane. "We will not meet again," it told her.

Cara touched its gentle, shifting muzzle. The thick lips, now warm, enfolded her hand. The Dead could bring only one thing with them from Life. Cara had brought her mission. The horse had brought only thoughts of Cara. "I love you, Dear Daughter," it said. "I will always love you. Forever and forever and forever . . ."

The white horse and everything around Cara faded away, giving her only enough time to think how much the Flower looked like a pair of warm white hands.

Chapter 7

Flower Power

Disruption, Epesu had said. Disruption, had rejoiced the Serpent.

A great wind followed Cara back into the world. It slammed into the tents and the fires of the pilgrims at the base of the cliff, flattened the fires down to the ground and extinguished them, ripped the hides from the tentpoles, lashing them into the faces of the men who tried to hold them down. The people rose to their feet, and howled.

For the wind was piercingly cold. It stilled the heart and sucked the breath from the lungs, for it was a wind that blew through the soul as well, the wind of loneliness and loss and regret. There was a flickering of blue-white light in it, like lightning, and all the moisture in the air began to fall as snow.

From somewhere in the darkness, through the rent between the worlds that Cara had made, silently, like smoke, shadows for eyes, came the Dead. Their mouths opened and closed like fishes. The Living cried aloud in fear, and covered their faces, and the Dead stumbled through them and the remains of the camp. The snow fell, tiny particles of white that were driven almost horizontally through the air.

An army of the Dead, held by the Flower of Life, were hauled into the Land of the Living. They filled the valley, like a forest of swaying trees seen in fog. They crowded about the base of the cliff, crowded their way up the rock, covering it like spiders, slithers of snow winding their way up the cliff between them, crowded their way through the rock, into the fortress of the Wensenara.

Despite the iciness that cut into their souls, and the storm, and the marching Dead, one by one, the people of the camp fell still. They stood, uncaring, backs to the wind, as their tents were torn from the ground, as their barley and oats were blown away like dust, as their bedding took to the air like winged beasts that wrapped themselves around other people. They stood, gaping and as silent as the Dead.

Above them, the Flower of Life shone steadily. Clear through the walls of Epesu's chamber, clear across all that distance of snow-filled air, its shape sharply defined, its light strong and pure without aura or halo or refraction, even through the water that filled the pilgrims' eyes from the cold. The people, as soon as they saw it, felt what it was and fell into reverence and awe.

The wind boomed through the halls of the Wensenari. Its prizing fingers tore the gold from the walls and sent it spinning in sheets like paper in wind, or sliding along the stone floor like scythes, cutting the ankles of the sisters of the Secret Rose. Their heavy black robes rose up over their heads, whipping their shoulders; they fought to close the heavy doors of their rooms; they saw the Dead and thought the world had ended.

The Dead thronged, hissing, into Epesu's chamber. Perched on its stilts, out from the wall, the room pitched and groaned like a ship at sea. Epesu came for Cara, stumbling as she walked, holding out a mug of tea. "Drink this," Epesu said, voice full of concern. "It will warm you."

Cara kept her eyes dim and befuddled, as if she could not think clearly, and cradled both the Apple and the Flower to her breast, one in each hand. She held out only the Apple. The Dead reached out.

"Better give me the Flower too," said Epesu. "The Dead want it from you."

Cara and Epesu faced each other, neither one of them moving. Cara pretended to drift in and out of consciousness. Words were circling inside her mouth, behind her lips.

Epesu put the tea as near to Cara's hand as she could, ready to put the mug into it as soon as she had the Apple. Nimbly, she picked the Apple out of Cara's grasp.

The moment she took it, she hissed sharply, as though burned, an intake of breath, and her face froze in horror; and Cara, wide awake though newly back from the Dead, ducked out and away from her, saying, "Cast no spells. Do nothing I do not tell you to do."

The room rose and fell, buffeted by the wind. The mug of tea Epesu held turned with its own weight, on the handle around her finger, and the tea poured scalding down her legs, scattered into droplets by gusts of wind. The Apple clung to the very tips of her fingers, unfalling.

"Release Stefile," commanded Cara.

There was a sudden collapsing in the corner of the room, and Stefile fell forward. Cara caught and held her. The spindle dropped to the floor, and rolled back and forth across it with the movement of the room.

"Days and days," Stefile wept. "I've stood for days and days. Cara! I saw you die. She cut your throat. I thought you wouldn't come back. She's a witch, Cara, a witch. The tea, it had the spell of No Wind in the Branches."

"I know, I know. It's on her, now."

"If you'd taken it, she would have had you, taken the Flower. The tea was poisoned, and she would have made you drink it. And I couldn't speak, I couldn't say anything! Punish her, Cara. Punish her!"

"She is punished enough. She will stand like Hawwah, forever, wanting the Apple."

"No," Epesu pleaded, in a voice like the wind.

Stefile and Cara stood together, for a moment, the Flower pressed between them, shining through their breasts. The Dead shuffled around them, clutching at them with fingers that felt like branches of pine needles.

"We have to be away," said Cara, standing back. "Can you walk?"

"Yes," replied Stefile. The warmth of the Flower had healed her.

Cara strode to the window, and looked out, and saw all the valley revealed. She saw the pilgrims looking up, the Dead moving in their midst; she heard a great sigh rise up from them. As Cara stood in the window, some of them dropped to their knees.

"The Flower," murmured Cara, to herself. She turned back to Epesu. "We cannot go back that way. Is there another way out?"

Epesu fought not to tell them. Her lips worked against each other, struggling to keep still. Then suddenly, stuttering, came the single word, "Y—yes."

"Where?"

"B—behind. Up the cleft in the rock. Through the gardens. Behind!"

Cara picked up their furs, and slung them over herself and Stefile, the Dead yawning after her in a slow silent mime.

"Don't leave her here. Kill her! They will find her!" insisted Stefile, suddenly savage.

"Will anyone take the Apple from you, Epesu?" Cara asked.

Tears welled up in Epesu's eyes, and spilled down her cheeks.

"They will know what spell it is, Epesu. You scorned love. Does anyone here love you enough to take the Apple so that the spell falls on them? After all the things you must have done to make yourself Great Mother?"

"No," whispered Epesu.

"It needn't be love, Cara," warned Stefile angrily. "Just greed."

A new fear came into Cara's eyes. "When does the spell fade?" she asked. "Tell the truth."

Epesu pressed her lips tight, until they were pale, and fought not to speak. The flesh on her cheeks began to quiver from the effort and the tears quaked in her eyes, and she snarled with the strain. "Ahhhhhhh iffffff," and suddenly the words tumbled out of her, unwilled, "if you unsay the words!" She bit her lip to prevent it speaking. Blood welled up from the corners of her mouth, and the lip began to blubber, "B-b-b-b-b-b-b . . ."

"Tell me!" ordered Cara.

The lip tore itself free, a patch of velvet red flesh dangling loosely. "When you die!" she wailed, and the secret was free.

When Cara died, the Apple would be loose in the world. Unless, of course, Cara never died. The Flower glowed, next to her heart.

In the Land of the Living, the Flower was transparent, but solid, like crystal, glowing with a gentle, irresistible light, each petal soft and plump and lucid. It shone through Cara's fingers as if they were not there. Nothing could dim or bend its light.

"Why is it so beautiful?" Stefile asked, quiet, bewildered.

"Because it is a piece of God," replied Cara, her voice hollow with remorse.

If she ate of the Flower, she would be immortal, never die, be as a goddess. The Flower brushed her heart, made it sad with love for it. The Flower was everything that was good and warm, everything that was as it should be, without violation. Stefile's fingers approached it, gingerly at first, then touched it too. The fingers of the Dead gathered round it.

Then Cara saw the face of the Serpent, grinning.

"No!" she said, and snatched it away from her eyes. "It's not for that. It cannot be used for that!"

"You've earned some reward!" blurted out Stefile.

Never to have to die, never to have to return to the Land of the Dead. She had been there once, surely that was enough. The Flower drew Cara back. Cara faltered.

"Kill me," said Epesu in a calm even voice, because it was not something that Cara had to fight to make her say. Epesu's eyes were hard. She did not want Cara to be immortal. She did not want to stand, starving, flesh dropping from her, as long as Cara lived—which might be forever. She did not want to stand, an empty skeleton, her soul held to it undying, feeling the wind stir in the sockets where her eyes had been. "Kill me, and I will take the Apple with me, back to the Land of the Dead."

Breath escaped from Cara, with relief. She and Epesu looked at each other's eyes. "Yes," Cara said. "That will work. By the hold I have on your soul, I tell you to die quickly and without pain, and take the Apple with you, back to Hawwah. Stay in the garden with her, and take all the good things of your life with you." Looking away from her, Cara swung the sword across Epesu's neck. The head fell backward, looking up. Blood gushed upward in a pulsing fountain, slapping the floor in sheets, droplets spraying in the wind, against the walls and over Cara and Stefile. The body stood for a very long time, held either by Epesu's will or Cara's. Finally it fell, and when it dropped, the Apple was gone, back into the Land of the Dead.

Cara turned, arm around Stefile, and pulled open the door. The corridor beyond it was thick with the Dead, reaching out for them, mouths working in silent unison. "They can't hurt us," Cara said, and together she and Stefile plunged into them. They broke through them as if through thick shrubbery. The hands of the Dead, given some substance by the Flower, could hold them for just a moment.

Disruption followed the Flower. As it was wrenched from Epesu's chamber, as Cara and Stefile stepped through the door on to the stone, there was a roar of wind, and a cracking of wood, and suddenly the entire structure of the chamber, beams, planks, shingles, loom, mats, parchments, shutters, were burst apart, smashed away from the wall, as swiftly as an explosion. Cara and Stefile ran, eyes closed against the torrent. The air was full of chips of wood, and dust, and bits of precious metal like knives. They gasped for breath, heads turned, groping their way along the corridors, brushing aside the hands of the Dead. They crawled up the steps, out of the temple, feeling their way.

Outside, on what had once been the roof, the great wooden arms that hoisted up the carriage were being rent apart. With long painful screechings, sheets of gold were being torn up from the domes of the towers. Plates of metal bobbed, glinting in the air as if on wires. Beaten by the wind, hands covering their eyes, Cara and Stefile stumbled up to the narrow stairway between the towers. Cara, feeling the smooth warmth of the Flower, thought of Epesu and thought of herself, sinner, murderess, and felt tears start in her eyes. She was crying for the contrast, between the dark worlds that were, and the world that the Flower promised. The Dead followed them, out of the Wensenari.

Chapter 8

The Wound between the Worlds

The Flower was Life itself. Everything that lived wanted it. They followed Cara too.

The rats from the kitchens of the Wensenara, plump and brown, waddled after the Flower, and clambered up the steep stone steps. In the light of the Flower, worms rose out of the soil of the vegetable gardens. They were made translucent in the light, and were driven wild, thrashing. They reared up on each other, into a wave of pale flesh. Cara and Stefile waded through it, kicking. The wave slipped sideways on itself, tumbling away from them.

They climbed out of the crevice in the cliff. As they pulled themselves over the rocks, into the plateau forest, something white shot straight at them. Cara had time to glimpse its heavy-headed shape, two dark eyes in front, before she turned and ducked, hunching over the Flower. Claws scrabbled briefly against her armored back, before the white shape soared away, over the valley, veering helplessly in the wind. It was an owl. Overhead, in the light of the Flower, great spirals of predatory birds—hawks and falcons and a single eagle—turned on the columns of air that rose up from the cliffs. Cara and Stefile ran for the shelter of the trees.

The wind in the forest blasted between the trees, swirling dust and needles up from the forest floor. The wind made a sound in the branches like the sea. The branches whisked Cara's and Stefile's faces like brooms. Insects, driven like the rain, pelted into them. Suddenly, screeching, a flock of starlings, caught in a funnel of air, whirled around Cara and Stefile, slamming into the trunks of trees and through the branches. Beating their wings, they entangled themselves in Stefile's hair; she tried to haul them free, shouting something to Cara that she couldn't hear. They fought their way into a clearing, and there was a sudden drop in the wind.

The starlings settled over Cara in a blanket. "Stef, get them off!" she shouted, trying to cover the Flower in her hands. The birds pecked at her hands, at the Flower that shone so clearly through them. Birds covered Cara's wrists, swarming over each other's downy backs.

The light of the Flower could not be dimmed. Its light pierced Cara's back and armor, showed clearly through all the layers of dust and branches. In the sky overhead, the birds of prey folded their wings behind their backs, and plummeted out of the sky as if they were spears. They tore through the tender upper branches, and broke apart on the larger ones, explosions of blood and feathers against the trunks. The single eagle, larger than any, crashed through all, eyes blazing with the light of the Flower. The branches raked its feathers out, and cracked its sides, and it slammed into Cara's back with all its weight, at blinding speed. Cara was thrown on the ground, with a cry. The birds covered her, seething. Beetles worked their way up from the ground, and squirrels, too anxious until now, bounded forward on to her back. "Get off!" shouted Stefile, and tried to beat them back. The silence, had she noticed it, might have seemed ominous.

Then from behind them came a rumbling and a crashing, and low rising moan. A wall of dust seemed to advance across the forest. Suddenly, like a breaking wave, it swept through the clearing. Stefile howled as it hit them. The wind tore a strip of her heavy hem loose from her skirt. It pulled the beasts away from Cara, sent them rolling over the ground. Cara and Stefile huddled, low to the ground, covering their faces from the dust and needles.

They waited until the wind was merely strong and steady before standing again. When they did, Stefile hissed "Cara!" and clenched her hand.

Crouched at the base of each tree, sheltering, were wolves. Their fur blown in the wrong direction, their faces screwed shut at it, the wolves smiled, either with the wind or aggression, unsheathing yellow-rimmed fangs. Their thin slit eyes seemed to burn with the light of the Flower. Stefile gasped and looked behind them. She saw a wolf, as silent as a shadow, dart from one tree to another. They were being encircled. She heard Cara's sword being drawn.

She also saw, through the trees, a giant elk, gamboling like a fawn, tossing its great antlers, dancing. Stefile could see every hair along its back. The conifers swayed in the wind, and it was as though everything in the forest were marching toward them.

Stefile felt herself lifted up, the torn flap of her dress lashing. As if caught in a vortex, she and Cara were rising. The wolves closed in under them, like water. They sprang up into the air on powerful hind legs. One of them caught the loose strip of cloth and tore it free. The rough bark of a tree crept slowly past them as they rose. In the light of the Flower, it looked like continents, with valleys and mountains. On the ground, out of the blowing dust, as though part of it, came the Dead.

Halfway up, the tree had split with its own weight. Humming with the spell, Cara lifted them both up into the crevice, and left them leaning against the raw wood and sticky sap. The shield clamped itself over Cara's chest, over the Flower, like a tortoise's shell. Her mind and body felt like lead. Circling, circling, the magic would keep circling inside her head, even as she slept. Fatigue that even the Flower could not heal lay like a metal bar across her eyes. Cara discovered she yearned to be free of the magic, yearned for her year to be over. She listened to the wind, and cradled Stefile under her arm.

"What manner of thing?" Stefile wondered aloud. Her eyes too burned with the light of the Flower.

It was the silence that woke Cara. Silence, and the sudden, sickening knowledge that the Flower was gone. She leapt forward with a start that nearly pitched her out of the tree.

"Stef!" she cried out in panic. Stefile was not beside her. Cara pulled herself to the edge of the crevice, her feet wedged into it, to lean out.

The wound Cara had rent between the worlds had healed. Everything was still and radiant with light though there was no sun or moon. All around her, covering the branches of the trees, were birds, silent and calm. On the wide, heavy branch that had pulled the tree open, Stefile sat.

"I've got it," she said. Her face was mournful, baggy, and her hands were stained with sap gone black with dust. "Don't worry." Listlessly, she swept away the insects that crawled toward her and the Flower.

"I ate some of it," she added.

"Oh, Stef," groaned Cara, feeling only sadness for her.

"All these birds came, and the insects. You were asleep. I thought to keep it safe, the shield let me take it. And I ate. Just one petal."

"Poor Stef," said Cara, knowing how the Flower pulled. "I'm sorry. It's all right."

"I didn't do it for me!" said Stefile, quick anger in her voice, and then went still, hanging her head, and picking at the bark.

"For who, then?"

"For the child," she replied in a pale, bitter voice. "Our child."

It was a moment or two before Cara said, "Oh, no."

"For the last time, Cara, is it true what you tell me about yourself?"

"Yes," admitted Cara.

"That you go back? After a year?"

"Yes! Yes, it is."

"Then what happens to the child? A child that you father, after a year? Does it live? Does it die?"

Cara shook her head, helpless with guilt.

"Then you shouldn't have stuck yourself up me if you didn't know, should you?"

"No," replied Cara, so softly that even she could not hear it.

"Anyway, that's why. I thought the Flower could save it. No other reason."

"How long have you known?"

"Oh! Since the Unwanted Way. I knew in the pass, in the mountains. When the witch held me, I kept hoping it was the spell that was stopping the blood. But it hasn't come, Cara, and it won't. I can feel the thing move."

"I'm sorry, Stef."

"So am I. How can I be a mother, living the way I am, like a vagabond, thieving. With the Galu, and all of this! Where am I going to live? What am I going to do with it? Take it home? I don't know my grandparents' names, and my Ata wouldn't have me. If I can still find him, after we killed the bondmaster. Tell me what I can do! You've eaten from Hawwah's apple, you're the great sorceress who turned herself into a man, you're its father. Tell me! What can I do?"

Cara could not answer.

"Tell me what I can do, or I'll throw this thing to the wolves!" She held the Flower out over the air.

"We'll send you to my aunt at Long Water."

"Oh!" sobbed Stefile in outrage. "Oh, that is good. Home again, to some woman I don't know, patient little wife-to-be. And what will I get at the end of that? A husband? A life? I'll get a squalling brat, like all the others, and maybe not even that. Nothing! Not even you!"

"Would you rather have the child in the middle of a battlefield, with all the Galu about it?"

"I don't know about the Galu. It's you who hate the Galu, I don't care about the Galu, it's you who want to bring them down and be Sir Hero, Haliki. Cara Haliki. Sir Dear Daughter Hero."

"I am very, very sorry this happened," Cara said, her voice clear and calm, but darkening.

"So am I. By the Gods, I'm sorry. I wish you'd left me at home."

"Whose child would you be having then?" asked Cara. "How much time would the bondmaster let you have with it, before he made you give it over to the crones, or made you work with it tied to your back, or even sold it. I told you what I was. You chose not to believe it."

Stefile's eyes were narrow. "That does not leave me with much, Cara."

"I'll help you all I can. It's all I can do." Cara looked at her, trying to draw softness and surrender out of Stefile's eyes. Stefile picked at the bark, and did not look up.

"You want to be rid of it," stated Cara.

"Yes."

"You ate the Flower for it."

"Fool of me."

Cara thought of the Destroyed Woman, Cara with the broken face, who would never marry. "I'd want it," she said.

"Then you go have it," replied Stefile with an angry sputter of a chuckle. "What will it do to me, the Flower?"

"You're going to live forever," said Cara, as if by stating it as flatly and as baldly as possible, she could somehow make it comprehensible. "You're never going to die. You're never going to age."

Stefile gave a chortle of amused fear. "What am I going to do with forever? Sixteen years has seemed long enough in this life for me. Cara? I'm alone, Cara. I'm frightened and I'm more alone than I ever thought it was possible to be. Look at me!" She gave another shivering laugh. "Stuck up a rotting tree, with a baby inside me, and a man for its father who is really a woman, telling me I am going to live forever, because I have just eaten part of the living God. Me?" She began to sway back and forth with laughter, shaking her head. "I want to go home . . ." she began, and couldn't finish, couldn't speak with laughter. Finally she was able to gasp out, as if it were a joke, "*and there isn't any home!*" She was crying too.

"Stef," said Cara quietly. "Give me the Flower."

"Why?" she replied, wiping her cheeks. "Are you frightened I'll drop it?" Then she saw why.

"Just give it to me, Stef."

"Oh, no," said Stefile. "No. I don't want the role of Hawwah. I don't want to be blamed."

"No one will blame you."

"Really? Not you? Tell me that you are not doing this for my sake, or I really will throw it to the wolves. May the wolves live forever!"

"It is true. I am doing this for my sake." She was. Desire for the Flower flooded over her. "But I think I do love you anyway. And I will love the child."

"Oh! They all say that. I've seen what comes next. Here." She stretched across the space between them, and gave Cara the Flower. A thrill of expectation shivered through Cara as she took it. She really was going to do it.

"Maybe," said Stefile in a weary, hopeful voice. "Maybe it will stop you going back."

"Maybe," replied Cara, without much hope. The Flower, like warm, clear water, was in her hand. She slipped her thumbnail under one of the petals, and ran it up to the top and tried to prize it free. She pricked herself on the thorn, shook her thumb, sucked it. The petal she had chosen clouded over, suffused with blood. She tried again, more carefully, and with a slightly moist sound of breakage, the petal came free. She put it in her mouth. It sat on her tongue, heavy, cool, and soft, without fragrance, tasting of nothing at all. Then very suddenly it melted, even the thorn. Without Cara swallowing, the Flower became part of her.

Nothing changed. There was no thunder or rising wind. Cara felt as she had felt before. She held out her hand to Stefile. "Come on, come on, love, sleep at least."

Stefile looked at her, across the space between them, exhausted, emotionally cold. Cara was suddenly frightened that their love had run its course. The fear made her go very still and patient and accepting. "I want to stay here and think, Cara," Stefile answered her. "You sleep."

Feeling somehow defeated, Cara pulled herself back into the crevice, hugging the Flower to her. She would just have to see, just have to see about everything, everything was in balance. She could lose to the Galu, Stefile could leave. She settled back against the wood, and swirling in her, kept in abeyance only, was every emotion.

Fear of loss, fear of loneliness, fear of having sinned. Pride in the power of her loins, jealousy. Cal Cara Kerig could have no children. Guilt and concern: it was Stefile who would have to bear the pain and pressure. And love, love for the child, love for Stefile, Stefile who might not want a woman with a ruined face; child, child with no name yet who might yet die. Life everlasting. Knowledge. And the mystery, Hawwah's mystery, which still did not feel solved, as if the womb were a cavern that extended all the way back to God, a portal through which each human being climbed into life. Women were closer to life. Cara was glad, after all, that she was not really a man. Magic. Magic and fear and something that was sweet and clean and wholesome, the life that people yearn for and which never quite comes, even to immortals.

Sleep.

Chapter 9

The Beast That Talks to God

Stefile was shaking Cara awake. "Cara, Cara, get up. Get up!"

Cara lurched awake. "What? What is it?"

It was day now, almost afternoon, with a high sun, and a light breeze. The crevice in the tree seemed deeper and wider, and the whole tree seemed to lean backward. Cara thought, in the confusion of half-sleep, that it was she who was lopsided.

"Cara," said Stefile, her face tense and expectant. "Cara. The Wordy Beast." She grabbed Cara's hand and pulled her. Cara's back was covered in sap, strands of it followed her, as she stood up, wondering what Stefile meant.

The Wordy Beast, which she had seen defaced on the walls of the palace of the Galu; the Wordy Beast that Stefile yearned to see, Asu Kweetar, the Most Noble Beast, which Cara had never quite believed in, until now.

There, on their wide branch, weighing down the entire tree, sat the Most Noble Beast, on white haunches, four or five times the height of a man. It was all white and beautifully muscled like a lion. It had a mane of white feathers, and enormous white wings that were held outstretched for balance. Its eagle face was fierce, its beak was hooked, and its eyes were silver, like metal, with a vertical iris like a cat's. Over one of its lion shoulders a bow was slung, with a quiver of arrows behind it. Around its neck, it wore a necklace of purple amethysts. It sat, unmoved and unblinking.

"Are you Kweetar?" Cara asked, still unsure. "Can you speak?"

"Yes," the beast said, like a knife in Cara's mind. Its beak did not move. Its mind spoke, with the clarity of a blade.

"When I was a girl, I dreamed I'd see you, Wordy Beast," said Stefile, beaming with delight. "And I have. Is it true that you whisper stories to children, in the night?"

"Only if they are very young, and tender, and have made no choices. They are enough like my cubs then."

"Oh!" whispered Stefile in wonder. Transfixed, she stepped around the trunk, and onto the branch, hand outstretched to touch the beast.

"Stef, come back," said Cara in fear.

"Do not touch my beak," warned Asu Kweetar. "I snap." His beak was much longer than a man's forearm. Stefile withdrew her hand, but she still gazed at the beast, with a half-smile. She sat on the branch, legs around it, to see it better. "I would not mean harm," Asu Kweetar continued. "But I am a beast."

"Why are you here?" asked Cara, pressing the shield closer, unable to hide the Flower, even in daylight.

"I am here to carry you, over the mountains, to the City. The Dead are below. The Dead, and all the animals of these mountains. They spread out from this tree, all along the Dragon's Back. The Flower shines. It is seen for miles all around, like a star. There are caravans of gypsies coming here, and all the people of the hills, and the farmers who first saw the Flower at the base of the Wensenari. You will never carry the Flower through them. That is why I am here. To carry you over, and to hold and protect the Flower, until you decide how it should be used."

"Is that the only reason?" Cara asked. The beast was silent. His massive tail twitched. "How can we be sure that you won't take the Flower for yourself?"

"AS YOU HAVE?" roared Asu Kweetar, in silence, booming only in their heads, and covered the distance between them in one forward lunge, tearing off a shower of needles and small branches with its wings, his back legs staying in place. The entire tree dipped and swayed; Stefile gave an involuntary cry, and grabbed the branch. The head of the beast was just in front of her, longer than a man was tall, his eyes depths in which to fall. "Do you not think that if I wanted the Flower, I could take it?"

The tree still rocked. "Do you not?" Asu Kweetar demanded again.

"Yes," replied Cara, only whispering. "Yes, I think you could."

"The Flower is nothing to me," said the beast, settling back on its haunches. "I already have what it can give. I am the beast that talks to God."

"It was a question that had to be asked."

"And it has been answered." The beast began to preen his neck feathers with his beak.

"If . . . if you speak to God," began Cara, faltering, "can you tell me, Asu Kweetar, if the Galu are as terrible as I think?"

"They are. I hear their minds at work. They are rigid like clocks, regular with hatred. I do not think they are quite alive."

"Was I right to take the Flower?"

For some reason the beast was suddenly possessed by a sneeze. It made him toss his head, and hiss through holes in his beak. As he sneezed, his unspoken voice replied, "You are a human being. Your race has taken the fruit of Knowledge, only you know about right and wrong. I am a beast. I cannot make choices. I am very glad of that." The beast's eyes were suddenly full on Cara, like lamps.

Cara found she could not look him in the face. "Carry us then, Asu Kweetar," she said. "Carry our thanks as well."

"Sit on my neck, not my back," said the beast, "or my tail will lash and brush you away. Hold on to my necklace. Not to my feathers, or you will pull them out, and I will turn and bite off your legs." Then he lowered his head toward them, on the branch.

Stefile and Cara looked at each other, and Cara nodded for Stefile to go on ahead of her. Stefile stepped over its beak, holding up her skirt, and crawled up the flat of its head. The feathers were stiff and clean, like fresh sheets, and as Cara climbed round behind her, the light of the Flower glinted on the fibers, refracting for the first time, as if in a waterfall, arches and swirls of rainbow.

"Cara," said Stefile, her head bowed, glancing over her shoulder, speaking while there was still time. "I never knew my mother. Can you understand? She was killed just after I was born, she left me to run away. I don't know what a mother is supposed to be like. I don't know what a mother is supposed to do."

"Neither do I." Cara smiled gratefully, relieved, kindly. "We'll each learn, Stef, eh?" Stefile did not look sure. Cara hugged her from behind, pressed her face up against the side of her neck, and breathed in the smell of her hair.

"Duck low," the beast advised them. "Hold on to the necklace. Do not look up until I tell you." Carefully, he turned on the branch, one white paw crossing over the other. He stood still for a moment, shrugged his wings.

Then he began to run.

The giant branch plunged down and sprang back with each ponderous stride of the beast, flinging even it up into the air. Cara and Stefile felt the smooth surge of muscle; their stomachs dipped and rose; they buried their faces in the feathers of the beast's neck, and felt branches scrape over them and the showers of bark thrown up by the beast's claws. There was a sudden crackling, a series of loud retorts behind them. The branch dropped away beneath them. It and half the broken tree had peeled away from the trunk and, held by wrist-thick strands of wood, had swung back into the main body of the tree, crashing through all the foliage around it. The beast was in the air.

Cara and Stefile felt Asu Kweetar droop in the air, sag with their extra weight lower and lower, felt the fierce beating of its wings, and its breath rippling down its throat, under their legs, and heard its lungs like bellows. "Now," the beast told them, and they sat up, felt the wind slam into their faces and slice through their layers of fur, and saw themselves soar between the ragged tops of the trees. The beast's beak opened wide and he let out a piercing shriek of triumph.

He turned in the air, leaning, and Cara and Stefile saw below them, covering the land, clinging to the trunks of the trees, all the animals together: mountain goats and mountain lions; bears and fawns; worms and birds; eels and even fish that had crawled out of the streams on their fins, silver and half-dead on the land. There were tortoises, necks straining out of their shells, and squirrels moving in brisk little flickers of alertness. Standing among them, still like morning mist, were the Dead. All of them, beast and spirit, craned their necks and turned their heads, following the Flower as it departed. All of them together moaned or bellowed or roared or chattered or bleated or lowed in dismay. A cloud of birds, roused at last from the calm the Flower had spread among them, rose up. Bees and flies and butterflies; geese; and two large swans, mated for life, the long necks held straight out and their wings whistling; squirrels leaping from tree to tree; they followed Asu Kweetar. Asu Kweetar was faster. The beasts of the land tried to follow, loping along the forest floor, or running with long, hungry, elegant strides. The Dead opened their mouths to cry out, but no sound came. They took each other's hands, and gazed into the shadowed pockets of each other's eyes. When the Flower, like a star, dipped below the horizon, the last of its power was cut off from them. Its light no longer held them in the Land of the Living. It was as if they were burned away by the sun.

The wolves saw the goats and remembered their empty bellies, and ripped life out of the herbivores' throats until blood drenched the needles that carpeted the ground. The order of this life, such as it was, had returned.

Cara and Stefile passed over mountains so high that there was only rock and ice beneath them. They howled with the cold and clutched each other, as Asu Kweetar's breath billowed over them like thick smoke. "We will drop lower soon," the beast promised them, "unless the Dragon wakes."

"Drop low soon, then, Most Noble Beast," said Cara.

"When I can, little brother. I am cold too. You will learn to believe that cold can no longer damage you. You are immortals." The feathers of his neck were puffed out, soft white down underneath. "Put your hands there. Do not pull them out by mistake. If you find a tick, oblige me by exposing it to the cold. They let go then."

"Do—do you really talk to God?" Stefile stammered with the cold.

"Yes," replied the beast.

"What does that mean?"

"It means I can hear God, all around me, in the high air, when I fly. I am a thinking beast and, next to human-kind, I am most beloved by God. I ease God's pain."

"God's pain?"

"God loves. Could you love this world and not feel pain?"

"What—what does God say?"

There was a long silence, full only of the roaring of air in their ears. "I cannot tell you," said the beast. "Do not misunderstand. It is not given to me to be able to tell you. Besides, I am only a beast of the air, as you are of the land. I do not understand myself. It is like music that you cannot remember."

They passed over the mountains, and swooped low, as Asu Kweetar had promised, over marshy bogland.

"We are extremely hungry, Most Noble Beast," said Cara after a time. Without speaking, Asu Kweetar grabbed his bow with his front paw, and pulled it over his own and his passengers' heads. He reached behind and slipped an arrow from its quiver. "I am a beast of the air. I do not like the ground. I cannot eat what is of the ground," he said.

Asu Kweetar swung low over the reeds, and mal-lards hidden in them. He chased the birds over the surface of the marsh until they rose up high into the air, flying as if in migration. Then, in the air, he pulled back the string of his bow, and loosed an arrow. Its shaft was curved. It swooped low, coming up below the fowl, driving up through its stomach. The arrow arched up and over in the air, carrying the mallard with it, back toward Asu Kweetar. He caught it in his beak, mumbled it in his mouth, and spat out the arrow. The arrow flared into flame in midair, carried on as a sheet of fire for just a moment, then disappeared, dribbling away through the air as ash. The beast passed the bird back to Cara and Stefile. It was black with burn, and hot and cooked inside.

"I am brother to the Dragon, who is the Earth, rock and fire," Asu Kweetar explained. "I will be there when he awakes, and rears up, the Earth uncoiling."

Cara and Stefile ate, as the beast hunted for himself. Stefile noticed, as Cara pressed against her, that the armor, pink and flecked with white, was warm and seemed to throb very slightly. It occurred to her that Cara's armor was always warm.

They passed into Cara's country, along the river, over the watery lands of decayed irrigation, to the heart of the state, and it was all in ruins.

Chapter 10

The City from the Better Times

It was night. Over Hapira Izamu Pa, no light from lamps or celebration fires was reflected on the low clouds. The City from the Better Times was silent and dark. The land all around it was black, with smoke rippling up in thin trails from mounds of ash. The reeds were gone from along the banks of the river and marshland. So were the floating villages that had hidden within them. Ash floated on the water. Bodies of men were splayed on the banks, bleached and swollen.

In the light of the Flower, those bodies began to stir, to shudder and sigh.

"How?" wondered Cara in dismay. "It has only been a season, from the end of summer to the end of autumn, how could they do so much evil?"

"There are many more of them than you think, and they have many more powers than you think, almost as many as you. Their time is ripe. They are about to march. They know you are coming. Do you want me to come with you?" Asu Kweetar stood on the tips of the claws of his hind legs, trembling, wings aloft, holding himself aloof from the ground. He lived at the Top of the World, where everything was made of ice and air.

"No," said Cara, scowling. "No. It is better that you keep the Flower safe until we know. Stef?"

"I come with you," said Stefile firmly.

"Then pick your way carefully to the gate, and beyond," said the beast. "Beware of serpents and flies. They are the servants of the Galu, and live in their throats and ears. It causes me distress, as if a cub has died, that I cannot answer your most important question. But not even the Galu themselves know the answer to that. I will be near, and know when you need me, and return."

"Thanks. Our thanks," said Cara.

"I am a beast. I have no choice. I do not need thanks," replied Asu Kweetar.

"We have need to give them," said Stefile.

Asu Kweetar turned, the Flower shining through his front claws. He ran a few steps only, on his hind legs, and launched himself powerfully into the air. He hung there, legs drawn up, his wings beating, billows of ash mushrooming up around him. Slowly he began to rise, then faster, almost straight up, the Flower shining out through his back, as if it were a glowing heart. It seemed to rejoin the stars.

The blistered bodies on the bank fell still, covered in darkness. Cara and Stefile took each other's hand, and walked across the ruined earth.

Underfoot there was a grinding of ash and bone. Tiny, harmless creatures, hamsters and hedgehogs and ground squirrels, lay smoldering. Where grass had been, puffs of soft gray ash spurted out from under their boots.

In front of the City gates was a crowd of people, raised up in a mound where they had fallen. Their arms, light and crisp, were still pushing against the gates, melded to the wood, as if admittance to the City could have saved them. The gates themselves were charcoal, and gnawed away completely along the top by fire. The tiles of the walls had gone yellow, or black, or had finally fallen. The tips of someone's fingers still burned like candles, with a blue flame.

Cara and Stefile had to march up and over the dead, to the gates, their legs suddenly sinking through layers of matted cloth. They too pushed against the gates, grinding the charcoal first onto their hands, and then onto their shoulders. There was a screeching of metal as the hinges broke away from the heat-crumbled stone, and there was a shower of mortar. "Get back!" shouted Cara. The gates began to fall inward.

Behind the gates, more of the dead were heaped into another pyre that was smaller, more thoroughly consumed than the first. The gates fell on it, balanced on it like a seesaw, the bottom edge rearing up into the air, scooping up Cara and Stefile, throwing them from their feet. The gates fell, and rose again, like a sigh, the bindings that held the logs bursting. The great cedar trunks settled separately, cushioned by the dead, with a muffled rumble and belchings of ash.

Cara and Stefile lay still for a moment. The logs covered the inward mound of bodies like a ramp. Unsteadily they stood, and walked down it, through the silence, into what was left of the Better Times.

It was like a city on the moon. Soft dust covered everything. The buildings were dark, without doors. Nothing moved. They waded through the dust, through what had once been the main market square. In the tiny, domed shops that lined it, the fabled wares of the merchants remained, as if in bitter caricature. The famous glass had burst apart in a shower of icy slivers that glittered in a glimpse of moonlight. The metalwork had melted and warped. The brass statue of a girl was still lithe and graceful in form, though burned rough, her copper robes an exfoliating, creamy green. Loaves of bread and cake were lined up in the ash, the shelves underneath them having burned completely away. The trelliswork that sheltered the market, from which passersby could pick grapes (always mindful, lately, of the serpents) had utterly disappeared. Cara and Stefile came upon the remains of a horse, still standing in front of a collapsed cart. All the water in its body had boiled away; its flesh was brittle and latticed.

"The Spell of Fire," said Cara, standing before the horse. "The first and simplest of the spells." She began to weep. "They used it, Stef. Used it to burn everything. The air. The birds would have fallen, burning. There would be no air to breathe; a great wind would blow through the streets. The soil itself would turn to ash.

Basements into ovens, flesh into bread. There will be a great scar, Stef, even in the Land of the Dead." They left the horse, no ears, its eyes as hollow as a sad question, waiting as if life or its master could return to it.

Cara and Stefile walked on into the streets where people had lived. There were ghostly rooms in the houses, with blackened tables that could barely balance upright, with cracked and yellow plates still waiting for dinner. There were burned beds, with children still asleep in them. A woman, like a loaf of black sugar, huddled over a bundle to protect it. A dog had lain next to a man, peacefully it seemed, its head on its paws. The air was sharp and bitter, and there was grit between Cara's and Stefile's teeth.

Beyond the mud brick houses of the ordinary people were the houses of the rich, with many floors on wooden beams, which had fallen in. Cara and Stefile had to climb over piles of broken stone that had sprawled across the streets. In places only the corners, and the stalwart chimneys, still stood.

They came to the common ground. The beautiful trees had been burned into coral shapes. The grass was gone, only dust was left. A goat, still enchained, lay bald and half-buried in a drift of it. In the center of the square was a long low building with royal crenellations along its roof.

"The Library," groaned Cara. "Oh, Stef. The Library."

They walked over dunes of ash toward it. The Library had belonged to the greatest of the ancient kings, who had given it and its parklands to the City. Its door had been burned through in its middle. The doorkeeper sat in his box, one shoulder wrenched above his ear, his lips burned into a perpetual smile. Beyond him, in a corridor, a Librarian lay face down, a bucket in his hand with the bottom burned through. The scrolls of the kings were gone, the wonder stories and the sacred texts. Their silver caps lay scattered about the floor, half eaten away. There were no shelves left, anywhere, in any of the chambers. The clay tablets lay in rows, like dominoes, some of them shattered, others baked into a smooth, almost glazed-looking brick. Cara knelt before one of them, and picked it up. It was still warm.

"Perception in his heart, command on his lips," the tablet said. "The river arises from the grotto under his sandals. His soul is Mu, his heart is called Tefmut. He is Hakarati, who is in heaven. His right eye is day, his left eye is night. The warmth of him is breath for every nostril . . ."

The tablet was not complete. Was it reciting the praises of a king? Or the praises of a God? Who would now know? Cara thought of all the patient labor that had evaporated in the flame, all the names and history that were now lost. The Better Times. Cara tried to imagine the stones freshly cut, white and clean, and the king, proud of his gift, full of faith in the future, in his purple, tassled robes, and oiled hair. Lives rising and falling like the tide. And were they all wasted?

Carefully, Cara lay the tablet down in the dust. "Come on," she sighed, and grunted, as if with the effort of standing.

Outside, on the steps, Cara howled. "Galu! Galo gro Galu! There is something in your City that still lives! Galo! Here we are! Gro Galu! Worm!"

The echoes rolled away, all the way to the high, blank walls of the Most Important House. No answer came. There was a well in front of the Library, in the grove of small trees shaped now like arthritic hands. "This is a good place to wait," said Cara. She dropped a stone down the well. It had boiled completely dry, and all the way down it, the stone rattled. Like a serpent.

There was a silvery laugh.

"No need to shout, Cara. I've been here all along," said a voice that seemed to come sideways, out of the shadows, and out of the shadows, sideways, stepped Galo gro Galu, sauntering through currents of dust about his feet. "You have become so clearly visible, Cara. I would have thought that put you in danger." There was a clinking of spurs.

"Hello, Galo." Cara found that she was smiling. Cara was not afraid, or startled, in the least. She felt something akin to amusement and pity. The Galu looked ridiculous, small and frail, naked again, smudged over with ash, like an urchin, streaks of it where his fingers had rubbed his face and belly. He smiled his horrible smile. His teeth had always been the color of ash.

"Oh, Cara, I'm so glad you remember. I like things to be personal. Our last meeting was so quick and abrupt. I'd like this one to be longer. I'd like to talk."

Cara laughed at him, shaking her head, leaning against the well. "Would you?"

"We know about the Flower, Cara."

"Do you know what it will do to you?"

"No. Neither do you. I think that is why you are here?" The Galu laughed, darkly, and turned away as if in scorn. "Do you like my City, Cara? Isn't it calm, isn't it still! When the gods destroyed the world the first time, in the Flood, it was because humankind made so much noise the gods could not sleep. They said the next time would be by fire."

"And the gods restored humankind because they found there was no one left to do the world's work. Who will work for you, Galo?"

"Oh. The unlucky ones who are left. Have you seen my new carrier, Cara, Cal Cara?" The Galu twitched reins in his hand, and made a wittering noise. "Here, boy, come on, don't be shy. You know Cara."

The human bearer of the Galu shambled into the moonlight, moving in a series of jerks. "I'm afraid he's not much use as a trainer now," said Galo, and chuckled.

It was Galad. Eyes wide and stupid and uncomprehending, he worked a metal mouthpiece in his teeth, trying to spit it out. The top of his head was gone. Without another thought, without a cry, Cara stepped forward, and slammed her sword into Galad's neck, the practiced stroke, cutting the vital cord, and Galad fell, back into the shadow.

"May the two halves of your soul be reunited, Galad," Cara prayed, kneeling beside him. "Take my love with you into death, if you have no one else's."

The Galu thrust his head next to Cara's. "We did it because of you, Cara." Cara flung him from her, against the well. "You're not smiling now," the Galu said, in a silken voice. "Not smiling at all. Do you feel rage, Cara?" He draped himself along the edge of the well. "Look at me. I have no sword. You could start there, and work your way up." The Galu traced the line, delicately, with his finger. "Or have you forgotten violence?"

"No," said Cara grimly. "I remember it."

"Yes, but you know, don't you." The Galu sat up in disappointment. "They all learn, and lose heart, poor dears. Oh, not you, Cara, you haven't lost heart, far from it. But the others. Faced with something they can't kill, they do not know what to do. Without murder, human-kind becomes as tame and confused as sheep. Make no mistake, Cara, all of this, all those Better Times. They were built on murder, or the threat of it. All those great, benign-looking statues, with their great, smug, greasy smiles. They were meant to frighten, meant to bully. Awful, noisy, seething, bloody creatures, Cara. I don't know why you want to help them. Seeing that you are what you've become." The Galu chuckled. "You are much more like us now, do you know, Cara? Much calmer, much quieter, altogether less anxious. Even Dirty Little One Dress here. Such a change."

"Why," demanded Cara, "did you burn the City?"

"Oh, it was *time*," said the Galu. "Time to burn it, Cara. These people. They had lived long enough in their decaying comfort. Blister them clean, silence them, bring stillness and peace."

"How did they discover what you are?"

"Oh," said Galo airily. "No reason you shouldn't know, I suppose. There was a revolt. The warriors came to the House, to kill us, in the ancient way. Some of the warriors. Some of them were loyal to us." A sudden thought lit up the Galu's eyes. "Oh, yes! Haliki! That was *very* good! Which one of you killed Haliki, the Prince of Angels?"

"I did," replied Stefile, and the Galu clapped his hands, and roared with laughter.

"Oh, I thought so! How delicious! Oh, he deserved it, that rigid-backed little prig. Did he know? Did you tell him it was you?"

"Yes."

The Galu's laugh was low and insinuating. "You must have had our Father for an inspirator."

"The warriors revolted," said Cara calmly. "And then?"

"Oh, yes, you're supposed to be drawing me out, aren't you. Well, they killed us. They were rather surprised at how many of us there were. Three hundred and thirty. Roughly. Three hundred murders, all at once, cut after cut, metal sliding through us lubricated with blood, slippering about our intestines, slicing our hearts so that they shuddered to a halt. We laughed at them, laughed in their faces. You should have seen their faces! You thought there were only fourteen of us, didn't you, Cara, fourteen in the Family. Well, on that day, there were fifty-four of me alone. Fifty-four Sons of the Family. Do you know how many of us think of you as a kind of grandparent? We have a great deal of affection for you, Cara. Oh, but I must tell you this! They left us to rot on the stone, and the next day there was a thousand of us. And do you know what they did? They did it again! They actually did it again!" The Galu spun on his heel with glee. "They had to use gardening scythes because there were not enough swords. And a rich harvest they had of it, my love!" The Galu hopped up on the well wall and did a little dance. "They made three thousand of us, Cara. Three thousand! What are you going to do about that, eh? How will you save them from that!" He shook his fists with delight. "We burned this place because we are *done* with it. We are about to march, Cara, upriver, across the mountains, over the seas, killing and being, luxuriously, killed. Broad-limbed, handsome young farmers will take their axes to us. And after we have manipulated them into interesting shapes, their sweet young wives will be made murderesses, taking blessed revenge. Then the land will be burned free of them, and we will move on. Oh, but none of them will be like you,

Cara." The Galu jumped down from the well, and pressed his face close up against Cara's. "It is as personal to be brought to life by hatred, as by love."

"Life?" said Cara, and pushed him from her. "You call it life?"

"What else would you call it? Except, of course, that I cannot die."

"What your father hates about life is that it is always new, always changing. You always stay the same. You are dead, Galo."

"Oh, I am born again the same each time, yes. Same memories. But isn't it tiring, Cara, to have to start over again each time? How do you know who you are?" His voice took on a note of genuine interest. "The time you have to spend learning about the world! Learning how to speak! The inefficiency of it. And the idea of coming out of someone else! How can you stomach that? How strange your relations with each other must be. In and out of each other, in out, and out pops a new one, as shapeless as a lump of dough with about as much character, half yours, half someone else's, something that must depose you, if it's to have a life of its own, boot you out of your own house. It's a wonder you don't all kill your children at birth. And the act itself! All those moist clicking noises and secretions. No wonder it is counted as a sin." The Galu shuddered. "Our way is much cleaner."

"*Cleaner!*"

"Swifter, then."

"Why did you burn the marshes?"

"Oh, Cara. Don't be so relentless. I'm not going to tell you anything you need to know."

"Were there rebels hiding there? Can you starve, Galu? Can you die at all? What will you eat, now that the fields are gone?"

The Galu gave a low chuckle. It was a question he would enjoy answering. "We eat the dead, Dear Daughter. We crack open their bones and make soup. Sometimes we eat the living."

Cara gave a shivering laugh. "You make me very angry, Galo, but I am angry in a new way, and I have new things to do with my anger. You are coming with me."

"Am I?"

"Yes. I came here to kidnap one of you." Both of them grinned, as if at a shared joke.

"Kidnap," repeated the Galu, enjoying its absurdity. "Why?"

"So that I can find out how you react to the Flower."

The Galu gave a mocking laugh. "We hate everything it stands for!" Then he added, almost pityingly, "Kidnap me? Look around you, Cara."

"I know, Galo. I've seen them. Do you really think they are a threat to me?"

"We can't kill you, Cara. But we can overpower you. There are enough of us to hold you down. You will make a very good carrier, Cara, to replace the one you killed."

Leaking out of all the shadowed doorways, into the central garden, came the brothers of Galo gro Galu. "We all love moonlight, Cara, and wells that have gone dry. We all love you. We are never alone, because we move in unison."

There were five hundred and seventy-six Galu who bore the name and face of Galo, and they had his mind as well. They all came forward, with the unanimity of bees, all with the same hard smile, all making the same clacking, crackling noises, over and over with their tongues. The Spell of Fire.

Cara struck Galo across the face, all her great weight behind her fist, and slung him over her shoulder. She too was muttering spells. She leapt up on the lip of the well, and took Stefile's hand. There was a spark of flame at the tips of the Galu's fingers, and suddenly a shaft, not of wood, but of living flame, flew out of them at Cara. It cracked open the armor over her breast; Stefile involuntarily screamed. Like a dog scrambling in dirt, the fire clawed out scraps of flesh, searing them black. Cara fell backward into the well, pulling Stefile with her.

The Spell of Fire was the first and simplest of the spells, but the third, and therefore stronger, was the

Spell of Rain. Rain fell, drenching, out of the low wispy clouds that could not hide the moon. There was a hissing of steam on the Galus' fingers, and they yelped, and shook them. They sprang forward to the edge of the well. There were mutterings of confusion, and a cry of "Light", and murmurings of spells. By the time a tongue of flame, sheltered by a saddle, burned over the mouth of the well, all it showed was a dry, stony shaft, which was empty, all the way to its bottom pavements. Empty, that is, except for the fading echoes of laughter.

Chapter 11

The Secret Rose

And Galo gro Galu thought:

Why are they laughing?

He lurched from side to side, only dimly aware that he was being carried.

A male voice boomed close to his ear. "It makes no difference! It makes no difference at all!"

Being carried? the Galu wondered.

"How does it feel?" asked the female, concerned.

Strange, the Galu tried to reply, but his jaw flapped lopsidedly, and made a grinding noise inside his head.

"Good, good, it feels good. Touch the hole," said the man.

Disgusting, thought Galo. Do they think of nothing else?

"It's healing shut!" squealed the woman.

Does it do that? wondered the Galu, his knowledge of human anatomy sketchy at the best of times.

"Now you may truly call me heartless," said the man, and roared again with laughter.

I don't understand what is happening, Galo realized. His hand struck rock, as they ducked low.

"Well, hello, Galo," said the male. "You're awake again. The One Book talks about this place. Keekamis built the wells of the City by tunneling underground to the river. That is where we are going."

For a swim? thought Galo. He regretted the beautiful ash on his body. It would wash away. He heard splashing underfoot and wondered if they were already swimming, or not.

"I am going to learn from you, Little Galu," Galo heard the voice promise him. "I'll learn what the Flower will do to you. I'll learn many other things too, I'll go on learning. Nothing can kill or hurt me. I am a very powerful sorceress. You made me that." Galo felt himself kissed on the cheek. He tried to wipe it off. "I will be your undoing," the voice added. "I will also save your soul."

Galo heard the splashing of water deepen, and he felt himself plunge into it, felt it close, green and cold over him, felt a thick-fingered hand clamp over his nostrils and mouth.

He felt the lurching and the kicking of the body that held him, felt his hair floating, felt himself floating, as if dropping off to sleep. Perhaps he did lose consciousness for a time, for very suddenly he was gasping for air, his head held under the neck above water. "Seagulls," he thought dully. All about him was a flock of seagulls, bobbing on the water. They seemed to accept him as part of the floating garbage on which they fed. Instead of flying away, they sat on the water, their hooked bills turned sideways with their heads, their alert eyes looking upward at the light. The light was descending.

Suddenly the Galu felt himself shot through with pain. The light seemed to pierce him in rays, and he tried, awkwardly, to scream. His mouth and jaws flapped, and a part of his mind made suddenly clear by a shaft of light understood that his jaw was shattered and his palate cleft.

He began to rise. Dazed and sickeningly confused by a pain he did not understand, the Galu thought it was the seagulls who lifted them all out of the water. Seagulls circled about him in the air, screeching, beaks open. Drops of water glinting with light fell off his legs through a space below him that was suddenly vast.

"I can't swim," he said, bewildered. He remembered someone speaking—or was she speaking now?—it was the girl, One Dress, saying, "I tired to breathe underwater and my lungs filled with water, but it didn't matter."

"Keep still!" another voice commanded him, slicing into his skull like the barbs of light. How was it that he was not cold, wet as he was in this wind? What kept him warm? The countryside below him was a ghostly gray. It flickered past, so quickly, in a blue-white light. They passed over a great fire. "My brothers have started without me," he thought. Streams of white smoke rippled out of black fields that sparkled orange and red in lines that were crinkled with ember. Farmers burning stubble. Harvest. Where are we? he wondered, and looking up saw a great, white, fierce face, like an eagle's. As if in the middle of a dream that he did not like, Galo wanted to lose consciousness again, and he did.

Galo gro Galu awoke in breathtaking cold, hearing thunder and strange music.

Light, dazzling, stung him, and he held up his hand, turned his head away. The thunder seemed to crackle under his feet. The walls, away from the light, were smooth and glossy and white and blue. They were made of ice. Light filtered through it, following cracks, catching on bubbles in it. Beyond the walls of ice, something moved.

Distorted by the ice, rippling, the shape filled Galo with unease. It seemed to billow like a cloud, and it flickered with light. He looked away and up. Another shape, overhead, seen through a ceiling of ice, was black, surrounded by what looked like lacy swirls. Enormous feathers perhaps, or fins. The blackness gaped. Galo gave a little gasp, and pulled his eyes away, his heart pounding as if at a narrow escape.

"You are very wise to look away," said a voice. It was too close, nauseatingly close, inside his head. Something was in the room with him, ahead, where the light was most blinding. "Those are my brothers and sisters. They are unknown to you and humankind, and have no interest in either. The few men who have seen them clearly have been struck dumb and blind." Amid the whiteness, a white form sat, wrapped in loose white robes. Dimly,

Galo made out an eagle's head, in a haze of reflection, and lion's paws. Dimly, he heard music, sounding like a lyre, pierced by a whistling, a sweet sad dying fall, from somewhere within the honeycomb of ice.

"Where . . ." the Galu began, and felt a raw scraping of bone inside his jaw that made him squeal in pain.

"Do not try to talk," said the voice. "This place is Siretsi Takan, the Top of the World. The Flower is there, in front of you."

The Flower? Galo simply could not see it. It was lost in light. He screwed his eyes shut, and covered them with his hands, but the light was as searing as before. Turning his head, he felt for the Flower with his hands, finding a table made of ice. Its top had melted into a rough, pockmarked surface. In the center of it was the Flower, plump and slightly warm. He could cover it over with his two hands.

"That is it?" he thought. "The Flower? This great thing, that is all it is?" It made him angry, disappointed in a way, and scornful. He wanted to shred the thing, and scatter it. But his hands, laid over it, did not move. He turned his head and opened his eyes to the light, for just a moment.

Suddenly he was aware, with a sense of just having woken, that he had been staring at the Flower for a very long time. The flesh about his eyes was shivering with pain, and streaming with tears. But he could see the Flower now, dimly, an outline of blue.

Cara and One Dress were in the room. They weren't there before, when had they come in? Galo felt a stab of vivid venomousness that almost revived him. Wrapped in furs and breathing out steam, they were as damp and hot as their genitals. He was cold. It was the cold that was so confusing him, and the pain in his jaw, and the awful light, bruising his eyes. All the room around him seemed darker now, like twilight, his eyes were so burned by the light.

"How long has he sat there?" Cal Cara asked.

Asu Kweetar replied, "Since the sun first struck the ice and made it boom and batter."

"The Flower holds him?" asked Cara.

"Completely," said Asu Kweetar. "He loves it. He loves it beyond words, beyond thinking, more than any of the smaller beasts, more than any human. More than you, Cal Cara Kerig. It is very strange."

"Lies," thought Galo. "Nonsense. I feel none of that." He was staring at the Flower again. He could see it very clearly now, each petal of it. "There," he thought with satisfaction, finding little flecks of bright light in the midst of its crystalline softness. "Imperfection. Even there. Everything was botched by this God. This is a universe that has been ruined by its maker. The universe is a cage that God has trapped us in, and we do not have the strength to unmake it, to tear ourselves free of it." Then, unbidden, a thought came to him. "Still, anything that was perfect would not change. It would not be alive."

"How long has it been since he took it?" Cara asked.

"What does that mean?" Galo asked himself angrily. "Took it! I don't want it. Took it? What does that mean?"

"His heart has beaten four thousand times since he ate of it," replied the beast.

"Ate it!" thought Galo, with disgust. "What an absurd thing to do!"

"Has he slept?" the girl, One Dress, was asking. "The change seems to take hold when you sleep. It is a smaller death, in which the Flower takes root."

A smaller death in which the Flower takes root! Oh, the simpering pretentiousness of it! *Why* did peasants always think that power consisted of being kind and half-awake? All regal doziness, being oracular and vague, as though creatures that ruled never had to have a clear, hard thought. Oh, she was a vulgar sow, immortal or not. "I think they probably call each other 'Sir' and 'Lady,'" writhed the mind of the Galu in impotent hatred. "I'll stake a thing or two that for all their immortality, they'll go back to live on a farm. They'll raise ducks and geese, and give them pet names. Then they'll eat them."

Love the Flower! Eat the Flower? That? It was as bad as the sun. Promising light and warmth, but it raised blisters on his skin, and was followed in this God's universe by winter. Love the Flower! By the Serpent, he wished he could get away from the Flower! A sudden fury seized him. He would show them how he loved the Flower. Love? Was this love, Cal Cara?

He grabbed the Flower in both hands, and pushed his fingers into it, between the petals. Cara and Stefile shouted and sprang forward, dim in the dim room, and Galo gave a squeal of pain, struck perhaps by a fresh blaze of light; there was a sudden crack; the Flower broke down the middle, and heedless of the blood on his fingers from the thorns, the Galu shredded it.

Was it night? Suddenly, everything was dark, except where the Flower was. The Flower was on the table. Galo blinked to clear the water from his eyes, which seemed to be sore from grit. The Flower! Reminded that he hated it and had meant to destroy it, he lunged forward, rose to his feet, pulling out fistfuls of its petals, growling, sobbing as he rent it apart. Flakes of it settled like snow, twists of the Flower gleaming on the table like broken diamonds. Panting and wiping his eyes, he watched them glow.

The Flower was on the table, and the Galu was full of confusion and dread. Something terrible held him. How long had he been sitting there? Hadn't he been standing before? Shreds of the Flower's destruction were all about it on the table. They moved, drawing themselves up in the middle, using their thorns like hooks to pull themselves, migrating, as disgusting to the Galu as slugs. He swept them off the table, and following the sweep of his hand, he saw them on the floor, the petals, writhing and turning and suddenly burgeoning, a clear line of division appearing down their middles. The floor was covered with them, small, roiling larvae. With a yelp of horror, he began to grind them under his feet, kick them away from him.

Then he saw . . . Oh, sweet Serpent, sideways winder, defender against God . . . saw what he had done. Shifting, growing, steady with light, clear and pure, one after the other, after the other, were many Flowers. They were piled in the corners, nearly to the ceiling, penetrating each other with warm light. Everything else was lost in darkness. He turned, and in terror this time, savaged the Flower, hands clawing at it, but before he was done, he screamed, and let it drop, and buried his hands in his armpits. The Flower rolled, to join its brethren. The Galu felt something shiver and shrink in his chest, felt a wizening and a weakening. His three eggs, his children, his other selves, were dying, like apples withering with age. He opened his mouth, nearly healed now by the Flower, to scream, and felt their souls, so like his own, escape like vapor.

"Father Serpent, coiled at my breast!" he howled. "Help me! help me!"

"Come, Galo," said a voice out of the darkness. It was Cara. Hands helped him to his feet. "We'll let you rest now."

Galo felt his hair floating free from his forehead. He awoke in warm water, looking out over a coral reef. It fell away beneath him, in tormented pinks and greens and whites, rippled with sunlight, to blue depths where all other color was lost. Straight ahead of him, deeper than the deepest jewel, the blue extended into the heart of the ocean, layers of light going out mile on mile. There was no sound.

Galo tried to stand up, but couldn't. He tried to look down and couldn't; he could only lower his eyes. There was no body beneath him, only coral, as though all the reef had become his body. "Odd," he thought, scowling with puzzlement. Water, salty and warm, filled his mouth and throat. "Oh. I see. Well, it was *one* way of disposing of us, I suppose." He felt no fear, or panic.

A parrot fish, a brilliant turquoise, lazed along the reef just below him, its tail idly stroking the water. Galo marveled at the perfection of its beak, open shut, open shut. Small black fish moved in a flock with a geometric precision, all to the left in unison, then all to the right. They did not swerve or scatter as the parrot fish swam up behind and then over them, leaving behind a gap in their formation. So gentle, so orderly, thought Galo. He heard a strange hooting, something like an owl, but more resonant. A trumpet fish swam by, its mouth a long horn of crusty tissue. Its hooting was taken up all along the reef. Light, sweeping the reef in rays like searchlights, struck the trumpet fish and its translucence, and Galo saw the fish's spine, and the twisting of blood vessels around the spine, and the brown clumping of its heart and its bowels together, all of it precisely, delicately in place. Far off in the ocean, a pallid white like a moon in daylight, swam a shark, its shape as simple and ferocious as a spearhead.

A shadow settled over Galo, beside him, and heavy, sandaled feet crushed the coral near his face. It was Cal Cara Kerig. She carried an old barnacled chest with her, and adjusted it on the sloping reef, somewhat in front of Galo so that he could see her, and sat on the chest, holding on to it so that it would weigh her down.

"Well, Galo," she said, amused. "You did it, didn't you?" She spoke clearly through the water, no bubbles garbling her words. Her lungs were full of water. She could not drown.

Galo pouted.

"I know this might seem somewhat extreme," Cara continued, "but we had to find some way to make sure you could do no harm. I tried to find an interesting place for you. Are you comfortable?"

"No," mouthed the Galu silently in the water, and felt it wash, cooler, through his mouth and out through the opening of his neck, where his head had been severed. A small fish began to tug experimentally at his cheek. Cara brushed it away.

"Don't worry about those," she said. "We heal rapidly, us immortals." She tapped her chest, where the hole had been. The armor too had healed.

"Go away," mouthed Galo.

"Oh, Galo, now, now. I'm here to keep you company. I thought you might be bored. I'll visit you often."

"Yuck," mouthed the Galo, and stuck out his tongue.

"Then I'll bring some of your brethren to you," said Cara, more darkly. "You did us a very great favor, Galo. You showed us that the Flower is inexhaustible. Do you know what I think, Galo? I think the Serpent has been caught, himself. Secret Rose, every action is another. He thought he would use you and me to destroy the Flower. Instead, the Flower has used him, to set itself free in the world again. Humankind will be lost to him. He has lost, Galo."

Galo sucked the small fish into his mouth and chewed it, vengefully. He squirted it out, cloudy remains and shreds of flesh, sideways at Cara.

Cara chuckled underwater. "Goodbye, then, Galo. You'll have all eternity in which to think, and a brain that will not age. You will come to some very interesting conclusions, I think."

And I won't be able to tell anyone about them, thought the Galu in cold anger. He had loved words, and now he had lost them.

Cara let go of the trunk, and it rolled down the reef, making a clicking sound through the water as it struck the coral. She kicked her way farther up the reef, breaking the surface, dancing, floating as she walked. Bubbles marked her passage, twirling in the water, round and white like pearls.

Galo watched and listened for a very long time.

Chapter 12

The Warriors Who Carried Life

Culmination came swiftly, in winter, through snow. Snow fell over the South, like the Food of the Gods, in flakes. The people of the South had never seen snow before. It came at night, in a high wind, and some of them thought that the stars were falling. Overhead, the greatest of the stars seemed to be carried aloft, across the sky. Those who saw it felt their hearts leap up, unaccountably, and they saw, as if it were day, all the land around them, covered in white, sparkling where the light hit it. Had the world changed forever?

Culmination came where no human eyes could see it, save for those of the warriors who had remained to serve the Galu. They were called the Loyal Dogs, encamped with their masters in the Most Important House, in the heart of the City from the Better Times.

Snow fell, shreds of cloud, the warriors thought, and the strange cold, as unnerving as fear itself, had driven them inside. The beautiful songs of murder were played to soothe them, and they all sat together, all persuasions of warrior, in the main hall of the School of Angels. There were still flowers on the table, grown as always by the women in the garden of the School. Ravening birds had eaten the butterflies. Charcoal braziers smoldered, to keep the hall warm. Shadow Men played dominoes with the Men Who Advance like Spiders. They tried to keep each other hearty, with murmured jokes and wine. Their women sat together, in postures of civility. They knitted, or dandled on their knees beautiful children from the

158

villages, who had taken their fancy for a day or two. They dressed the children in the costumes of princes or gods or sailors. They treated them to sweetmeats and watered wine, until they had to pass them over, regretfully, to the kitchens to be killed. It was considered a delicate, harmless hobby for the wives of warriors with such work to do.

At one table, the Masters of the Fighting Schools sat together, poring over maps, speaking in restrained voices, making marks. The villages beyond the marshes, outside the destruction made by the Fire, were being divided up and scheduled for extermination. The Galu would go in advance, and the Dogs would follow. The Dogs took a certain subdued pride in the work. The human race was to be superseded in an efficient, orderly fashion. Now that the armies of those who had deserted the Schools were destroyed—the Baked Men had been the least Loyal of all, and the Poison Man had led them—the work could proceed. The Loyal Dogs felt themselves to be instruments of a great change, part of a grand process that transcended their own feelings or scruples. They felt sorry for themselves, having to overcome such scruples. It was a terrible struggle for them. Even the inarticulate Men Who Cut Horses talked long into the night with the Angels, who felt it their duty to guide and to advise.

The Loyal Dogs spoke of Heart. They meant the kind of courage it took to face the things they had to do. They raided villages upstream to collect women to do work. They collected the children, to eat. That took more Heart than anything else. The herding and killing of children was done in shifts to spread the unpleasant chore. To make sure they all had a hand in it.

They worshipped their masters, reveled in them. Trained, disciplined, taught to love war, they loved the power and the invincibility of the Galu. They danced for them, sang for them, tried to speak like them, dress like them. The Angel Warriors discarded their spotless white for purple. When the Galu ached to be hewn, their other selves heavy in their breasts, the Loyal Dogs killed them, and thought of their own glorious death that would come—by immolation, by the sword—when the work was done.

There was a tremendous sense of companionship among the warriors; the old boundaries between the Fighting Schools had been lowered in an effort to fill the black pits that would open up in their souls at night. They would cry out then, and comfort each other. "Helping each other across" it was called, and spoken of no more directly than that.

"We are the last," the Angel Dogs intoned, "the last of humankind. We must behave with reason and with dignity. This is necessary, this thing that has happened. We must be sure that it is done swiftly, cleanly, with a minimum of trouble. It must be done with regret, and sorrow."

So they sat, that winter's night, trapped in the Angel hall, nervous, impatient, trying to keep their spirits up, trying not to hear the insinuations of the wind.

A warrior entered, a Shadow Man. He and his mechanical doubles stomped their feet and shook their heads to shake off the snow. Only his head was covered by a hood. Glancing self-consciously about him, he made his way as unobtrusively as possible to the table where the Master of his school sat.

"Salmu, Isshas. There is something," he said.

"Yes, Capesi, yes," said his Master, without looking up.

The man did not want to speak. "There is something. In the sky."

"Yes, Capesi, we know. It is called snow."

"It is a great light, Isshas. A great light." He was murmuring now, thin-lipped. "Like a new star."

"A new star. You have been draining the cup, Capesi!"

"No. It comes from the North, toward us. It is very close."

"Well, let it come!"

"It is being carried by Asu Kweetar. The Wordy Beast. And two warriors. I could see them from a long way off."

"The Wordy Beast! Did he talk to you, then?" an Angel said, leaning back on the bench, smiling.

"Yes," said Capesi, quietly. There was a roar of laughter. "He said he was coming to destroy us."

"You are frightened, Capesi," said his Master, chuckling. "Come, come, we can't have you frightened. We must send Asu Kweetar and his two masters away! Aye?" There was a murmur of assent. "Well? Up then!" roared the Master, and the warriors gave a boisterous yell, and leapt to their feet. Here at last was sport, in the long night.

Holes had been knocked through the walls between the Schools. The word spread quickly. "Ho, ho, Capesi," the warriors teased. "There best be something in the sky after this!" They snatched arms from the storerooms and strode out into the night, hands on each other's shoulders.

"Aiee!" they cried, and pointed, for the sky in the North was ablaze with light. The snow, as it fell, gleamed with it, twinkled with sudden pinpricks of it. Snow was already gathering in drifts in the corners of the courtyard. The warriors scooped handfuls of it up, and chased their women, who shrieked, and darted away, laughing. As a joke, they gave piggyback rides to the Baked Men, who laughed like idiot children. The Men Who Fight like Turtles walked upright into the courtyard, balancing their armored shells on their shoulders. The playful Spiders, who scorned their earthboundness, gleefully rang their shells like gongs.

"So where is Asu Kweetar?" smiled the Shadow Master. He was keeping close to Capesi; they would have great games with him, later.

"He is coming," said Capesi. "I stood on the walls, and could see farther than from here." He cast his eyes on the ground; there was one thing he could not bring himself to tell his Master. Capesi knew what the light was.

Then it was upon them. Silently, the white beast swept low over the walls. The warriors turned as it passed, cheering, because there would be a fight. Then they saw the Flower. Its light flashed on the snow, as if reflected from a thousand mirrors. They felt the light too, and the cheer went sour, and fell away. The light pierced the crystal water of the snow and broke into colors. The snow was like pieces of rainbow, and before they could call up a name for it, the Loyal Dogs knew from where the light had come.

"Lamps," suggested one of them. "Lamps for the storm." But no one said, yes, that was it.

They could hear the whistling of the great beast's wings. They could see two warriors on its back. They saw something else, held in a net, but linked by filaments as well, which glowed. There were flowers, many flowers, linked by light.

"It *is* a Flower," admitted one of them. "But that one is clear, not white." There was a murmur of assent.

"There's more than one there," another corrected him. "There weren't many Flowers." He meant in the Book.

As suddenly as if she had been clubbed, a woman fell to her knees, covering her mouth, sobbing, mewing out words no one could understand. "Up, woman, up!" her husband shouted and tried to haul her to her feet.

"But there were! There were many Flowers," she told him. "There were! On the Tree!"

The beast began to keen, like a great bird, and it circled, over the roofs, beating backward with its giant wings, reaching down with its hind legs to land on the highest point of the Most Important House.

"On the temple! On the temple!" the woman wailed, for the temple had been neglected. She hid her head, and her husband stared ahead, silently. On her knees, she began to claw at the snow as if to hide.

Asu Kweetar settled on the roof of the ziggurat, where the Family were supposed to worship. The beast walked upright on its hind legs, striding the peak of the temple, giant wings held aloft, light in a white arc across them. Then the beast spoke, into their heads.

"Why?" it said. "Why did you choose to do this? Why did you choose to follow the Galu? I don't understand how, or why?"

The Loyal Dogs found they did not know either. They were silent, watching.

"Was it fear? Was it worship of strength? What did it, when there is a God, and you can choose to believe, if you want to?" The beast held up one of the Flowers, with tendrils of fire, over its head.

"There grew a Tree in paradise," the beast began. The Dogs groaned aloud. The words were from the One Book, and they knew what was coming next. "And the ancients called it the Tree of Life, and on that Tree, the Flowers grew"—the voice of the beast twisted with loss and longing and anger—"until the Snake destroyed it. Now! Look!" The beast threw the Flower down.

The warriors on its back emptied their nets, in a tangle, and there was an avalanche of light on the roof of the temple, and with it, rumbling, came the sound of a great fall, a booming noise.

The sound gathered strength; the air and stone surrendered to it, and everything shook, the air and stone moving in waves, until something seemed to give, to split. The beast shrieked and whistled, beside itself with excitement, spinning round and round itself like a puppy, its tail lashing. There came a crackling from the fabric of the temple. Branches of light forked up from it, like lightning; roots forked down. Then, with a gentle rustling like leaves and a tinkling like thousands of icy bells, the Flowers rose up together onto the limbs of Life.

"The Tree! The Tree! The Tree!" screeched Asu Kweetar, leaping up, and snapping.

The Tree stood, a blistering white in all its parts, branches and trunk, a young tree, heavy with blossom.

"Oh!" said the beast. "It shines." The beast crouched low, quivering, its front legs outstretched. It circled one more time, and then settled, under the Tree. It laid its head on its paws, and looked up at it.

"Can you hear its voice?" the beast asked softly. "Like wind in the branches. Like rain on leaves. Can you hear what it says? It says that it's come back. The Garden

is restored, here. No more voices in the night. No more
fear. It says there is time now. You don't have to die."

The beast fell silent, and everything was held in sus-
pension. The snow fell hissing. Everything was white,
illuminated, silver. The clouds overhead were silver, glistening, and the snow turned and twinkled like sequins,
reflecting crisscross shafts of light. The patterns of the
crystals were illuminated, and could be seen. The air and
the stone and the gusts of snow seemed as orderly as the
streets of a city that have been planned. The Loyal Dogs
stood silent too, not sure what they felt, not wanting to
move.

Then came a sudden, hideous blare of noise: crude
trumpets and bashing gongs and cymbals. Faint and far
away, but harsh enough to break the peace, the music of
the Masters.

The Dogs did not know what to do. They loved the
Flower: should they take it? Should they defend it? They
loved the Galu, loved their Masters. Should they defend
them? The Dogs began to run. They ran in all directions,
away from the temple, toward the temple, toward their
barracks, or back and forth between them. Some
grabbed the arms of fleeing comrades, and spun them
around to face them. "Fight! We fight!" they shouted,
and their comrades only shook their heads, weeping.
The light had made everything they had done poison.
Some drew swords, and in a kind of blind panic, slew the
deserters. Some suddenly stopped, as though weary, and
stared. Others, full of bitterness, without quite realizing
it, turned, swords drawn, and began to stumble toward
the Flower, not sure if they wanted to destroy or preserve it. They began to gather, in the scattering of the
Dogs, like strands into a single thread.

"Go back!" wailed the beast, in dismay. "Go back,
you don't understand! The Flower is yours by right, you
don't need to fight us for it, but you must get away from
this place until our work is done!"

The discipline asserted itself. The Spiders recog-
nized each other, and fell into their ranks. With a sudden
dipping of the knees, they picked up their polished col-

umns of metal, and began to jog with them, carrying them toward the Tree.

"No!" said the beast, pacing the temple. "Don't be deceived, Dogs. We are prepared to fight you. We don't want to but we will. And if you try to take the Flower now, I can tell you that we have a dreadful, dreadful, unexpected ally. Go back!"

The Dogs still came. Their breath shot out from their nostrils, a blazing white, obscuring everything they saw, except for the Tree.

"Fools have no eyes! Fools have no ears!" wailed the beast.

Then it gave a snarl, and shook itself, and lowered its head. The two warriors on its back slipped down onto the roof of the temple. They stood beside the beast, a quarter of its height, both of them armored, one in white metal, with a dome of armor over her swollen belly. Later, in the few songs that were sung and largely disbelieved, there was no telling which of the two was meant by the name Warrior Who Carried Life.

Cara stood on the top of the temple, and the light of the Flower was like a beam through her eyes that she could train. She could see the Loyal Dogs as they surged into the square; she could almost count them: too many, too many to hold back for long. The Spiders planted four towers around the temple. Clawed buttresses bit into the pavement and gripped, and the towers rose with a sound like flutes, one section telescoping out of another. The Turtles, who fight with patience, crouched under their shells to wait. The rest of the Dogs charged up the ramp. It was the only way to surmount the seven giant levels of the ziggurat. It was smooth, clad in limestone, with no steps, forty times the height of man. Cara saw leathersoled sandals flattening the snow, polishing it.

"Cara," said Stefile, fear rising in her voice.

"They'll slip," said Cara. "They'll fall." Her thoughts were murderous. She wanted to cut them all down. In her mind she glimpsed a Dog, made immortal by the

Flower. He grinned at her in vindication. You won't get that, my lovely, she promised him. Either way, you won't get that. The Galu will have you.

She was depending on the Galu. The Galu would not let anything else have the Flower. They would burn their own Dogs to prevent it—at least as far as Cara knew. She heard their horrible music, and wished it closer. There were stars overhead. God had returned, surrounded by death. She, Cara, was yearning for the Galu to kill again. The snow swirled around them, like all the contradictions, and somewhere amid them was God. The Dogs were nearly upon them.

The shield and the spear leapt out at the Dogs, ringing against their heads, pushing them back. Asu Kweetar screeched inside their heads, so loudly they dropped to their knees and covered their ears, but the sound didn't stop. They slipped on the snow, feet flailing. A Man with Wrists of Steel fell backward onto his comrades, and rolled, with a rumble and a clanking of metal. A Shadow Man slipped, and grabbed those ahead of him. His doubles grabbed as well, pulling men off their feet. A Man Who Cuts Horses drew his sword, and his overarching backstroke slashed those behind him. A rank of Angels, fearsome, impatient, seeing only the Flower so clearly ahead of them, flung themselves forward. Dervishes, they broke through the men ahead of them, and very suddenly spun themselves into pieces, a flurry of blood and flesh, on the drawn swords they did not see.

Cords of braided metal were thrown, arching through the air between the towers of the Spiders. The cords hung low over the top of the temple. The first of the Spiders launched himself into the air, sailing down the length of the cord, with a sizzling sound, on a pulley. Asu Kweetar turned to him. "You serve nothing," he told the man, and drew his bow, and let loose an arrow. Its tip was white, and it plunged through the head and helmet of the Spider, and ploughed a furrow along his spine.

The most nimble of his comrades, Angels and Horses, were just then gaining the top of the ramp. The Spider swept low over it, his hanging legs smashing into

the heads of his companions, the scythe that was bound
to his hands slamming into the backs of their necks. He
somersaulted, a helpless mass, across the stone, and up,
slightly, across into the opposite tower.

The arrows of the Beast were curved like
boomerangs, and returned to him, to be plucked from
the air and sent out again. The shield and the spear
pushed back the Dogs in the advance. Those behind
them pushed forward. The line up the ramp swelled in
its middle, and suddenly overspilled its edges. The column of flesh, seething, began to slide helplessly, irre-
vocably backward, on slush that was hardening into a
ruby ice. Those who fell dragged down those in front of
them, and together, they slid sideways into the legs of
those behind them. With a slow sagging from the knees,
those behind settled on top of them. The descending
weight of even more men above them pushed them to
one side. Slowly, helplessly, they seemed to ooze toward
the edge of the ramp. In a tangle, like holly, they pulled
each other, rolling, over it. Some were able to cling, for a
time, to the slope. Others judged the distance to the
layer of the temple beneath them, and jumped. The
clacking, wailing music of the Galu ground closer.

Cold had made both metal and stone more brittle,
and grease was thick. A Spider on his pulley squealed to
a halt overhead, halfway down a cord, blocking it. There
was a sudden, spreading crackle through the stones of
the square. The buttress of a tower sprang free from shattered pavement. With a tortured creaking, the tower
leaned toward the ziggurat, held only by the web of
cords that linked it to the other towers. The Spiders who
clung to its lower sections jumped down from it. There
was a prinkling sound of breakage, as the wires of the
cords snapped. Then the cords burst apart, lashing
through the air. Slowly, as if with great deliberation, the
tower fell, trailing men after it who plummeted down,
kicking, on to the stone. The tower fell on the ramp,
crushing one side of itself, bending from the top. The
tower began to slide, wiping everything out of its path,
or gliding over it. As it fell, the crumpled top moved

farther and farther out from the ramp; the entire, massive edifice began to roll, gathering speed, whipping the metal cords round with it. Like a barrel down stairs, it began to bounce, rising up and dropping down, rising up again, and hammering the limestone beneath it. The Dogs scattered in front of it, hurling themselves off the ramp, kneeling under its shelter, hands over their heads. Some of them on the ramp were miraculously passed over as the tower, hollow and elastic, sprang up into the air, making whiplash, metallic noises all along its length. It reared up one final time before sweeping into the Dogs still at the base of the ramp.

Then silence. The Dogs had been trained not to cry out in pain. They had also been trained to regroup. They stirred, struggling up through the limbs of comrades. A Baked Man pulled a length of metal from out of his leather skin, and walked on, barefoot on frozen blood and water. The Turtles began to creep forward under their shells.

"No!" snarled Asu Kweetar. "You defeat yourselves! Go back!" He launched himself into the air. He flew low over the ramp, gathering up straggling warriors in his front and rear paws, beating others with his giant, soft white wings.

Cara watched bemused. It was almost funny, this sudden collapse of the Fighting Schools, like watching a clumsy giant fall.

"I'm almost disappointed," she said. "I have not yet had to strike a single blow."

A Man Who Cuts Horses was suddenly standing in front of her. Cara whinnied at him, mocking. He struck. His sword dipped and swerved around Cara's, rose up, and was driven down. He severed Cara's arm clean away. She barked out a nervous laugh. She fell backward, and sat on the stone.

Stefile called her name, and leapt forward. The Man Who Cuts Horses wiped aside her blow almost casually. A Man with Wrists of Steel lumbered up behind him, ponderous in his armor, and swung at Stefile. She danced backward, out of the way of his heavy downward stroke. Then, untrained, she jumped as hard as she could on the blunt back of his sword. There was a grating of metal on metal as the sword slipped out of his grasp. He blinked at Stefile for a moment through the slit of his visor, and then snatched Stefile's sword from her, grabbing it by the blade with his metal-shod hand.

The Man Who Cuts Horses lifted up his sword. I still haven't struck a single blow, thought Cara. Her arm was beside her on the stone, still holding the sword. The Horseman swung down. With a sudden humming sound the arm somersaulted into the air and blocked the blow with Cara's sword. It rose in the air, flipped over the Horseman's head, and slapped him across the buttocks with the flat of the sword. Outraged by the dire insult, the warrior spun around to find himself facing the sword alone, pink and white-flecked, floating in the air. He swung at it, and it ducked out of the way. Then, very carefully, it inserted the Horseman's blade into its handle, and wrenched it out of his grip. Cara yelped with laughter.

The Steel Wrists swung at Stefile. Suddenly a shield descended from above, and absorbed the blow. It stayed in front of Stefile, blocking her view. She heard the Steel Wrists give a little cry of surprise. This was followed a few moments later by a clattering, spreading crash from below. The shield was raised. The Steel Wrists was simply no longer there. Stefile felt a tap on her shoulder and turned. Cara's arm presented her with her own white sword, gave a little wave, and then darted off, swimming through the air like an eel.

Cara gave a fresh howl of laughter. "Stef! Stef!" she cried. From out of the stump of her shoulder, baby fingers emerged, wiggling. "The Flower!" Using her left arm as a prop, she jumped to her feet. "The Flower! The Flower! The Flower!" she roared, and hopped up and down with delight. She grabbed hold of the Man Who Cuts Horses and, although somewhat asymmetrical, swung him around in a little dance. Aghast, the Horseman pulled himself free, his bearded cheeks puffed out at the impropriety. They were supposed to be fighting!

Shrieking with laughter, possessed with it, Cara reached up and wrested a handful of petals from the Tree and crammed them into the Horseman's mouth. Infuriated, the Horseman spat them out. Then he realized what he'd done. His jaw drooped open. Shaking his head, muttering, he simply turned and walked away, back down the ramp.

Cara felt something in the air all around her that was like the buffeting of many small wings. Stefile was beside her. Cara could feel her hand. Cara swung her around too in a kind of stumbling peasant jig. All she could see was the light. It seemed to form highways up through the snow and sky, big and broad enough to walk on. The beams shone through her, tickling, making her want to giggle. The snow all around her was like thousands of bells, rolling.

A Baked Man stomped toward her, stiffly, with wattled knees. Like a baby, Cara thought. He jammed a long sliver of metal into her neck. Cara left it there. She had not been made immortal to give blows, but to absorb them. Feeling a thin, wide grin spread across her face, she reached up into the Tree, and peeled away a petal of the Flower. She pressed it into his hands, and held them. His encrusted mouth was a tiny straining circle of surprise. That made Cara laugh aloud. He was at other times a cheerful soul, and without quite knowing why he laughed too, a brief, hearty chuckle, the light of the Flower illuminating the velvety black of his eyes.

"This's yours," said Cara, her words slurred. "Alway's been. Now go. 'Fore the Galu."

The Baked Man stared back at her, confused, almost hurt.

The music of the Galu screeched and bashed and rattled overhead.

"Run!" hissed Cara, and gave him a push.

Yes! she suddenly thought, with a thrill, as the Baked Man skittered down the icy ramp. Something caught up both of them, both Cara and the Baked Man, and suddenly he was lifted up as he ran. He squawked, kicking, and squealed, and he soared up and over the walls, out of the square. There was a roaring in Cara's ears like a wave, and it seemed to carry her down the ramp. She advanced, arms outstretched.

An Angel smashed his fist into her chest. She grabbed his hand without looking, and pulled it out, and held it by the wrist, and pulled the Angel with her. A kind of warrior she didn't know ran toward her and rammed his spear into her gut. She walked forward on the spear, smiling. She patted his cheek—a child's trick to distract him—and kicked his feet out from under him. Armored, he tobogganed down the ramp. The Angel she held began to scream, staring at her arm. The arm had began to glow, like the Flower. He broke free, and ran.

"Time to go home now!" said Cara, in a high mocking voice that was hardly her own. It filled the square, it shook the stone. "Time to go home now!"

A flight of arrows rose up against her, and she turned to welcome them. They dug into her shoulders and chest and arms.

"Dance," she whispered.

All the weapons of the Fighting Schools rose up against them. The swords, the shields, the spears all danced in front of her like a curtain, prodding, slapping, poking, herding their masters backward. The metal duplicates of the Shadow Men wrested control from them, and made them walk backward. Tossing her head, Cara danced on the ice, arms still held outward, snapping her fingers, flicking off the blood. She whirled and stumbled down toward the Dogs.

The stones of the pavement began to shake. With a hollow scraping sound, like the lifting of a grate, the first of the great stones began to rise. The men on top of it howled, and dropped to their knees, and clasped its edges as it swept upward, bearing them away.

"Whee!" Cara cried, feeling everything race past her. She looked up at her arms against the sky. They were as clear as water, and they flowed around bones that were like ice, light bending and rippling through them. Magic swelled, unbearable within her, aching like love, until she thought she would burst. She opened her mouth to howl, and it was like something rupturing; a torrent seemed to pour out of her, with the weight of the universe behind it. She felt it sweep across the square, and break against the old walls, rearing up, and then surging over them. Dimly she saw all the warriors and all their goods rise up too, like a flock of ravens, borne up, lifted over the walls. She saw the giant towers turning in the air, glinting, like ships.

She heard the music just over her head, like an empty mechanical contraption. She felt a giant claw grab her, felt its reptilian scales under her hands. "Enough!" commanded a voice inside her head. She felt warm feathers, and a sudden weightiness in her stomach as she was hauled upward. Her head drooped weakly and she saw the square below, suddenly so small, with its little cake of a temple, with a line of little black insects, so shallow and insubstantial, on the walls all around it. The only real thing there was the Tree.

"That," said the shadows, the deluded Galu, "is for us!"

There was a sparking of orange light from their fingertips, and fire—solid, livid jets of orange flame—leapt out of them, joined into one, and poured into the square, filling it to the brim. All the bloody snow on the pavement billowed up, hissing, as steam, rising up through the fire, flickering pink and ocher on its roiling underside. The falling snow turned into feathery streaks of vapor as it hit the heat. In the middle of it, the fire and the steam, the Tree stood, untouched and steady with light. No soldiers had been left behind.

"We didn't kill them," said Cara.

Asu Kweetar hugged her to his breast. Like a fire her mind seemed to flicker and go dim.

"No, we didn't, Little One. We didn't," said the beast. He was weeping.

Chapter 13

When the Dragon Wakes, We Will See Him Together, Each of You, and Me

Cara awoke, because there was no movement. The beast beneath her was still. Her head was in Stefile's lap, who was tugging at her hair, untangling it. Cara's body was caked in black, icy blood, and she felt weak and shivery, feverish. She groaned and sat up.

The light of the Flower filled a chilly mist, all around them, blue-white, in wisps and wafts. All around them, on the roof and down the ramp, knelt the Galu, in serried ranks. Their eyes were wide and unblinking, streaming with tears. Cara stumbled down from the warmth of Asu Kweetar's neck. Dazed, she moved among the Galu, toward the Tree. Stefile followed anxiously, silently.

"It was all joy," said Cara, in confusion. "Why does it feel like sorrow now?"

"Cara, I thought you'd gone mad," said Stefile with relief, and took her hand.

"I . . ." Cara began and couldn't finish. It hadn't been madness, but what had overcome her? She only very dimly remembered the dancing and what had happened to the Loyal Dogs. What she did remember, heart-stricken, was the light, and the snow like bells, and the sound of the magic. Everything seemed very dull now, and ghostly. She felt as if something had been broken inside her. "I was being carried," she said, and walked on, toward the Tree.

The silver leaves rustled as she approached them. She reached up, almost absentmindedly, and picked one of the Flowers. Holding it in her puffy baby arm, she pulled off one of its petals with her older hand, and held it out toward the nearest of the Galu. She knew his face.

"Hello, Galo," she said. "You wanted this." His eyes were upon her as she moved the petal toward his mouth. He opened it.

Then suddenly from out of that face, from all the other faces around them, shuddering out from under the skin of their faces, came a single, gigantic voice. It roared, harsh with anger. "All *right*!" it said. "You've won!"

The face in front of Cara began to blister and swell, crispening, bubbles of oil seething under the skin. Then very suddenly, it burst, spraying Cara. There was a split down its forehead and nose, black liquor welling out of it. The flesh on the shoulders began to bruise, blacken, and to peel off in strips, falling away from the bone. The bones charred and crumbled. Something was destroying the Galu, in rage.

"Serpent," said Cara weakly. She didn't want to see him again.

The Galu collapsed, their flesh tumbling onto the stone. The flesh flapped, like carpets by a door with a draft blowing under them, belching out dust and ash. Their black blood trickled in streams down the ramp. The streams joined together, winding and sinuous, flowing up and over the uninhabited flesh, slipping over the edge of the ramp, dropping down into the square, gliding across the pavements. The darkness cohered into a dark pool.

The pool heaved in place, and shivered, and with a sudden leap, like pieces falling into place, he rose up, the Serpent, in the Land of the Living, and he tossed his head from side to side.

"No! No! No! No!" the Serpent wailed, thrashing. He looked more human now, his scaly disguise dropped, a skin-colored column of flesh, on fleshy coils. His blunt, round head had a human face, a white beard, and ruby lips. He filled the square.

"You destroyed them, not us," whispered Cara, fearfully.

"I'm going to have to take it back!" the Serpent cried, and shrugged himself forward. "I'm going to have to take it back!"

"Leave it to us. Leave us Life," begged Cara, beginning to weep. "Hadam? Father? Don't hate us. Why do you hate us?"

The Serpent simply howled. He lunged forward, his vast bulk and heavy head shooting up the ramp, knocking Cara and Stefile aside. He was cold, like a block of ice, and his breath was chilly vapor. He opened his human lips, bloated and red, and closed them about the trunk of the Tree of Life.

Asu Kweetar shrieked, and sprang forward. He lanced out the Serpent's eye with his beak, and there was a bursting outward of clouded jelly. The Serpent hissed, and turned, and Asu Kweetar leapt back, and clambered up on the Serpent's hide, which was creased in folds. The beast scrambled up the Serpent's head, and leaned over his face, and snapped his beak shut across the black circle of the Serpent's other eye, ripping out its clear covering.

The Serpent was blinded. The blue and yellow backs of his eyes were illuminated, in empty sockets. He screeched and tossed his head, and Asu Kweetar was flung. The beast rolled across the stone, and there was a crack. The coils of the Serpent rose up all around the temple, and dropped, lumbering onto the top of it, groping blindly. Asu Kweetar hobbled out of their path as they fell like fleshy trunks of trees. The beast dragged one wing, broken. He stood on his hind legs and charged again, claws outstretched to gouge at the Serpent's exposed throat. He slashed at it deeply, red blood spurting over white feathers. The Serpent knew then where he was. The coils looped, and arched and gripped.

He lifted Asu Kweetar up, and beat him against the stone, hammering him up and down, the coils crushing and twisting the beast with a sound of snapping wood, but it was the Serpent who was shrieking in pain.

"You won't have him, God!" the Serpent cried, jerking his head up blindly toward the sky. "You won't have him anymore." He stretched the beast out, gripping him by the legs. The Serpent placed his lips, like a kiss, on Asu Kweetar's belly. The Most Noble Beast squirmed, and turned his head, and snapped on empty air. The Serpent's teeth, great flat plates as long as Cara's arm, closed, scooping out all the inner workings of the beast's stomach. Asu Kweetar squealed like a pig. The Serpent pulled back, hauling out strands with him, tore them free, and then spat. The Serpent shuddered, and threw Asu Kweetar from him.

Then with the speed of a whip, the coils wrapped themselves around the Tree, and as he touched it, the Serpent howled as though burned. The Serpent clenched, and the Tree buckled, and then broke, like glass, cutting his sides, and light burst forth, crazy light, sweeping through the mingled steam and ash like searchlights. The Serpent heaved himself backward, and the temple shook as the Tree was uprooted, and the air seemed to open with a gasp so cold, it seemed to slice through Cara's heart, and stop it for a moment, immortal as it was. Cara saw the Tree and the light retreat, as the Serpent, rigid with pain, threw himself back and forth amid the light. Then the air seemed to fall shut like a curtain, and the Serpent and the Tree were gone.

Stefile was already beside the Wordy Beast. The animal's heart and lungs had been left to him, but out of the crater of his belly, fountains of blood gushed out, slapping the pavement with rich red droplets. He lay gasping on his back, his claws still fighting, feebly.

"Oh, no," said Stefile, in a tiny, wounded voice. "Oh, Wordy Beast, oh, no."

Asu Kweetar was a beast, long lived beyond understanding, but they understood then that he could die. He was dying. His silver eyes stared, growing dim and dry, and his beak hung open, sideways. Stefile knelt and moved her hands toward his stomach, as if to close the arteries as thick as her fingers, through which life splattered, wasted. The ruin was too great.

"Pity God, whose work is spoiled," they heard a dim whisper from his mind. Then, a promise. "When the Dragon wakes." Then Asu Kweetar tried to stand. He lifted up his head, with its dim eyes, and his claws tried to close, and his one whole wing thumped against the stone. They saw into his mind.

He thought he had stood. They saw how, deluded in his death dream, he thought he had risen, and was flying, free in the air. They felt his heart beating, and the surge of warm air in his lungs, all delusion, and the wind ripple across his wings, white and firm and strong, and he screeched with delight. At last, he was away from the ground! He soared fast, into wafting white cloud, higher, higher, until the water turned into drifting crystals of ice, where the thunder boomed.

They seemed to hear something else through him, something warm and welcoming and infinitely sad, which enfolded him, which was steady and wordless and flowing, like a human voice singing, which was somewhere ahead in the white, white cloud. Then it all faded.

Stefile burrowed her face into the feathers that were still stiff and clean and warm. "Oh, Wordy Beast," she pleaded. "Don't die. Please don't die."

Cara felt something throb, in a tiny hand.

"Stef!" she screeched suddenly, and pulled her out of the way, on to the stone.

In her new, raw, infant arm, still clenched, was the Flower she had plucked from the Tree. "Dear God, if you love anything, make me not too late!" she prayed, plunging her good arm down through the open beak, deep into the beast's gullet, past the stiffening tiny blade of a tongue.

"Cara!" cried Stefile, jumping up, grabbing her. "Cara, Cara, Cara!"

They watched in silence. The beast was still. "Too late," sobbed Cara, the words rattling with the shudder of her breath. "Too late."

A strand of flesh, as thin as a thread, leapt across the great wound. Very quickly, as if on a loom, threads of flesh crossed and recrossed each other. The torn edges plumpened, and reached out. "Help to close the stomach, eh?" whispered Cara, and they knelt, and tried to ease the wound shut, as a net of white was woven with blinding speed. They had to pull their fingers clear of it. Cara's severed arm reached across to help. And a third pair of hands joined, to help them. The Baked Man knelt with them, and Stefile gave him a silent nod of thanks. Under their hands, they could feel the stomach fill, flooding with the organs of life.

Suddenly there was a rasping of breath, and the white chest rose up, heaving. The flesh about the dim eyes strained to blink, and finally did, and the eyes, freshly moistened, gleamed. The beast lolled his head, and sighed, and then, limply, rolled on to his side.

Stefile whooped with joy, and jumped up and down, and swung Cara about, and hugged the Baked Man. "*Jarwe! Jarwe, Jarwe, Hallu!*" she cried.

"Oh! I saw!" They felt the beast's mind brush theirs with wonder. Then, disappointed. "I was flying."

"Where is some water? Where is some water?" demanded Stefile, weeping.

"Can you hear it? Can you?" asked Asu Kweetar, raising his head, and looking all around him.

"No," whispered Cara, stroking his feathers, making him lie down again. The snow had stopped, and in the East the sky was silver, like his eyes.

They each knew, of course, what Cara had done. If she had kept only one petal of it behind . . . But none of them spoke of it. It was enough. They saw Asu Kweetar fly again. He rose up white as a cloud, and slightly pink with the dawn. He circled over their heads, making high and wild sounds.

"When the Dragon wakes," he promised them, "we will see him together, each of you, and me."

It was a long, slow walk out of the City. The Dogs wandered through it, dazed, their faces covered in ash, their minds somehow wounded. "What do we do now?" one of them asked Cara.

Cara was moved to pity. "Go home, back to your villages. Live there. Forget this," she told them.

Beyond the City was a wide, marshy plain. The bogs were black with ash. They found a charred wooden barge and used that to find the river. The Baked Man went with them, playing jolly marching soldier songs on a small pipe. It was many days before they saw another human face. The face, a young fisherman's, fell in amazement to see, floating in the air behind them, a human arm.

The Baked Man said goodbye to them at the Lower Falls, to see his people. It was he who sang the songs that told of what had happened. They were largely disbelieved, save for the fact that their singer resolutely refused to die.

Chapter 14

After Magic

Life returned to what it had been, neither better nor worse. The next spring, the reeds began to grow again along the banks of the marshes. Villagers who lived beyond the reach of the consuming Fire fearfully took canoes through the expanses of waste. The rich farmlands were singed black and deserted. Younger sons with no inheritance and some courage began to resettle them. How the fire had started, where the Galu had gone, no one knew. God, it was said, had destroyed them. Hapira Izamu Pa was shunned, and given a new name. Da Nata it was called, which meant Emptiness, or Ruin.

In the Village by Long Water, a warrior and his supposed bride were suddenly seen to be living in the Important House. Liri Kerig, who had left the house, would not say why she accepted them, or who they were. The Old Women tapped their noses. "A tale there," they said and nodded. "Given only to us to understand." Then they told their tale and no one believed them. Four months after the outlandish people came, when the last spring began to turn into summer, a child was born.

Aunt Liri was its midwife, and Cal Cara Kerig, the true daughter of the house, watched and waited in the hushed and familiar rooms that were candlelit and warm. The child shrugged its way headfirst into the world, already with fine, lank hair, and a wise and wizened face. It looked about it blinking, and coughed to clear its throat.

"Hello, Mother," it said to Cara, in a high-pitched, piping voice. Then it arched its head back, and looked over its pink and red shoulder. "Hello, Mother," it said again. Then it pulled, and wriggled, and stepped out, walking, still attached by the cord. They saw then that it was a daughter.

Gently, Cara lifted her up. The child had a pleased, amused expression, like a wry old woman being carried on a sedan. Cara placed her on Stefile's soft stomach. "I have waited such a long time to be born," she said in a birdlike voice, and rubbed the moisture and buttery grease from her eyes.

They tried to call her Wisdom, or Knowledge, but Our Tongue was too crude and simple. The word, Sykantata, also meant magic, and sometimes, sex.

At three days old the child called Knowledge, or Magic, could run. She ran flapping her arms, keening, naked, up and down the stone steps that led to the house.

"She can run. Let her," shrugged Stefile, through teeth that held her pipe. Faced with the facts of it, Stefile found that she was not a mother to worry. The severed arm faithfully followed the child, lowering her down the highest steps, carrying her over boulders. "There, see? All right," said Stefile. The child swung on the arm as though it were a branch, and walked by the river, holding its hand.

Cara spent her days at the foot of the cliff, digging the gray, baked earth. Somewhere, she knew, her father was trying to dig ground that would not break. "I'm here, Ata," she would whisper. Syki and the arm would help, pushing flowers into the ground.

"There is a white horse in the garden," Syki said once, climbing onto Cara's lap. "No one can see it but me. It is standing there with big black eyes and it weeps."

"The flowers are for her too," Cara said, and kissed the top of Syki's head. She turned and looked up at Cara, smiling, shaking her head in tolerance, as if her parent had much to learn.

A week after she was born, Sykantata disappeared for a whole day. The arm returned alone, disconsolate, dragging its hand, shrugging when asked questions.

Stefile marched up and down the irrigations, hugging herself, her face closed against pain, haggard and steely. It was Cara who saw the child's return, at dusk.

A magpie glided into the hollowed-out courtyard by the doorway, and in a flurry of beautiful black and gray landed in the window of the winter stable.

"I have been all the way out of the canyon!" piped the magpie. "Down the river! I flew! I saw a very large place with three big buildings. Was that the City?"

"Syki!" exclaimed Cara, and stepped forward, and then stopped, frightened suddenly that she might scare the bird away. "Is that just your voice?" The magpie let out a joyful, mischievous chuckle and leapt down into the stable. Sykantata came running out of its dark doorway, her cheeks bulging, her eyes grinning. She spat out a single purple amethyst at Cara's feet.

"A present!" the child exclaimed. "Magpies always bring presents. Did I see the City, Cara?"

"No. It was Canyon's End, not the city."

"Then I will fly even farther tomorrow. I will be a cormorant. They fly farthest of all."

"Why do you want to go so far away?" Cara asked, wounded somehow that they had created such a prodigy, another wonder. She reached out for her, and the child laughed, and ducked away.

"To see it!" Sykantata answered. She ran to the edge of the hollow, and leapt out into the air, and there was a sudden fluttering, and she flew, as a bird.

Stefile stepped out from the shadows of the kitchen. Cara silently passed her the amethyst.

"I've always wanted to do that myself," Stefile said. "Run and fly." She watched the distant silhouette of the bird. Suddenly another bird seemed to climb out of it, and there were two of them, wheeling together on an updraft. Then Stefile asked, "Are you going to tell me, Cara?"

"Tell you what?"

"What's going to happen."

"It's hard to explain."

"Explain it." Stefile's voice had an edge.

Cara moved like an animal in a harness it does not like. "There are threads," she began, and lost heart for a moment, and began again. "We are made of very small threads, like weaving, one strand from the man and one from the woman, and they come together when the seeds mingle." Her hands were pointed toward each other, fingers wriggling, and she brought them together, interlocking. "That's how we grow. Like weaving. The strands are in every part of us, half from one, half from the other." Cara looked at her hands.

"And so?"

"And so." Cara ducked, and smoothed down her hair, quickly, with one hand. "And so, at the end of my year, I think. I think that everything that is like a man about me goes back to what it was. The seed in my loins, and the seed out of my loins. I think that part of Syki that comes from me will go back too."

"What does that mean?" Stefile's mouth twitched, in anger.

"I don't know," Cara replied, and felt Stefile's anger gather.

The birds in the sky had divided again. There were four of them now, weaving in the wind.

Cara added: "What happens to cloth when all the warp is taken away?"

"It falls apart," said Stefile, looking at the sky. Like a turn of a kaleidoscope, the birds divided again, and again. There was a flock of them now, calling to each other, in the sunset.

"They're not all the same," said Cara. There were crows and sparrows, heron and egret, hawk and pigeon. They flew screeching and cooing and hooting, in a great spiral concourse, dividing again, and again, until there was a cloud of birds, dark against the orange sky. Cara was certain of something else.

"She knows, Stef. She knows it's going to happen."

Stefile tossed the amethyst back at her, and stood up, hands pressed together, and went back into the house.

Stefile went to work the next day, on a doll. Silently she carved a block of wood, with deep angry strokes of the knife. She knitted a dress for it. She crushed berries to make ink, to paint eyes and a mouth on its rough head, and she took yellow thread and embroidered flowers on the dress, with quick jabs of the needle. The doll stood on the kitchen table, lopsided and lumpy, waiting for the child to return.

They found her the next morning, asleep on the kitchen floor, so small that Stefile could lift her up in one hand. They gave her warm milk to drink. "You can't fly away from the Earth," the child murmured. "You go very, very high, and then something stops you." Quietly, Stefile gave her the doll. Syki took it wordlessly, cradled it to her, and fell asleep, her head on the table.

Syki said nothing about the doll, but she took it everywhere with her after that. "What's the doll's name?" Cara asked her once, in the kitchen.

"Hawwah," replied the child.

"After the story in the One Book?"

"No!" said the child, as if Cara was being very stupid. "Because it's your mother's name." She stirred her soup in a very adult fashion, pretending to cook. "And Stefile's too."

Stefile spun around from the stove. "What?"

"Your mother's name," said the child, her voice going thin.

"Could she know that, Cara?" Stefile demanded.

Cara raised her hands, and said, "Can you, Syki?"

The child looked worried. "I only know," she said, helpless.

"I didn't," said Stefile. "I didn't know." She lowered herself carefully onto the chair beside Syki. "What can you tell me?"

"She was called Hawwah. She didn't have a last name. She was very small and pretty, and when she was twelve she was traded to your father, and she had three children, but she didn't like him, so she ran away, and the dogs got her. She was fifteen then, fifteen summers. That's all I know."

"One year," said Stefile. "One year younger than I am."

There was no calendar exact enough to tell them how much time they had left. They lived as best they could. Some days they saw the child, some days not. Wading through the river, Stefile tried to snatch a fish, and there was an eruption of water where the fish had been, and the child rose out of it, shrieking with laughter. "Don't catch me! Don't catch me!"

"Yes I will. Yes I will," said Stefile, laughing breathlessly, "I'm going to catch you and eat you." The child squealed again, and ran into the reeds, and Stefile chased her into them. But she wasn't there. Stefile knocked the reeds aside. "Syki? Stay here. Please?" There was a dart of silver, across the river. "Syki? Stay?" Stefile was alone on the mud, reflected sunlight playing on her face. Her lower jaw shook for a moment, and then was thrust forward, hard, and Stefile turned away.

In the evenings, in the kitchen, they ate without her. Stefile tried to be brisk about things. Patches of damp would suddenly open out across her clothes. "Uk. It's my motherhood again," she would say, and mop herself. "I feel like a spring." But at night, she would pace the house. Cara would get up to look for her, and find her asleep on a hard kitchen chair, or in the library, amid the smell of ash, looking out of the window over the valley. "I'm all right, Cara," she said once. "I'd rather be here. I'd rather be here when she gets back."

Then one night, Stefile came back to the bed, and stood over it. "Cara?" she said. "Cara? There is something you should see."

"What?"

"Syki."

Dazed and flat-footed, Cara followed her. From down the long corridor, there came a ghostly, childish giggling. There was a light, flickering in the library.

Inside there was a small blue flame. It floated in the air, dipping and weaving and diving, and it was the fire that was laughing. It squealed when it saw Stefile, and wrapped itself, glowing, around her arm.

"I think it's just a part of her," said Stefile, her voice dull and even. "I think it's here to let us know she's well." She let the light writhe and flow about her, and brush against her ear, flickering slightly, as if nibbling it.

"It doesn't burn. It feels like breath," said Stefile, "It's not like a fire at all."

Cara could see Stefile's face in the flow, and saw there was a new quality in it. It had become heavy, as enduring and unmovable as stone. Cara feared it. Stone can break. "Come to bed," she said. Stefile turned, and her movements had become heavy too, lumbering, like a great boulder rolling.

One day, after Syki had been gone for an absence of a week, an old woman hobbled, swaying, up the ramps of the steps to the house. She clutched the hands of two dirty, naked children. One of them carried the doll.

"Cara! Stefile!" called the old woman, in a child's piping voice. "Come and see your great-grandchildren!"

"Who was your husband, then?" Stefile asked, arms folded.

"Oh, I didn't need a husband," the old woman said proudly, straightening the silent children's wild hair. "Or a son-in-law either." Then she spoke to the children. "Sari, Mari, these are your great-great-grandparents who are many days old."

The children sat on the steps, and Stefile tried to get them to smoke her pipe. The children looked back at her, numb and slightly uninhabited. "They're not very good at playing," said the old woman. "They're shadows."

Stefile wordlessly held out her arms to her. The old woman limped forward and settled on Stefile's lap, nearly as big as she was, with a sigh. She lowered her ancient head, supported on leathery strands of muscle, onto Stefile's shoulder. "Oh, Ama," she said. "It's been so long since I've seen you." Stefile rocked her gently back and forth. The old woman fell asleep. Cara and Stefile laid her out on one of the broad steps, and went to get pillows. When they came back, there was a baby in the folds of the long brown robe.

It was a real baby, nearly bald, with downy hair and a pudgy face, and no words. Stefile rocked her too and fed her.

"Oh, my aching bags," said Stefile ruefully, as the infant suckled. "Why do you leave them so alone, ah?" The baby gurgled and grinned, as toothlessly as the old crone. Stefile began to hum to the child an old, gentle song that she thought she had forgotten, and as she sang the two silent children began to peel away. Each white flake was a butterfly, until there was a cloud of butterflies in the garden. Suddenly they clustered, fluttering, around Stefile, and rose up, and the child was gone again.

That night, as they lay beside each other, Stefile started to speak. "I feel like I'm on a rope bridge," she said, "the kind that only have a single cord to walk across. And I have to keep very calm, and look only straight ahead, and not look down. I just have to keep walking, straight ahead."

Summer ripened. It got too hot to work outside during the day. For fun, Cara tried to teach Stefile her four spells. Stefile stood over the stove, making clicking and clacking noises in her throat, and chuckling. The embers remained cold.

"There's no need," Cara said. "The world doesn't want it."

"I don't. Not in this heat. You try."

Cara did, making the spell of fire, and nothing happened. "Ah, well," she smiled. Like a cold dew, realization settled over her. The magic was going. She was not a great sorceress any longer. The realization grew, in silence, filling her days, filling the house, one more unspoken thing.

In the library, Cara began to teach Stefile how to read. They were rehearsing the word signs, when the arm floated in through the window, and lay on Cara's lap. It had gone suddenly gray, its severed edges white and crinkled and soft.

"It's dying," said Cara immediately, as if by jumping to a conclusion, she could make it wrong. She took its hand, and felt the fingers feebly close around hers, felt them throb. The arm folded itself up, like a baby in the womb, and its brother arm cradled it. Syki came from nowhere and knelt beside Cara, and watched, tense and wide-eyed, the process of death. The arm would twitch and shudder fitfully. It lay still for a very long time before Cara finally admitted that it was dead.

They buried it, like a favorite animal, in the garden. "Another place to plant a flower," said Cara bitterly. She could not persuade Syki to leave the grave.

"But what will *happen* to it?" Syki demanded, scowling.

"Nothing. It's ceased to be. That's all."

"But it was part of you. Why did it die? You won't die."

"No," said Cara, quietly. "But everything else will."

"I won't," said Syki, firmly.

"You won't?" said Cara, something flaring in her breast. She knelt in front of the child. "You won't die?"

Solemnly, the child shook her head.

"Then what will happen?"

"I don't know. But I can feel it under my skin at night. Like fingers. Like they want to get out. It makes me want to move."

"Are you frightened?" Cara asked.

The child looked up, lips pressed together, and nodded yes. She took Cara's hand and walked with her up to the house.

That night, Syki ate with them again. Cara let her drink some wine, and she fell asleep on Cara's lap, her ruddy cheeks squashed flat against her, her tiny red mouth agape. Stefile knelt, and stroked the disordered hair on the head that still seemed too large for the infant body. She pressed her face against the child's. When Cara felt Stefile's cheeks, they were slippery with moisture. They carried the child to bed, to sleep between them.

The next morning, Cara awoke in a disordered bed, with a great sense of well-being. In a kind of daze of comfort, she watched dust swirl in rays of sunlight. Cara's mother had always said something very strange about dust: that it was the remains of the dead, and should be respected. "The air is full of other people," she had told Cara. The dust in sunlight looked like stars.

In the center of Cara's head, as though a fist had unclenched, there was a marvelous sense of relief and release. She relished it in the warm bed.

She would have to be up soon, and make Tikki's breakfast. She would make porridge and shake thick wads of goat butter from the knife onto the porridge to melt. Father would already be out in the fields. It was getting late. With sudden decision, she threw the quilt from her, and stood up, her body slim and strong like a reed, and flapped barefoot across the matted floor. She had to hiss to suck back the spittle that tried to escape between her teeth. Her face. She ran her fingers over it, ridged and furrowed and rigid like dried leather. Somehow, this morning, she felt so good she didn't even mind about her face. She'd grown used to it, perhaps, and besides, there was sunlight and porridge to be made, and her books to read. She slipped on her racki, her morning robe. It was light and cool and white. She had forgotten how much she loved it. Who, she wondered, had repainted the fresco on her wall?

She padded down the long silent corridor. "Tikki?" she called. "Tik-ki."

In the kitchen, sitting desolate on the floor, in a rough woolen dress, was a woman.

The world was a wall, with Cara's shadow on it, but the shadow was cast by two different, strong lights. There were two shadows, pale and wan. They were dark and clear only where they intersected. With a kind of lurching nausea, Cara seemed to see them move together, until they made a single shape.

She remembered her father, Ata, what had happened to him. I am the earth. Abomination. Kill me, her brother had asked her. And the dream thing, was it possible, manhood. And the Galu, and the Serpent, and the Flower, and this woman.

Who was she?

Harsh-faced, thick-lipped bondgirl. The first time Cara had seen her, she had been slapping a child's face as hard as she could. Then blowing dust and magic. She had been a man, and had left part of herself irreparably behind, to mingle more intimately with the girl than the rest of Cara could, to engender life.

"Ste—Ste—Stefile," she stammered, remembering a name.

The woman stared back at her, steadily, hollow-eyed, head leaning back against the wall. Cara lowered herself, trembling, on to a kitchen chair, squinting with confusion. Was this a dream? Dreams were like this, everything familiar, but horrible. It was as though she had been away on a long voyage and returned to ruin. It was as though she had been away no time at all, only to find everything, everything changed.

"There was a child," Cara remembered.

The woman only stared back at her, unblinking.

"Where? Where is it?"

"Gone," the woman said. The word was a weight, and Cara felt what it meant before she understood it.

"She was torn apart," the woman said calmly. "Like you were. Only you came back. How much have you forgotten?"

Cara stared back at her, numbly. There had been a child who could run. There had been love. "Torn apart?"

"Oh, well and fine," said the woman. "You don't remember. I wish I didn't either. We had a child. Or rather I did. I don't suppose it is yours, any longer. It doesn't matter. Babies die. Only, of course, this one didn't quite die, did it?"

"I-I-I-I-I-I-I," stammered Cara, stuck on the word, or rather, the idea. "I-I-I-I-I-I-I-I-I"

"Bite on it," said the woman, wearily.

Cara did. They sat in silence. Then something stirred in the woman's face, and she spoke again, sour lines down either side of her mouth.

"She spun round and round. Like a spindle. The quilt got tangled up around her feet. It was like you said. The threads were being pulled out of her. They went back into you. She spread out." The woman's hands made a smooth, spreading motion. "All red."

"I-I-I-I-I-I-I," Cara began again.

"I can't stand that," the woman said. It was simple fact.

"I—I'm sorry," Cara was suddenly able to say. "Oh, Stef, I'm sorry."

The woman's mouth twitched. She pulled in air, and expelled it again. "Yah," she said, looking down at her hands. "Yah. I think so." The hands made a small, helpless gesture. "You told me it was coming." Then she looked up, and looked at Cara with the same unblinking stare.

"Hello, Cal Cara Kerig," she said. She flicked a finger toward Cara's face. "Did the change do that?"

Cara sucked in spittle with a startled hiss. She realized she had never told Stefile about her face. Why? Why hadn't the Flower healed it?

"No. The Galu did that when they came."

"You look about the same. Around the eyes. The rest is a ruin."

"I know," said Cara, looking away.

"I'm sorry," said Stefile. "Not that saying sorry helps."

"I know."

"How much do you remember?"

"It—it's all coming back."

"That's a shame," said Stefile. "I don't suppose you can go back?"

Cara shook her head. There was a decorative groove along the back of the chair, and she was running her fingernail back and forth along it. "No."

"No. You told me that too. You told me everything. And me not quite believing all the while. Oh. It's been a strange year you've led me, Cal Cara Kerig. Quite gaudy in its way. Not as gaudy as yours."

"Gaudy?" Cara thought of the afflictions of her family, and the Land of the Dead, where there was no color.

"Sorry," said Stefile, her voice still dull. "It's a peasant word. It means I was happy."

"So was I." Cara glanced at Stefile, surreptitiously. When the magic had gone, it had taken lust with it too. But Cara remembered love.

"Oh, no," said Stefile, in a small, weary voice. Milk came spreading from out of her breasts out across her rough wool dress. She sat on the floor, unmoving. "Damn. Damn eveything," she cursed. As if exhausted, she fought her way to her feet, pushing herself up from her knees. "Damn the world."

Cara stood up too, and did a phantom dance toward her, uncertain she was wanted, wanting to hold and comfort.

Stefile suddenly shouted, "Stay there!" and waved Cara back with her hand. "Just . . . stay there!" She turned her back to Cara, and tore open the top of her dress, and mopped herself with a rag from the table, and suddenly flung it across the room, and covered her face. She made a creaking noise, which was wrenched from a clenched, constricted body. It was not the sound of weeping. Stefile was stopping herself weeping.

Cara stood where she was, watching helplessly. Stefile gathered breath, and quickly wiped her cheeks.

"Stef?" Cara asked.

Stefile's hands played nervously with each other, clasped in front of her belly. "I didn't tell you," Stefile said, her voice thick with struggle. "She was pulled apart . . ."

"You told me."

"No I didn't." Stefle shook her head. "Not this. She was pulled apart, but it was like when you clean your pens, the ink spreads out on the water and it was like that. She spread out, like that, into a kind of mist, in the air. It started to move. And I tried to hold it, keep her to me. Just like always, always, always. And I felt it tug. I felt it tug away. It was still alive. She was still alive." She turned toward Cara, her hand over her mouth.

"I don't need to know this," said Cara.

"But you do. You do. It started to move, out of the window, out under the door, and I followed it, into the yard, down the steps, into the garden. And it filled the garden. It filled the whole valley, getting thinner and thinner. It went up into the sky, like red clouds, and filled that too. It spread everywhere, very faintly. I can still see it. Very faintly. Everywhere I look I can still see it."

Something terrible was happening in Stefile's face. It seemed to be pushed to one side, and the teeth were bared like a snarl. Then, she tried to look happy. Her eyes tried to sparkle, and the snarl tried to twist into a smile.

"So I tell you what I think. I think she has become a kind of spirit in the world. I think the animals will breathe her in, and the fish will swallow her. She'll go into the soil, and into the plants, and into the clouds, and the rain and the birds. Just like we all do, only she will know it. She'll be everywhere, in all things. She'll know everything. And that's what she wanted, isn't it? So I can't be unhappy, can I? Not for her. So it's all right, Cara. All of it. You see, it really is all right."

The eyes were wide, and the head was shaking back and forth very quickly, to show, really, how right it was.

Then simply Stefile fell. She dropped on to her knees, and curled up into a tight knot on the floor, her forehead pressed against the polished stones. Her hands were cupped around her eyes.

"Stef," said Cara, truly alarmed. "Stef. Get up." She took hold of Stefile's arms and tried to hoist her to her feet, but Cara was not as strong as she had been. Silently, Stefile knocked her hands away, drew in tighter.

"Come on. Up on your feet. Up." Cara pulled again, and Stefile whimpered, and then suddenly, with a howl, rose up.

The face seemed plumper, swollen and red, and it quaked, and its mouth was open, howling, lines of spittle between the lips, and the eyes were open, and full of water that was shaken out of them. "I can leaf yall oh!" it wailed, words dissolved.

Cara grabbed her, and pulled her to her, and hugged her. "Oh, Stef. Oh, Stef," she said and began to weep herself.

"Aiee nont stan!"

"You cry, Stef. You cry as you can." She felt the little body jerk and shiver, as the weeping escaped in yelps. "You haven't slept," said Cara, stroking her hair. "You haven't slept in months." They knelt together on the hard floor, rocking silently, Stefile's face pressed against Cara's.

Finally, after some time, Stefile was able to say, "She was beautiful, wasn't she?"

"Yes. She was."

"And strange. Oh, Cara, I feel like I've left the world and I don't know where I am."

"Me too."

"What's going to happen now?"

"I don't know. We'll just have to see."

But the question had to be faced. Stefile patted Cara's arm. "I'm getting you wet."

"Doesn't matter," murmured Cara, and held her.

Stefile still pulled free. "My knees hurt," she said, and managed to smile. She stood up, and Cara followed, clumsily, somehow abashed. "I want to think for a bit, eh?" said Stefile. "Just for a bit. I want to go to the river."

Cara nodded. She no longer looked at Stefile. She saw, on the table, face-down and crumpled, the doll called Hawwah. She saw Stefile's hands pick it up. Cara was running her hand along the groove in the chair again, and suddenly she remembered: she had always done that as a child. Patterns. She heard Stefile walk across the kitchen floor. She heard the door close behind her.

"Duhdo duhdo genzu," Cara murmured.

She wandered through the rooms of her life like a ghost. She sat in the room where she had been a little girl, and felt the bed that was still warm, from Stefile, or perhaps only the sun. She went into Tikki's room, where there was a cradle, as empty now as a womb. She remembered that once she had made Tikki draw a picture on the stone floor, and he refused because that was not what boys did. She kept pushing the stick of charcoal and wax at him, until in a kind of rage, he had drawn a horse on the smooth limestone. It was a miraculous drawing, ready to move, better than anything Cara had drawn. The bondwoman had scrubbed it away. Now Cara knelt, and tried and tried to see any trace of it. She heard a sudden noise, birds at the boxes, and turned. She was still expecting to see Syki come back once again. If she did, bright and brittle and sometimes slightly heartless Magic, it would be no surprise. If Tikki, handsome and smiling, should step through the doorway, it would be no surprise. Death was the surprise.

She stood in the garden at the foot of the cliff. "Ata? Ama?" she called, because it seemed that they were with her. The words alone had the power to make her feel small and tender, to call up from the core of her being, the child from which she had grown. "I hope you can hear this . . ." she began and did not finish. The tears came then, aching out of her eyes, as though her eyes were her heart. Was it enough that love had once existed? Could that be comfort enough? It suddenly seemed to Cara that everyone in the world was still partly a child. That was why they followed a God. Or the Galu. Wave on wave of them.

I am Cal Cara Kerig, Dear Daughter of the Important House, so named because my parents loved me, and they were important people. That is who I am, and that cannot be changed or taken away from me, not by anything, not even death. That can never be destroyed.

She sat in the soil of her parents' garden, and looked out over her valley, which had not changed. Mist and moonlight and rock would not change either. She plunged her hands into the soil. It was warm from rotting.

This is what it is like to be old, she realized. You lose beauty and strength and friends, and you are left with only the memory of love. But you still have yourself, and that must suffice. She suddenly felt cantankerous and old. This was what everyone else had to put up with. What did it matter that her face had not healed? It was healed, as much as it needed to be. What did it matter that the magic was gone? She had done without magic before. All she had to do was live, and that was guaranteed to her. "Come on, Cara, up," she told herself.

But the house was dark inside and empty and silent and still, and she did not have the heart to cook any food, not for herself alone. There was something terrible in that silence. It was as though the house were going to be that empty forever. And the young would grow old and die, and the young after them would die, until everyone she had ever known was gone, until the world she had known was gone. Without Stefile there would be no one to remember with, or understand.

Dear God of the world, she didn't want to be alone.

She heard the latch of the door behind her, and turned, startled. "Oh, hullo," she said, too brightly, embarrassed at standing alone.

Stefile kicked the front door shut behind her. "I caught a fish," she announced, with a quick, nervous smile. She marched across the kitchen, holding it out in front of her. She knelt, and pulled out the baking brick, with a great clatter. "We can eat fish for free," she murmured, half to herself. It was what she had said the first day, on the riverbank. She stood up, back to Cara, and began, without success, to look for the knife. "I tried your spell," she said. "The one that changes."

"Why . . . why did you do that?"

"To make myself a man. I thought it would be a way. It didn't work. As you can see. Then I understood why. It didn't need to."

Cara found herself running her hand along the back of that cursed chair again, and felt tears spill, unbidden, out of her eyes. Why am I crying, she thought. I don't feel that bad. "Are you going to stay?" she asked. She had meant it to be a hard and direct question, but it came out a thin, almost wheedling plea.

Stefile's back went still. "Yes," she said.

Stefile glanced over her shoulder, and saw Cara, small with a ruined face, picking at the chair, and what struck her about the figure was its bravery. "Yes," Stefile said again, and went to her. "Yes. Yes. Yes. Yes."

That night Cara dreamt that they were all reunited at the end of the world. They all sat together on the hill by the wells of vision, her father and brothers, even the warrior in his shell of armor, who Cara had come to love too, in a way. Sykantata sat on his lap, with the doll. The head of Galo gro Galu looked out over the valley, held by the Baked Man. Cara saw herself and Stefile, and almost didn't recognize them, they were so changed. They looked wise and powerful and ancient, rugged companions, victresses of a thousand lives. They wore strange clothes that were not made out of thread. Cara knew somehow that together they had seen mountains worn down to rubble, and cities built of that rubble rise up higher than mountains. They had seen other worlds.

There were two other women there, and they danced together. Cara could not think who they were at first. One was plump, with very fine skin and red cheeks, and something about her made Cara's breath catch with recognition. It was Liri, Aunt Liri, when she was young. Liri had been beautiful. Cara hadn't realized that. Beautiful and round and bobbing and full of chuckles. What else had been lost?

The other woman was not beautiful. She was tall and gangling, too gangling to dance well, all long veined arms and elbows. She wobbled and tottered in a red dress, and a crown that Cara somehow knew was deliberately tipped low over her forehead, to add to the absurdity.

The woman looked up, and saw Cara, and stopped, and smiled, as if there were nothing wrong in the world, or if there was, there was no point in spoiling fun. She was pop-eyed, and thin, and she gave a quick, delicious grin, wreathed in stringy muscle, white buck teeth resting on her lower lip. Then she raised a finger to her lips. Sssh, Cara, ssh, this is our secret.

"Ama!" Cara wanted to cry out; her chest seemed to swell to bursting, but it was a dream, and she couldn't move. She had finally, finally, remembered her mother's face.

In her dream, Cara heard hoarse, deep-drawn breath, and all the clouds in the sky stirred, and were pulled one way, toward the mountains of the Dragon's Back, and were pushed out again, with the breath. The clouds were torn into shreds, tangled wispy strands, and the mountains stood clearly in the distance, farther than Cara had ever seen before, as if to the end of the Earth, layers of mountains, in blue distance. Then they shifted. There was a crumbling and slow falling away of rock. The ground shook underfoot, and Cara's mother fell backward laughing. The sound of thunder came, delayed, and from somewhere in the sky, a high delighted keening.

The mountains stood up. Snow avalanched from them, the rock beneath it buckling, splitting, yawning. The mountains slid away from something underneath them, as dust and debris burgeoned up in giant billows. Through the haze of dust, sunlight caught something round and burnished, glinting. Obscured, surrounded by cracklings of lightning, a hind leg, scaly, bronze-colored, broke out from under the ruins of the nearest range. It stretched out, like a cat just awakening, out across the horizon, delicately extending claws. Forested crags tipped from it in a ghostly tumble of stone. Then everything was lost in a haze of dust. Something uncoiled, loosened, and out of the heart of the earth, something the size of a continent stood up. It filled the sky, above the clouds, sunlight glaring harshly on it, as if it were a moon. Shadows moved across it.

"For I am the World," the Dragon said, "and I am Life as it is lived, brother to him who talks to God, and you, you are the Beast that Chooses."

Overjoyed, Cara awoke. Stefile was beside her in the darkness.

At the end of the world, together on a hill, they danced.

Coming in the spring . . .

THE
UNCONQUERED
COUNTRY

by Geoff Ryman

The full-length version of Ryman's World Fantasy Award-winning novella is the extraordinary story of a young girl who must try to make her way through a world she doesn't understand. Bantam Spectra Books will proudly publish this fine novel in the spring of 1987.